*When the heart
takes a chance,
all things
are possible...*

Keeping Faith

"I shamed you in front of your family." Faith hid her face in his shirt.

Reese touched the underside of her chin with his finger, tilting her face up so he could see her eyes. "Mary likes you very much. She chased me around the kitchen with a wooden spoon"—Faith smiled at the image—"and ordered me to come upstairs and make peace with my new bride."

Faith's smile died on her lips. "Well, now you're safe. I'm not your new bride. I'm only rented. Temporarily."

"Faith, I'm sorry." He tried to kiss her. She avoided his lips. Reese stared at her face. He saw the pain in her eyes. For the first time he damned his contract and his elaborate scheme. "Faith, please . . ."

Faith studied his face. She saw the look in his eyes, and for the first time she was glad of the contract and his crazy scheme. It was too easy to love him, and much too painful. She pulled his face down to hers and kissed him, telling him with her lips the things she couldn't say aloud. . . .

This book also contains an exciting preview of another DIAMOND HOMESPUN ROMANCE, Spring Blossom by Jill Metcalf.

GOLDEN CHANCES

REBECCA HAGAN LEE

DIAMOND BOOKS, NEW YORK

GOLDEN CHANCES

A Diamond Book / published by arrangement with
the author

PRINTING HISTORY
Diamond edition / August 1992

ISBN: 1-55773-750-9

Diamond Books are published by The Berkley Publishing Group,
200 Madison Avenue, New York, New York 10016.
The name "DIAMOND" and its logo are trademarks
belonging to Charter Communications, Inc.

PRINTED IN THE UNITED STATES OF AMERICA

10 9 8 7 6 5 4 3 2 1

For Brenda, for liking it right from the beginning

and

For Teresa, who read every word

and

For Steve, for enduring the process

Acknowledgments

I wish to thank the staff of the Wyoming State Archives, Museums and Historical Department in Cheyenne, Wyoming, for the information sent, the personal questions answered, and the prompt responses to all queries.

I also want to thank Mr. and Mrs. "Windy" Briese of Woodbine, Georgia, for information and maps on the transcontinental railroad.

Edna Earle Morris and Emilie K. Hartz of the John E. Ladson, Jr. Genealogical and Historical Foundation and Library in Vidalia, Georgia, were a tremendous help with research as were Barbara Eidson, Fred Hartz, and Sally Thompson of the Ohoopee Regional Library in Vidalia, and genealogist Clifford Dwyer of Gainesville, Florida.

A big thank you to Betty Bivins of Ailey, Georgia, who traveled to Richmond, Virginia, and brought me several reference books.

Thanks also to Dr. Ramon V. Meguiar, Ob/Gyn, who patiently answered my questions about pregnancy and childbirth and kept me healthy during the writing of this book.

And, to the Romance Writers of America, Kentucky Romance Writers, Georgia Romance Writers and Southeast Georgia Romance Writers who critiqued, judged, and contributed information and guidance, especially writers Susan Johnson and Teresa Medeiros who made me believe I could do it, then coached me along the way.

Heartfelt thanks to agents, Cynthia Richey, and Eugenia Panettieri, and my editor, Carrie Feron, for their friendship, talent, support, and belief in me.

Prologue

Washington City
December 1869

REESE JORDAN GRIMACED as he finished writing out the advertisement. He hoped it was right. If it was, it would change his life. He studied the lines for a moment, then scratched out a word here and there and inked in others. He smiled, satisfied with the results.

He'd done it. He'd found a way to gain his heart's desire without compromising his beliefs. Marriage was absolutely out of the question. A real marriage anyway. But this . . . It would work. This was the plan of a master strategist. His plan.

Reese handed the sheet of paper to the clerk, who placed it in the pile to be typeset.

"I want it in tomorrow's edition."

"That'll be an extra two bits."

"Fine." Reese produced the money, including a generous tip.

"I'll set it right away."

Reese nodded. Early in life he'd learned that cash gained him the respect and attention he would have preferred to garner on his own. Right now that was part of the problem. He swallowed hard. By tomorrow his plan would be set in motion. There would be no turning back.

1

He slapped his hat against his thigh. The sound seemed to echo in the room. The clerk looked up at him questioningly. Reese jammed his hat on and stalked out of the office.

A wagon rolled through a puddle near the boardwalk. Mud splattered Reese's boots and his carefully creased trousers. Reese cursed beneath his breath, damning Washington and its endless flood of traffic. The capital was readying itself for Christmas. People crowded into the city to see the sights. Greenery, red ribbons, and the sound of bells were everywhere, surrounding the inhabitants. Reese had little patience with the holiday. His mind was focused on his past and the important matter at hand. He sprinted across the muddy street to the telegraph office. It wouldn't hurt to send the same advertisement to the Richmond newspaper.

Reese scrawled the ad copy on a sheet of paper, then paid the telegraph clerk. The cards had all been dealt. Now all he had to do was play them carefully and wait for the results. Reese found himself whistling as he exited the telegraph office and walked back to his suite at the Madison Hotel, not some Christmas carol but a bawdy little tune he'd learned in the war. It suited his mood.

Plan and plan carefully. That was Reese Jordan's motto.

THE CLICKING OF the handset alerted the clerk in the telegraph office in Richmond. He quickly jotted down the words to the advertisement. The telegraph key quieted. The clerk hastily scanned the message.

WANTED: HEALTHY WOMAN BETWEEN THE
AGES OF 18 TO 23 TO PROVIDE HEIR TO
WEALTHY RANCHER. WIDOW WITH EXCEL-
LENT LINEAGE PREFERRED. ONE CHILD AC-
CEPTABLE. MUST TRAVEL TO WYOMING
AND REMAIN FOR ONE YEAR. EXCELLENT
SALARY AND BONUS. APPLY IN PERSON
TO DAVID ALEXANDER, MADISON HOTEL,
WASHINGTON CITY, DECEMBER 20.

He read the advertisement a second time. "That
can't be right," he said, aloud, "I must have missed
a word." He carefully penciled in the word "for"
in front of "heir," then read the whole thing aloud.
" 'Wanted: Healthy woman between the ages of
eighteen to twenty-three to provide for heir to
wealthy rancher. Widow with excellent lineage
preferred. One child acceptable. Must travel to
Wyoming and remain for one year. Excellent salary and bonus. Apply in person to David Alexander, Madison Hotel, Washington City, December
twentieth.' "

The clerk nodded, silently congratulating himself
for catching his error. He placed his fingers on
the handset, telegraphed his receipt of the message back to Washington, then handed the corrected copy to the errand boy.

Chapter One

December 1869
Richmond, Virginia

THE RAIN CONTINUED to pound the roof and the few remaining glass windowpanes in the Collins House on Clary Street. Inside, the members of the Richmond Ladies Sewing Circle shivered in front of the meager fire, the tips of their fingers numb with cold as they protruded from the open ends of their knitted gloves. Several women muttered beneath their breath as they wielded the sharp needles against the hated blue wool of army uniforms.

Faith Collins shifted in her uncomfortable chair and turned her head from side to side, stretching the stiff muscles and tendons in her neck. She laid her sewing aside and got up to empty three of the large pans scattered around the parlor floor to collect the rain that poured through the roof of the battered house.

Faith hated emptying the pots and pans. It was a boring, repetitive chore and a complete waste of time. The floor was already damaged by fire and rain. A few more drops wouldn't make much difference. And the sound of the water pinging against metal grated on her nerves. It reminded Faith of gunfire and death and everything she'd lost.

5

But her ladies insisted on using pans to catch the water, and Faith grudgingly obliged. She was fighting a losing battle with the inclement weather and the roof. She had been fighting the battle for years. Her own private war.

The firing of the nearby arsenal during the retreat had been responsible for the majority of the damage to her home, and the repairs she'd been able to manage since the end of the war had not included a new roof.

It was hard enough to keep food on the table, clothes on their backs, and shoes on their feet. She might have managed on her own, but Faith had to feed and clothe the other members of the household who made up the roster of the Richmond Ladies Sewing Circle.

The weather was the least of her worries. It was uncontrollable. Faith was concerned with the basics—food, shelter, and clothing. Those were the primary topics of interest on this cold, rainy afternoon.

"Faith, you really shouldn't lift that heavy pan that way. You'll strain your back."

Faith looked up at her aunt, Virtuous May Hamilton Jessup. "Yes, ma'am. I know that, Aunt Virt, but . . ." She shrugged resignedly, knowing help would not be forthcoming from that direction.

Virtuous Jessup, with her still-black hair and deep blue eyes, would have been a handsome woman if she could have stopped thinking about the past and finding fault with everything and everybody. Aunt Virt would never let them forget all they'd had and all they'd lost.

"I would be happy to help you, Faith dear, but you know I have lumbago in my lower back. I've had it ever since my son, Will, was born. I nearly died giving birth to that boy. He was supposed to take care of me in my old age, and what did he do but get himself killed on a dreary battlefield in the wilderness?" Aunt Virt probably would have continued to rattle on about her woes if Aunt Tempy hadn't entered the parlor and interrupted the oft-told tale of her sister's ruined life

"Here, let me help you with that, Faith." Aunt Tempy helped Faith carry a heavy enameled chamber pot to the wooden cistern. The house had been so heavily damaged that the upper floor was unsafe and off limits to the members of the household. Faith, her aunts, Virt and Tempy, Mrs. Everett and Mrs. Colson, who were sisters-in-law to Aunt Virt, and Faith's sister, Joy, occupied the first floor of the house, living in the front parlor, back parlor, library, dining room, and office. They did the cooking in the dining room on a cast-iron stove Faith had purchased secondhand.

Faith smiled at Aunt Tempy. "This would be so much easier if we just pushed the cistern into the parlor and opened the lid. Most of the rain would fall into it."

Temperance Hamilton laughed aloud. She was completely different in looks and character from her older sister, Virt. Petite and red-haired, Tempy was always ready with a smile, a helping hand, or a shoulder to cry on. Faith didn't know what she would have done without her. "I tried to tell you this barrel wouldn't blend with the style of the room."

"What style?" Faith glanced around at the bare walls and floors. The once magnificent dining room was unfurnished except for the stove, a rough pine table and benches, a broken cherry sideboard, three wooden crates, a battered copper tub for bathing, and the oak water barrel.

"I'm glad Mama and Papa didn't live to see this," Faith said, softly.

Even the huge crystal chandelier was gone, a victim of looters. The scavengers had used it for target practice, then cut the support rope and allowed the gilded frame and the remaining crystal prisms to crash to the floor.

"I don't know," Aunt Tempy teased to lighten the mood. "I'll bet that chandelier was the devil to clean. At least that's one less thing to worry about."

"I suppose you're right, Aunt Tempy," Faith agreed. "We have enough to worry about without that. What with the roof and the price of everything going up except what we get paid for sewing and our property taxes due next month, I just don't know where to turn. We'll never earn enough money to pay for everything."

"We'll manage."

"But the taxes are due at the end of next month," Faith said.

"What about the bank?" Mrs. Everett asked. "Have you tried to take money out of the bank? That's what my dear late husband used to do."

Faith looked at Mrs. Everett. She hadn't realized the others were listening so closely.

"Agnes," Aunt Virt scolded her sister-in-law, "you always were such a featherbrain. Even I understand that in order to get money out of the bank, you must first put money in it, and that's just what we can't do."

Faith rubbed her temples, trying to blot out the angry voices. Couldn't they see it did no good to argue?

The squabbling between Aunt Virt and her sisters-in-law was a constant source of irritation to Faith. She needed help and guidance, not quarrels and accusations.

"And why not?" Agnes Everett asked indignantly. "We can put all our sewing money together and open an account at the bank. Then we tell the banker how much we need for the roof and the taxes and all, and we just draw it out."

"I wish it were that simple, Mrs. Everett," Faith said, "but it isn't. Our earnings from sewing have amounted to sixty-eight dollars and thirty-two cents, and that includes Joy's ten dollar gold piece. The roof alone will cost more than that. A banker would be out of his mind to lend us money on the basis of sixty-eight dollars and thirty-two cents."

"Can't we use the house and land as collateral?" Aunt Tempy asked. "I seem to remember Papa using the farm as collateral to get the money to build the new barn and stables."

"We could try, Aunt Tempy, but I wouldn't want to do that unless we had no other choice. The carpetbaggers are eager to snatch up land, and if we can't pay back the loan, we'll lose the house and the land."

"If we don't pay the taxes, we'll lose the house and the land," Aunt Tempy pointed out.

"I know," Faith said miserably. "What we need is a miracle." She sat down and picked up her sewing.

"What we need," Aunt Virt said bluntly, "is a man."

"A man?" Faith murmured, perplexed. "Another mouth to feed?"

"No, a man. A husband. A provider. Someone to shoulder the burden," Aunt Virt elaborated. "Someone to get us out of this mess. Someone who knows how to go about things. A husband."

"For whom?" Aunt Tempy asked her know-it-all sister. "There are five of us, if we exclude Joy." She glanced to the settee where five-year-old Joy lay curled up sound asleep.

"Well, of course we must exclude Joy. She's only five," Hannah Colson replied reasonably. "I wouldn't mind getting married again. Surely one of us can find a husband."

"Within a month?" Mrs. Everett was incredulous. "That's impossible."

"I'm afraid Agnes is right, Hannah," Temperance admitted. "Most of the women in the South are looking for husbands. I'm afraid there just aren't enough men to go around. The war has made a lot of widows and left a great many girls waiting at the altar. There will be too many old maids and widows in the years to come."

"Yes," Aunt Virt chimed in, "look at Faith. I don't see any men beatin' down the door asking to marry her, and she used to be considered quite a catch."

Faith frowned at Virtuous. She knew she was getting older, losing her looks, but she was only twenty-four, not eighty.

"There aren't many men Faith's age left around Richmond, except Union soldiers and undesirables." Temperance leaped to Faith's defense. "Joy has a better chance of marrying a gentleman than Faith does."

"I agree, Aunt Tempy," Faith said, "but by that time we'll all be homeless and hungry."

"Or dead," Virt added ominously.

"As I said," Faith continued, "we need a miracle—and fast."

"I think we have one," Hannah Colson said in a voice that trembled with excitement. "I think we have it. Look!" She handed Temperance a folded newspaper. "I found it in Major Butler's overcoat."

Temperance held the newspaper up to the flickering kerosene lamp and read aloud, " 'Wanted: Healthy woman between the ages of eighteen to twenty-three to provide for heir to wealthy rancher. Widow with excellent lineage preferred. One child acceptable. Must travel to Wyoming and remain for one year. Excellent salary and bonus. Apply in person to David Alexander, Madison Hotel, Washington City, December twentieth.' "

"That's it!" Virt exclaimed. "We have our miracle."

"Wait a minute," Faith ordered.

"Yes," Tempy added, "slow down."

"What's the date?" Hannah asked.

"The fourteenth," Agnes answered quickly.

"Good, that gives us plenty of time to get Faith ready," Virt replied matter-of-factly. "She can pretend to be a widow."

"At least I look the part." Faith stared pointedly at Virtuous. She didn't want to get swept up into their plans to send her to Washington to answer a newspaper ad. Her parents would turn in their graves at the thought. But unless someone came up with a better idea . . .

"Faith," Tempy asked, "you aren't considering this featherbrained idea, are you?"

She hated to admit she was. The possibilities were going around and around in her mind. It was a chance. A slim one, but a chance just the same. Faith nodded in answer to Tempy's question.

"Stop right there!" Temperance ordered. "Faith, it isn't like you to be impulsive. Take time to think this through."

"I can't. I might not do it if I give it too much thought," Faith answered truthfully. Already she could see the drawbacks of the scheme and the ordeal of traveling alone to a city full of strangers. "Does anyone have a better idea?"

The ladies all shook their heads—even Tempy, though her brows were knitted into a frown and her mouth was a thin, worried line.

"You must go," Aunt Virt ordered. "You're the only one of us who fits the description."

"For your information, Virtuous May Hamilton Jessup, Faith *doesn't* fit the description. She's over the age limit; she'll soon be twenty-five. And she's never been married, so she's a far cry from an experienced widow," Temperance retorted.

Faith's heart began to pound. "Joy could go with me. She could pose as my child."

"You don't look anywhere near twenty-five," Aunt Virt said, studying Faith with a critical eye. "You don't look a day over eighteen." Virt was quick to see the benefits of a little deception.

"Faith, stop," Tempy pleaded. "You can't just jump into this."

"I have to, Aunt Tempy, unless you have a better idea."

"I don't, but—"

"Then it's settled," Mrs. Colson announced. "Faith'll take the sewing money and go to Washington and get this job."

"No, it's not settled, Mrs. Colson." Faith hated to dampen their excitement, but these wonderful women had to understand the consequences. "There will probably be hundreds of applicants—women who are better qualified than I am. I may not get the job."

"You'll get the job," Aunt Virt predicted. "You have no other choice."

"Even if I do, I'll have to take Joy and go to Wyoming for a year. Who will take care of things here?"

"We will," Aunt Virt said. "I'm sure we can manage on our own for a year, especially with the bonus money you'll be able to leave us."

"That's another thing," Faith began, far from convinced. "What if the bonus isn't enough?"

"You'll just have to get enough," Agnes said. "Bargain. You're good at it."

"I just don't know." Tempy sounded hesitant. "Do you think you can do it, Faith? Can you lie about your qualifications?"

Faith put aside the trousers she was hemming and walked over to Temperance. She put her arms around her aunt and stared into the gray eyes in the expressive face so like her own. "Aunt Tempy, I'll do anything I have to do to see that this family survives. Our men gave their lives for the survival of our way of life. The least I can do is lie if that becomes necessary. We need money, and I'm the only one of us qualified to get it. Why, I would work for the devil in Hades if that would provide the money we need." Faith straightened her back. "At least I'm going to try. I have to."

"All right, Faith." Tempy leaned her forehead against Faith's. "If you think it's best, we'll help you. You're the only hope we've got at the moment. Go to Washington and do your best."

"Yes, please, Faith," the others chimed in. "Go to Washington."

The small group of women looked at her with hope shining out of their eyes. Faith wanted to feel as confident as the others. It had been a long time since she'd seen hope in their faces.

Faith realized, even if her dear ladies did not, how many other women desperately needed jobs to feed their families. She knew that landing a plum of a job like the one in the newspaper advertisement would be the answer to the prayers of many southern households. Her chances of being chosen out of a multitude of younger, more attractive women would require a miracle.

But a year in Wyoming, a year far away from war-ravaged Richmond . . . Faith sighed as butterflies beat a wild tattoo inside her stomach.

Chapter Two

FAITH WALKED SIX blocks from the Washington station to the Madison Hotel on the most miserable day of the year. Sodden from the icy rain, her skirts wrapped themselves around her legs, slowing her pace. Crystal droplets clung to her eyelashes and coated the tendrils of black hair peeking from beneath her drooping bonnet. Her feet were numb with cold, her shoes and stockings soaked after trudging through the muddy rivers that Washington residents called streets. Sneezing repeatedly, Faith hesitated on the sidewalk in front of the Madison Hotel.

The massive brick structure glowed with care and money. Ivy flourished, clinging tenaciously to the brick walls. Faith stood in the stinging rain and stared at the building. It had been a long time since she'd entered a fine hotel, and she had never done so alone. Her father or Hamilton, her older brother, had always accompanied her. A southern lady never traveled without a chaperon and never dreamed of entering a hotel without one.

Faith recalled her upbringing with a sad smile. Since the war began, she had done a lot of things southern ladies didn't do. This was just one more example. She bit her lip, straightened her back in

15

an imitation of Aunt Virt, and marched up to the entrance of the hotel as if she owned the place.

A uniformed concierge in a long jade-green overcoat adorned with gold braid stepped forward to open the door. Faith nodded regally in his direction and strolled into the opulent foyer. She paused for a second, summoning her courage, then walked to the registration desk and informed the clerk on duty that Mr. David Alexander was expecting her.

The clerk looked her up and down. Faith did not flinch under his haughty scrutiny. She had seen the same scornful expression on hundreds of faces since the war. She knew he thought she lacked the necessary commodity for prompt, efficient service. Money.

Faith's gaze cooled to a crisp slate gray as she stared through the insignificant clerk.

"I'm afraid Mr. Alexander is occupied at the moment, miss," the clerk informed her.

"Madam," Faith corrected, "and he's not too busy to see me."

"He's very busy. He can't be bothered."

"Surely that's for Mr. Alexander to decide," Faith said. "Shall we go ask him?" She stood her ground.

He shrugged and rang for the bellboy. "Escort madam to Mr. Alexander's suite."

"Yes, sir." The bellboy started toward the stairs with no more than a mere glance to see if Faith followed.

He led her up the stairs, down a corridor, and into a suite of rooms at the end. "He's down there. At the table."

Faith slumped against the wall. A quick glance at the line of women waiting to enter the sitting room of the suite confirmed her worst suspicions. The place was literally wall to wall with women of all ages, shapes, and sizes.

Faith took a deep breath, then wished she hadn't. The atmosphere was thick with the clashing odors of washed and unwashed bodies, fine soaps, and cheap perfume layered with the contrasting smells of fried food and rancid grease. Her stomach heaved, threatening revolt.

It seemed the promise of cold, hard cash appealed to all levels of society. The war had left a great many destitute widows and orphans in its wake. Many of them, Faith was sure, were better qualified than she to care for an infant in the Wyoming wilderness.

The woman in line ahead of Faith turned and issued an order: "You might as well take a seat like the rest of us. It's been like this since eight this morning. He's taking his own sweet time about deciding. It'll be a while."

Faith nodded in mute affirmation, then looked around for an unoccupied seat.

The chairs lining the corridor were all taken. Many women sat on the floor talking quietly among themselves, their skirts modestly arranged around them. Faith followed suit and sank to the floor, standing occasionally to advance several steps as the line moved slowly but steadily forward.

Three hours later Faith had made little progress up the line. She was cold, tired, and cramped from sitting on the hard floor with her legs tucked beneath her. Her empty stomach rumbled hungrily.

The noon dinner hour arrived. Faith's spirits rose as many discouraged job seekers left their places in line and headed down the corridor, grumbling to themselves. Faith stumbled to her feet as the line surged forward. Several women hurried to claim the coveted spaces. She had hoped the dinner hour would force more of the competition to vacate the corridor, but she was disappointed.

All around her, women reached into their belongings and produced bundles of food. Faith swallowed a groan of dismay and settled into a more comfortable position against the wall, determined to ignore her stomach's angry protests. The competition had come prepared. She sat in miserable silence.

Mr. David Alexander continued to work through dinnertime. Faith hungrily eyed the tray of roast beef, biscuits, garden peas, and mashed potatoes with gravy that the hotel staff delivered to his desk. Her mouth watered, and her empty stomach knotted up as the enticing aromas slipped past her nostrils. She even detected a whiff of apples and cinnamon on the tray—an apple cobbler maybe, or a slice of pie. And coffee. Hot, steaming coffee. It was almost too much for her. She pulled her legs up in front of her and locked her arms around her knees to keep from marching up to Mr. Alexander's desk and drooling all over his meal. She glanced around at her neighbors on the floor, hoping for a handout, but not one of the other women offered to share her meager meal, and Faith was much too proud to ask. She'd come to Washington unprepared. She had allowed her family's optimism to affect her judgment. They had assured her she would march into Mr. Alexander's office and come out with the job in a matter of minutes.

At last the crumpling of oil cloth and newspaper signaled the end of the dinner hour. Hope surged within her. Surely it wouldn't take all afternoon to complete the interviews. She stood up to stretch her legs and looked around, gauging the length of the line and the strength of her competition. Around her other women rose and stretched their cramped limbs, some of them carefully moving softly snoring toddlers from their laps to the floor. Others tried to soothe infants and tired cranky children who loudly wailed their displeasure at the exhausting wait. Faith breathed a silent prayer of thanks that she hadn't brought Joy along, as Aunt Virt had suggested, to "help sway Mr. Alexander."

Faith had reached the limit of her own patience, and Joy would have lost it hours ago. She was afraid she might burst into tears at any moment and wail right along with the children.

She looked around and saw on the faces of all of the women in line the same look of hope tempered by desperate need. They needed work just as desperately as she did. Many of them had probably been needier for a far longer time and had lost as much as she. Perhaps more. Although Faith had lost parents, brothers, cousins, and a comfortable wealth, she had never known the loss of a child or of a husband or lover.

A low buzz of anxious whispers surrounded her, and she heard a rustle of fabric as women smoothed the creases from their dresses, straightened their bonnets, and patted their hair into place. Some of them even pinched their cheeks and bit their lips as if preparing to greet a beau. Faith wondered what had prompted this display of feminine energy and wiles until she spotted Mr. Alexander in earnest discussion with another man in the doorway of one of the suite's sitting rooms.

"Who is he?" Faith asked the woman ahead of her, awed by the sight of him.

"He's the one."

"The one?" Faith asked.

"The one doing the hiring." The woman removed her gloves, discreetly licked the palms of her hands, then patted her brassy blond hair into place. "You wouldn't happen to have any rouge, would you?"

Faith shook her head, watching in fascination as the woman adjusted the lace-trimmed bodice of her bright pink gown to display a scandalous amount of flesh. "I thought Mr. Alexander was hiring."

"Oh, no, Mr. Alexander is the one at the table taking down all the information. He's a handsome devil, too, but not like the other one." She bit her lower lip. "If Alexander approves you, you get to go in and talk with the other man. I'm looking forward to that!"

"Who is the other man?" Faith asked again.

"I don't know," the woman answered. "But Mr. Alexander is just his agent. The other man is the boss. Take a good look. Have you ever seen anyone like him?" she gushed.

Faith looked up. The answer popped into her brain. No. She had never seen anyone like him. He was beautiful. There was simply no other word to describe him. Faith let her gaze wander over him from the top of his head, across the wide expanse of chest, down the seemingly endless length of hard-muscled thighs and calves, to the toes of his gleaming shoes.

She had to force herself to look away from him.
Just the sight of him was enough to make her pulse
race. Faith slowly closed her mouth. If he possessed
flaws, they had to be on the inside, because the
outside of him was perfection. No wonder the room
was crowded with females seeking employment.
Word must have gotten around.

Faith wondered if he realized he was the drawing
card, the main attraction, that the amount of gold
he offered for the job of caring for an infant paled
in comparison.

It seemed to Faith that she stood mesmerized
by the man for hours, but it could not have been
more than a minute or two before he lifted his
head from his conversation with David Alexander and straightened up. His midnight-black hair
touched the top of the door frame. Faith could
see it was long and silky. He smiled at something
Alexander said, then casually scanned the corridor
bustling with anxious women and children. Faith's
gray gaze locked with his.

The sudden eye contact sent a shiver of pure
excitement racing across her nerve endings. His
eyes were brown, she noted, a delicious chocolate brown, flecked with gold and framed by black
lashes and brows. Her breathing quickened. Her
face felt warm, flushed. She moved back against
the wall and busied herself by studying the toes of
her battered shoes.

Reese Jordan stood unmoving as the young woman seemed to disappear before his eyes. One minute
she was there staring at him, and in the next instant
she had faded into the milling crowd and become
hidden from view.

"Who is she?" he asked Alexander.

David Alexander glanced down at the paper he was holding in his hand. "Mary Stephens, nineteen years old; three-year-old son named James; husband killed five months ago in a tavern brawl. She's next." David indicated the girl waiting patiently in front of the table, holding a blond toddler anchored to her hip.

"Not her." Reese barely glanced at the girl. "The other one. The one in the center of the corridor a moment ago."

David looked around the crowded hall, then back at his cousin and employer. At least a hundred women were milling about in the room, and at least forty of them stood in the center of the hallway. "Could you be a little more specific, Reese? Which of the multitude has caught your discerning eye?"

Reese Jordan scanned the crowd, searching. "She was here a moment ago. Dammit, she couldn't have just disappeared. Where is she? I don't see her." He looked at David. "Send the next one in, but keep an eye out for her—petite, black hair, dark eyes, very pretty."

David shot a glance at his cousin. Dark-haired, dark-eyed petites were not Reese's preference. Big, buxom redheads and hard-edged blondes were his normal choice. "Are you sure you want to continue? It's late and you must be tired. I know I am."

Reese fingered the gold chain dangling across the side of his waistcoat and removed his watch from its pocket. He flipped it open. "I have time for one more. Send her in."

David gestured at the girl in front of him. "Mary Stephens." He handed Reese the sheet of paper outlining the applicant's history.

Reese looked closely at the young woman for the first time and shook his head. "She won't do."

"Why not?" David was puzzled. "She meets all the requirements."

"Look at her, David," Reese instructed.

David gave the girl a cursory glance. "What about her?"

"She's obviously in the family way, David. She meets the requirements too well. She won't do," Reese said with finality.

David shook his head at the young woman. "I'm sorry, Mrs. Stephens, but—"

"I heard him," she said dully. "I won't do. But you coulda said something earlier. I been waitin' here all day just to see him. If you'd looked at me, you woulda seen I'm expectin'."

"I realize that. I just didn't realize . . . I mean . . ." David Alexander faltered.

"I'll pay her off and let her be on her way. We don't have time to waste arguing," Reese interrupted, reaching inside the breast pocket of his jacket to remove his wallet.

The woman shook her head. "I came for an honest job. I don't take charity from nobody."

"It isn't charity." Reese made an effort to curb his annoyance. "I'm reimbursing you for your time. I should've had Mr. Alexander inquire as to whether any of you were expectant mothers before we began. A woman in your condition—"

"A woman in my condition can get along fine without your charity," she informed him angrily.

"You said I wouldn't do and I won't, but I won't take no reimbursing or charity or whatever you call it from you neither." She turned on her heel and addressed the crowd. "All you other women in my condition can just forget about this job. He don't take expectant mothers. Ain't no sense waitin' around." She picked up her belongings and made her way through the crowd. Several other women followed in her footsteps.

"Well, that lets me out," the brassy blonde in front of Faith announced. "I'm not showin' yet, but I will be soon enough. What about you, honey?" She turned to Faith.

"Oh, no, I'm not . . . I mean, my husband died in the war. I couldn't be . . ." Faith stammered, blushing furiously.

"What's that got to do with it?" The woman laughed suddenly. "Mine died in the war, too."

Faith's jaw dropped, and the woman chuckled even harder. "A girl does what she can to survive and feed her family. Don't you know that yet?" She shrugged. "Oh, well, good luck, honey. Maybe you'll get the job."

She waved good-bye to Faith and followed the departing women down the hall.

Faith looked around her. The crowd had thinned considerably. She wouldn't have believed there were so many expectant mothers in the room if she hadn't seen for herself. Nor would she have believed they would calmly walk away from a job they all wanted after waiting in line all morning. Her sense of fair play was offended. They should have been given an opportunity to be interviewed. The job involved providing for an infant. Surely a woman about to have a child of her own was well qualified to care for someone else's. But this new development did increase her chances. All she had to do was wait for her turn to talk to Mr. Alexander and gain access to the man in the other room. She could wait a little longer. The last train back to Richmond departed at nine in the evening. Surely she would get in to see the man before then.

SOME HOURS LATER Reese Jordan looked down at his cousin and took pity on him. David had done a tremendous job under trying circumstances, and he was tired. Lines were etched around the corners of his mouth, and his dark eyes were lackluster. The usual sparkle had disappeared from their depths hours ago. He needed dinner and a good night's sleep. "Let's stop for the night, David. We're both tired. I never dreamed we'd have to wade through so many women to find what I want."

"I warned you about a newspaper ad," David reminded him. "I was afraid this would happen. These are desperate times, Reese. You should have used a more conventional method. Dozens of young women of your acquaintance would be willing to go along with this scheme."

"And dozens of fathers and brothers would hunt me down when it's all over. No, thank you. I'll take my chances with the newspaper and my own instincts."

"Are you absolutely certain you want to go through with this insanity?"

"Absolutely. And it isn't insanity. This method has worked for thousands of years in Europe," Reese informed his cousin.

"With one important modification," David reminded him. "Marriage."

"Granted," Reese agreed. "But that's one modification I'm not willing to make."

"Why?" David asked for the thousandth time.

"You know why. You above all people should understand how I feel about this." Reese ran his fingers through his black hair.

"I remember a time when you couldn't wait to tie the knot."

Reese's brown eyes narrowed into slits. "That was a long time ago. I'm not that stupid or naive anymore. This is the only method I'll consider. I've thought this through, David. I know what I'm doing."

"You want a son and heir."

"Yes," Reese said with a finality that warned his cousin the discussion was over—"Send the women home for the night. Tell them the qualified applicants may report here at ten tomorrow."

"Ten?" David asked. Reese habitually began his workday before dawn.

"I have to attend a reception at the British embassy this evening. It's going to be a very long night."

"That long, huh?"

"I plan to meet an old acquaintance after the reception, and I don't want to disappoint her." Reese smiled suddenly.

There was a wealth of promise in Reese Jordan's wicked smile, and David understood why women found his cousin so irresistible.

Reese gestured to David. "Go ahead. Send the applicants home. I have to dress for dinner. It's been a long day for both of us, and it's going to be an even longer night."

"For one of us." David chuckled. "All right, Reese. Until ten tomorrow."

Reese nodded, then turned back into the next room.

David Alexander moved forward to address the crowd of women. "I'm sorry, ladies, but that will be all for the day."

An irate voice resounded through the crowd. "What do you mean that will be all?"

"I mean that we've finished taking applications and interviewing for the remainder of the evening. Those of you who are qualified and still interested in the position may report here at ten tomorrow morning to resume the screening process," David said calmly.

"But we've been here all day," wailed a big-boned blonde in the back of the room.

"As have I, miss," David acknowledged, "and I'm sure you must be even wearier than I. Go home. Get some rest. I assure you I'll await you in the morning." David dismissed the women from his mind and began gathering the applications and handwritten notes scattered across his desk.

Faith stood rooted in place, too tired to move and too numb to think. Women jostled her on all sides as they made their way toward the stairs. She caught snatches of conversation and tired grumbling through the rustle of skirts and belongings, but little penetrated. Her brain struggled to comprehend David Alexander's words. Tomorrow. Come back tomorrow at ten. Tomorrow the screening process would resume. Faith was torn. She couldn't afford to stay overnight, but she couldn't afford not to. How could she abandon her plan? It was the only plan she had.

David placed his papers in his satchel. He looked up in time to see the young woman swaying on her feet.

"Miss? Is there something you wanted?"

"No," Faith answered. She continued to stare at him.

"Are you sure?"

I want the job! Faith's mind screamed at him. *I need the job!* But she couldn't form those words.

"Miss, are you all right?" David asked.

"I'm fine."

She didn't look fine. As David watched, she swayed again, and this time her knees came close to buckling beneath her. Her chalk-white face was tight and drawn, and her large, expressive eyes were underscored by dark circles.

David instinctively moved toward her. He started to speak, but Faith shook her head and turned to leave.

"Tomorrow," David called urgently. "Be here tomorrow at quarter till ten. I'll see you get in to see him."

Faith said nothing. She straightened her back and kept walking.

David's stare followed her as she trudged down the corridor.

Chapter Three

FAITH STRAIGHTENED HER tired shoulders and smoothed her rumpled skirts as she reached the bottom of the staircase and headed straight for the front desk.

"I will require a room for the night," she announced to the clerk.

"I'm afraid we're full, miss. No vacancies."

"At all?"

"None except the Vice Presidential Suite," he said.

"How much for the suite?" Faith looked around to make certain none of the hotel guests could overhear her vulgar question.

"Fifty dollars a day," the clerk answered proudly. "Naturally it's second in luxury and price only to the Presidential Suite."

"Naturally," Faith agreed, masking her disappointment.

"Shall we send up your luggage?" The clerk's round eyes assessed Faith's shabby dress in a manner that instantly reminded her of his morning predecessor.

"No, thank you," Faith told him. "I don't settle for second best. It's the Presidential Suite or nothing." She stared down her nose at the clerk, gathering her skirts in her hand. "Good evening, sir."

With her head held high, Faith walked out of the Madison Hotel.

"Cab, miss?" the doorman asked as Faith walked out of the hotel.

"No, thank you."

"But it's raining again, miss."

"I won't melt," Faith assured him. "I've been wet before."

"Will you be staying with us, miss?" The doorman was older than the haughty clerks inside the building and full of concern for the young woman.

Faith shook her head. "No vacancies."

"The lawmakers are all in town. Congress is still in session. There's not a room to be had in Washington."

"It doesn't matter." Her shoulders slumped. "Thanks anyway." She managed a half smile for the doorman and started off down the street toward the station and the train home to Richmond.

MINUTES LATER REESE Jordan hurried down the front steps of the hotel and climbed into his waiting carriage. He stared idly out the rain-splattered window. As the driver urged the horses into a trot, Reese focused his attention on the wet scenery.

It had been a disaster of a day from dawn until dusk. The response to that tiny ad had been much greater than either he or David had anticipated. It had been incredible.

Thousands of southern widows were looking for employment, and at least two hundred had found their way to the Madison Hotel in Washington in response to Reese's ad, much to the dismay of the overworked hotel staff. The hotel manager had expressed the disapproval of the staff and the other guests at the influx of unchaperoned unmarried women flocking to Reese's suite.

"We are a reputable hotel, Mr. Jordan, not a bordello."

Reese chuckled at the memory of the manager's indignation. As if anyone would confuse the women he'd interviewed with the luscious creatures he visited in the big gray house on G Street in the Tenderloin district on the northwest side of the city during his usual excursions to Washington.

Reese turned away from the window and looked down at his long legs stretched out in front of him. He had narrowed his possibilities down to two women following the day's interviews, but there was a problem.

Although they both met his carefully adopted criteria to the letter, he wasn't interested in forming a liaison, however temporary, with either one. He told himself the brunette was too cold and mercenary and the blonde was too warm and available, but the truth was much more basic. Neither of the candidates stirred his blood. Reese hadn't even considered that possibility until today.

He hadn't seen a woman during the entire day who appealed to him on that most basic level— until the brief moment when his gaze met and locked with her huge smoke-gray eyes. She had struck a chord within him; then she had vanished, leaving Reese unsettled.

He turned back to the window in time to see a man walking a few steps behind a black-skirted figure. As he watched, the man broke into a run and grabbed the woman's left arm. She stopped suddenly and swung her free arm at his ear. A flash of silver glinted under the street lamp as the thief slit her purse strings and shoved her to the ground.

Reese reacted instantly. Shouting to the driver to stop the carriage, he leaped out and raced after the man.

Minutes later the chase was over. The woman's assailant melted into the dark side streets before Reese was able to catch him. He spent several moments in a futile search of the area before he retraced his steps, hurrying back to the victim.

She sat huddled on the ground, cold, wet, and muddied. She turned as Reese approached and clenched her fists, prepared to defend herself from further attack with the only weapons available.

"It's all right," Reese assured her. "I won't hurt you. Let me help you." He reached out a gloved hand.

Faith looked up.

Those eyes. Once again Reese was devastated by the look in those haunting gray eyes. A rush of tenderness rocked him down to his toes. "You."

Faith stared at the face of her rescuer. She took his offered hand, moving as if in a dream toward the only secure thing she could find.

Reese pulled her to her feet. "Are you all right? Did he hurt you?" Angry, urgent words spilled from his lips as he ran his gloved hands over her face and down her shoulders and arms, anxiously searching for signs of injury.

"He stole my purse." Faith held her left arm up

for inspection. The cords were still looped around her wrist, dangling in the air, holding nothing.

"Your purse? Forget your purse. Did he harm you?" Reese held her wrist toward the glow from the street lamp and pushed back her sleeve. An angry red abrasion encircled the tender flesh around her wrist. "I was afraid he'd cut you." Before he could stop himself, Reese rubbed his thumb across her injured wrist as if to erase the damage.

Faith inhaled. Her pulse leaped in response to the riotous emotions bursting through her at his touch. She opened her mouth to speak, but words failed her. She stood before him without moving, her teeth worrying her full bottom lip, her deep gray eyes staring up at him.

Reese caught himself before he drowned in their depths. His fingers caressed the back of her gloved hand for a bare second before he abruptly dropped her hand and stepped back.

"It's freezing out here. Let's get you inside. Can you walk?"

Faith nodded and took a step forward, but her knees seemed to turn to water. She wavered in his grasp.

Reese cursed beneath his breath and swung her up into his arms.

Faith rested against him. Heat emanated from his flesh and warmed her through the layers of clothing separating them. She was astonished by the warmth. He took a step toward his carriage before she found her voice. "My purse!"

"It's long gone."

"But—"

"Forget it. It can be replaced."

"But my money—"

"Is only money. Not worth risking your life. I couldn't believe my eyes when you tried to fight him." Reese struggled for words. "Confound it, woman, the next time someone tries to steal your purse, give it to him. Don't lift a finger to fight him. You little idiot, he was twice your size and carrying a knife." Reese's long legs covered the distance from the sidewalk to the coach.

"But he stole everything." Faith's voice was muffled by the fabric of his coat. "He got away with it."

"And you got away with a scratch and some bruises. It could have been much worse." Reese paused as his driver opened the door of the coach.

"Is the lady all right, sir?"

"Aside from being cold and wet and a bit shaken up, the lady appears to be fine, Murray." Reese stepped inside the coach and settled Faith on the seat, tucking the lap robe securely around her. "Let's go."

"Yes, sir."

"Where are you taking me?"

Reese looked down at the woman beside him. Her face was a pale translucent ivory except for her straight little nose, which was reddened with cold, and her shimmering gray eyes. Her eyes were the largest thing about her, he decided, and the loveliest.

"I was on my way to dinner. Have you eaten?"

Faith shook her head.

"Then you'll join me."

Faith shook her head again.

"Why not?"

"My purse is gone. I have no money."

God, but she was persistent, Reese thought. "Forget about it. Worrying won't solve anything."

"That's easy for you to say. You didn't lose anything," Faith reminded him.

"That's true," Reese agreed, "but I have enough for both of us. I'll buy you dinner. You can pay me back when you recover your loss. Fair enough?"

"No."

"Why not?"

"I'm not hungry." Her stomach growled loudly.

He smiled. "What if I told you I don't like to eat alone?"

"I'd want to know how you know, since you've probably never eaten alone," Faith mumbled, trying to hold on to her dignity.

"What was that?" Reese asked. "I didn't quite hear what you said."

Faith met his eyes and knew he'd heard every word. "I said I would be delighted to join you for dinner."

"Smart girl." Reese banged on the roof of the coach and shouted out the change in destination.

"WERE YOU REALLY coming here to dinner?" Faith asked. "Or were you going someplace a little more formal?"

They were sitting in straight-backed pine chairs at a table covered with red-checked linen in one of Washington's little-known restaurants.

Reese glanced down at his black evening wear and grinned at his companion. "Guilty as charged. I was supposed to make an appearance at a boring reception given by the British ambassador."

Faith looked up from her menu and found his rich brown eyes fixed on her. "I'm sorry you missed your reception."

"There will be other receptions," Reese said easily. "What will you have for dinner?"

Faith remembered, suddenly, the tantalizing aromas from David Alexander's noonday meal and ordered from memory. "Roast beef, mashed potatoes with gravy, biscuits, garden peas, and apple cobbler for dessert. And coffee, lots of coffee. Do you have real coffee?"

"We have real coffee, ma'am, but no apple cobbler," the waiter answered.

Faith's eager expression crumpled in disappointment. "Apple pie?"

The waiter shook his head.

"Oh, well . . ."

Reese opened his wallet and, removing a bill, pressed it into the waiter's hand. "I'll have the same. And find some apple pie."

"That was very nice of you," Faith told him. "I haven't had apple pie in a long time."

Her compliment made him uncomfortable. "I didn't do it for you," Reese told her. "I did it for myself. I have a taste for apple pie, too."

"Oh."

"How long?"

"What?" Faith was confused by the abrupt question.

"How long since you had apple pie?"

"Since the end of the war." It had probably been longer than that, Faith realized. The apple trees on the plantation had been blasted to perdition by mortar shells shortly after the fall of Petersburg, and now that the war was over, apples were a luxury she couldn't afford.

"Your drawl is southern," Reese commented. "Washington, Virginia, or Maryland?"

"Virginia. Richmond."

"You're a long way from home, Miss . . ."

"Collins. Faith Collins."

"Reese Jordan." He extended his hand across the table. Faith placed her hand in his. She had removed her gloves, and the feel of his skin against hers jolted her. His hand was big and warm, the knuckles sprinkled with coarse black hair; his palm callused in several places. Seeing her hand engulfed in his made her aware of the difference in their coloring. His skin was bronzed by exposure to the sun; hers was smoother, softer, pale in comparison.

Reese, too, was struck by the difference. He felt her shiver and a vivid mental picture of Faith Collins lying naked beneath him, her smooth pale skin covered by his hard bronzed body, flashed in his brain. He abruptly withdrew his hand and cleared his throat. "Tell me about yourself. Why were you walking alone after dark?"

"I was on my way to the train depot. Headed home."

"To Richmond?" He arched his right eyebrow. "What brought you to Washington?"

Faith looked up at him. I came for the job, Faith thought, you know I did. You saw me. "I came to apply for a job. At the Madison Hotel." Her words were sharper than she intended.

"Why?" he wanted to know.

"Why does anyone apply for a job?" Faith countered. "I want to work."

"Interesting," he commented.

"What's so interesting about that? People apply for jobs every day." Her temper was beginning to assert itself.

"You mention work," Reese reminded her, "but you don't say anything about needing money. It leads to some very interesting possibilities." He lowered his voice to a husky rumble.

"Do you think I'd apply for a job if I didn't need money?"

"You might. It would depend on the job."

If he could pretend not to recognize her from this afternoon, she could do the same. "What's your interest, Mr. Jordan? Does it matter to you what my reasons are?"

"I understood that the applicants for that particular position would be returning tomorrow." He sounded nonchalant.

"I won't."

"Any particular reason?" Reese didn't like baiting her, but he sure as hell wasn't going to let himself go soft because she had beautiful eyes. Lots of women had pretty eyes.

"I don't see that that's any of your business." Faith picked up her gloves. "I appreciate the offer of dinner, but why don't we—"

"Eat," he suggested.

"What?"

"Eat, Miss Collins. Our dinner has arrived."

Faith wanted to walk away, to throw the offer of dinner back into his handsome face, but the smell of roast beef made her swallow her pride. "But . . ."

"We can talk after we eat. You must be starving."

She was. And since she'd already swallowed her pride and succumbed to the aroma of roast beef, she decided that she might as well eat it. If she didn't like his conversation, she would leave after dinner.

Faith fought her instinct to wolf down the food on her plate. She forced herself to savor each morsel. She took four bites of everything on her plate, then reluctantly laid her fork down.

Reese looked up from his own meal in time to catch the wistful expression on Faith's face as she placed her fork on her plate. "Is your dinner all right?"

"It's wonderful," she admitted before blotting her mouth with her napkin.

"Then why don't you finish it?"

"It isn't polite for a lady to clean her plate in the company of a gentleman." Faith recited her mother's axiom.

"Blast politeness," he said curtly. "How long has it been since you've eaten?"

"Breakfast."

"And when was that?"

"Before dawn this morning," Faith admitted.

"Are you still hungry?"

Faith stared down at her plate and nodded.

"Then finish your dinner before it gets cold. Even a condemned man is entitled to a good meal." He spoke harshly, but the expression in his eyes was soft. "If you don't, you won't get any pie."

She looked so wounded at this prospect that Reese instantly regretted his joke. "Where I come from it's impolite not to eat the meal a gentleman buys for you." He pushed Faith's plate back in front of her.

"I've never heard that before. Where are you from?"

"I'll tell you if you promise to eat your dinner."

Faith picked up her fork and resumed eating. He was quiet for so long, she thought he had forgotten to answer her question.

"The West," Reese told her.

"Wyoming Territory?"

"I live there now."

She prodded for an answer. "And before?"

"Indian Territory, Texas, and the Dakota Territory."

"During the war?"

"And before." He leaned back in his chair, allowing the waiter to remove his empty plate and replace it with a thick slice of apple pie and a cup of steaming coffee.

Faith eyed his pie and began to chew a little faster.

Reese smiled in spite of himself. "You'll get your piece. I promise."

Faith finished the last bit of roast beef and pushed her plate aside once again. In a matter of seconds, the waiter whisked her dinner plate away and brought her a slice of apple pie and a cup of coffee. Faith tasted the dessert. It was heavenly.

Reese couldn't keep his eyes off her face as she ate the apple pie. He sucked in his breath as she licked a speck of cinnamon-coated crust from her bottom lip.

"Aren't you going to eat yours?" she asked.

Reese looked at his own dish. He'd barely touched his pie. "Why don't you finish it?" he suggested, replacing her empty plate with his.

He forced himself to look at other things as she finished his pie, positive he wouldn't be able to withstand another assault on his senses if he watched. He was damned uncomfortable as it was. He pulled out his watch and flipped it open just to have something to do.

"What time is it?"

Reese turned his attention back to his companion. She had eaten the second slice of pie and was enjoying her coffee. "Time to talk."

"What about?"

"About the job you applied for."

"I didn't apply. I stood in line all day waiting to apply." Though her words were carefully chosen, her bitter disappointment was apparent.

"There's always tomorrow," he reminded her.

"Not for me."

It would be better to keep his mouth shut, Reese told himself, better for both of them if he ignored her obvious disappointment and let her go back to Richmond. He should choose someone else. Anyone else. Someone who was less innocent.

"Do you want the job?"

"Yes, very much."

"Then tell me about yourself," Reese told her.

"Why?" She knew why, but she wanted him to admit he had seen her standing in line.

"Because I'm the man doing the hiring." Reese fixed his brown-eyed gaze on her.

She lifted her cup and cradled it in both hands, savoring the warmth. Her left hand covered her right. Reese stared at the sight.

She wore a ring on the third finger of her left hand, a thin gold band. He noticed it immediately, a tiny slash of gold marring her pale hand. His dark brows drew together in a frown as he studied it.

Faith followed his gaze to the wedding band. Hannah had cried when she took it from her own finger and handed it to her. Faith hadn't wanted to accept it, but she was supposed to be a widow. Aunt Virt's ring was too big, and Agnes couldn't get hers off her arthritic hand.

"You're married."

"Widowed," Faith murmured. Her expressive gray eyes were shadowed, unreadable. She wished she hadn't worn the ring.

"The war?" Damn the ring. He wished she hadn't worn it. He didn't really want to know.

Faith nodded to keep from lying outright.

"Children?"

"There's only Joy. She's five," Faith hedged.

"Oh, a girl." Reese was vaguely aware of his disappointment. He had asked for an experienced widow. Why was he disappointed to have gotten one?

"Is there something wrong with that? Joy is well behaved and smart. She wouldn't be any trouble." He didn't reply, so Faith continued, "Your ad said a child was acceptable. I wouldn't think of going to Wyoming without her."

"No, of course not," Reese remarked. "Is there anyone else? Other family? Parents, brothers, in-laws?"

Faith shook her head and Reese breathed a sigh of relief. "I do have two aunts, but I'm sure they'll stay in Richmond."

Reese knew they would stay in Richmond. The little girl was bad enough. He wasn't about to get tangled up with more of her family. This was, after all, a business arrangement. "Tell me more."

Faith did. She talked through another cup of coffee, then stopped to smother a yawn and barely missed placing her elbow in her cup. Her eyelids were beginning to droop. Reese realized his companion was practically asleep at the table.

Faith smothered another yawn. "I'm sorry. I don't know why I'm so sleepy."

Reese pulled his gold watch out of his pocket once again and opened the lid. "It's nearly ten. You've had a long day."

"Ten? It can't be ten." Faith shot up from her chair, tumbling it over in her haste. "I have to be on the nine o'clock train. It's the last one."

"You've missed it." Reese fumbled with the chair as he attempted to extricate Faith from her place between the overturned chair and the table. "You'll have to get a room for the night."

"There aren't any rooms; Congress is still in session. And even if I had a room, I couldn't pay for it. I've lost all my money." Her gray eyes were wide with panic as she looked up at Reese. "Where's my cloak? And what did I do with my gloves? My aunts will be so worried. Take me to the station."

"Confound it, woman, you've missed the train. You aren't going home tonight." Damn her eyes! Did he have to solve all her problems for her? "You can stay with me."

"That wouldn't be proper," Faith replied primly.

"I suppose leaving you to sleep on a bench in a train depot, prey to all sorts of vermin, would be more proper?" Reese argued. "There's plenty of room in my suite. And David will be there to act as a chaperon."

"What about my aunts? They're expecting me."

"I'll telegraph them and tell them you've been delayed." Reese handed her her cloak and waited impatiently as she buttoned it up under her chin.

"Let's get out of here." Reese put his hand beneath Faith's elbow and led her out of the restaurant and into his carriage.

They settled into the leather cushions of the coach. Reese gave the lap robe to Faith. She snuggled into the warmth of the blanket and was asleep before they had gone two blocks.

Reese watched her from across the coach. She was slumped against the interior wall. The wheels of the vehicle rumbled through a deep rut. Faith's head bounced against the wall. Reese winced at the sight, but maintained his distance. Her head bumped against the coach three more times, but she slept on, undisturbed.

She continued to sleep as the carriage rolled to a stop in front of the Madison Hotel. And she didn't awaken when Reese lifted her from the vehicle and carried her inside and up the stairs to the Presidential Suite.

Reese laid her on his bed and undressed her with practiced ease. He was careful not to move her more than was necessary. He didn't want to risk waking her. He studied her features as he revealed the body hidden beneath layers of clothing.

God, she was thin. Too thin. Her collarbone and hipbones jutted out through the well-worn cotton shift. With her short stature and slight build, she looked lost amid the stark white sheets on the massive bed. But the sight of her lush, pink-tipped, breasts, visible through the thin fabric, and the shadow of the dark triangle nestled between her slender thighs reassured Reese. Faith Collins might be slim and petite, but she was not a child in any sense of the word. She was a lovely, desirable woman.

Reese slipped her ugly black shoes from her feet and drew the covers over her.

Chapter Four

THE LOW RUMBLING snore of a deeply sleeping man came from the depths of the sofa. David Alexander chuckled to himself. After the long night, Reese apparently hadn't had the strength to make it to his bedroom.

David tiptoed to the sofa and looked down at his cousin. Damn, but he looked miserable sprawled out on that uncomfortable couch. David decided to let Reese sleep a while longer. The women wouldn't be arriving for an hour or so.

David backed away from the sofa, then walked to the corner of the room and pulled the bell rope. When the bellboy arrived, he ordered breakfast and a pot of strong coffee.

Reese awoke to the sound of voices in the doorway and sat up on the sofa in time to hear David order breakfast.

"Double that order," Reese said quietly.

David smiled. "That kind of night, huh?" he teased.

"What?" Reese raked his hand through his thick hair, trying to restore order to the unruly strands.

"I said you must have had a busy night."

"Why?"

"Why?" David mimicked. "Don't pull that innocent act on me, Reese Alexander Jordan. When you sleep late, then wake up with a wicked appetite, it can only mean one thing."

"That I was tired and now I'm hungry?" Reese suggested.

"That your lady friend kept you up very late and that you did a lot more than carry on a polite conversation."

"Actually, I did have dinner and some polite conversation," Reese informed his cousin.

"Save that line for her angry father, brother, fiancé, or husband. I know you too well." David grinned at Reese. "You're still in your evening clothes and you were snoring on the couch. What time did you stumble in, anyway?"

"I stumbled in, as you put it, at half-past midnight, and please keep your laughter at a minimum and your voice lowered. There's a woman sleeping in the next room."

"In your room? Alone?"

"It was better than allowing her to sleep on a bench in the train station." Reese stood up and stretched, working his head from side to side to remove the kinks from his neck. "Where is that damn waiter with the coffee?"

"You spent the night on that god-awful sofa when you had a warm woman in your bed?" David answered the knock on the door.

A waiter stood in the doorway with a tray of steaming coffee.

"That's right," Reese muttered as he joined David at the door. He took the tray and handed the man a silver dollar. "Hurry up with breakfast," he ordered before David could respond.

David closed the door behind the waiter, watching as Reese set the coffee on the table in front of the sofa.

"Is that all you plan to tell me?" David couldn't hide his burning curiosity.

"That's it. At least until I've had my morning coffee. Sit down. I'll pour you a cup."

FAITH SNUGGLED DEEPER into the warmth of the covers, dreaming of the time before the war when the sound of her brothers' good-natured arguments filled the morning air and the tantalizing aroma of coffee wafted through the house. She turned and stretched luxuriously in the big bed, her warm arms sliding across the crisp, cool sheets next to her. She was alone.

Her eyes flew open to focus on the bedroom wall. The wallpaper was strange. The flowers on it were different from the faded flowers on her bedroom wall. And where was Joy? There was too much room in the bed. She could move around, even stretch, without touching the warm little body that was normally sprawled all over her. What was going on?

She smelled coffee, real coffee. It had been years since she'd been able to buy genuine beans.

Faith pushed the covers aside and sat on the edge of the bed. She shivered with cold and looked around for her clothes. Her dress was nowhere in sight, but a dark brown velvet robe lay across the foot of the bed. Faith slipped it on and padded across the cold floor to open the bedroom door.

She stopped dead at the sight of the two men seated on the sofa drinking coffee.

The memory of the evening spent in the company of Reese Jordan flashed through Faith's mind, and the warmth of a blush stained her face a vivid pink.

Reese lowered his coffee cup and focused on the vision before him.

David nearly dropped his cup. It wobbled on the saucer, sloshing hot coffee on his hand.

She stood in the doorway. Her dark hair had slipped out of its pins. It hung past her slim shoulders to her hips. Her gray eyes were wide; her lips were red and slightly swollen from sleep. She was engulfed by Reese's brown velvet robe, completely covered from her chin to her bare feet, yet Reese wondered if he had ever seen a woman look quite so desirable, so kissable. She looked as if she had just come from her lover's bed. His bed.

"Good morning," Reese greeted her in a voice that sounded remarkably normal. "Sleep well?"

"Yes, I suppose so. Thank you."

"You're welcome."

Faith's fingers tightened on the lapels of his robe, and her eyes studied her toes peeking out from under the hem. She was extremely aware of the intimacy of the situation, of Reese Jordan's hot gaze, and of her threadbare shift beneath his robe.

David cleared his throat, shifting uncomfortably in his seat. "Coffee, ma'am?" He indicated the pot and extra cup.

Faith turned a deeper shade of pink. "Actually, I . . . um . . ."

"Down the hall, last door on the right."

Faith managed a grateful nod and hurried out of the suite.

The door had hardly closed behind her before David began bombarding Reese with questions. "She's your lady friend? Your companion for the evening? You spent the night with her?"

"Not exactly. I spent the evening with her. But she spent the night here. With you," Reese explained.

"And where were you?" David wanted to know.

"Downstairs at the bar. Drinking."

"You left her here? Alone? With me in the next room?"

Reese nodded. "She was asleep. I figured she was safer alone with you than with me."

David glared at his cousin. "Did you ever think your confidence in me might be misplaced?"

"You're a gentleman, David."

"That doesn't make me a eunuch."

"I know," Reese told him. "That's why I didn't wake you when I brought her in. I thought she'd be a lot safer if you didn't know she was here."

"What about her reputation? She was here yesterday. I saw her in line with the other women."

"I saw her, too, when I was standing in the doorway talking to you. She disappeared in the crowd."

"But you found her at the British embassy? And brought her here?" David speculated.

"No, of course not," Reese replied. Then, seeing David's puzzled face, he began to elaborate. "I rescued her last night. She was walking to the train station when she was accosted by a thief. He knocked her to the ground and snatched her purse. I happened to see the attack on my way to the embassy. I jumped out to give chase."

"So you brought her back here before you left

for the bar?" David asked, wondering how he had missed them.

"I took her to dinner first. She hadn't eaten all day. She was hungry and had no money. She missed the last train to Richmond and it was either bring her here or have her sleep on a bench at the train station."

"She allowed you to bring her here?" David wondered aloud.

"She didn't have a choice. She fell asleep in the carriage after dinner."

"You could have awakened her," David pointed out.

"Not this one."

"Why not?"

"Because she's a southern lady," Reese answered, "and I don't have a signed contract in my hands. Yet."

"Then you talked to her about the job?"

Reese nodded.

"And she agreed?"

"She says she needs the job, but I get the feeling she doesn't really understand what I want her to do."

"How could she not understand? The ad was pretty clear."

Reese stood up and began to pace. "Who knows what goes on in the mind of a lady?"

"I thought you did."

Reese turned to look at his cousin. "What ever gave you that idea?"

"You did," David said quietly. "You've always been such a ladies' man."

"I don't deal with ladies. I deal with prostitutes,

tarts, whores, and the occasional neglected mistress. I don't deal with ladies anymore."

"Then, dammit, Reese, why advertise for one? Why not let one of your tarts have your child?"

"Because, dammit, my son is going to have a heritage he can be proud of. He's going to be respected."

"Then marry someone and do this the right way."

"Out of the question," Reese said.

"There are plenty of nice women—"

"Yes, there are," Reese agreed, "but not for us. We're mixed-bloods, David, and while we're proud of our heritage, most nice women are horrified."

"All women aren't like Boston society debutantes."

"Only the proper ladies," Reese sneered.

"I never realized your experience at Harvard had made you so bitter," David said thoughtfully as he refilled Reese's cup with coffee.

"I'm not bitter," Reese told him. "I'm realistic."

"You think this plan of yours is realistic?" David asked.

"Of course it is," Reese said. "With enough money you can buy just about anyone or anything." Reese broke off at the light tap on the door. He walked to the door and pulled it open.

Faith stood in the hallway clutching his robe tightly against her.

"Come in and have some coffee." Reese's voice was a soft, rumbling purr. "You must be freezing." He frowned at the sight of her bare toes curling against the cold floor. He should have remembered to leave a pair of socks on the foot of the bed along with his bathrobe.

"I don't want to intrude on your conversation," Faith said.

"It's no intrusion," David assured her. "We're just passing the time while we wait for the breakfast tray."

Faith's eyes sparkled. "You've ordered breakfast?"

"There should be enough for a small army. Will that be sufficient?"

Faith's cheeks colored with embarrassment. "Don't go to any trouble on my account. You bought my dinner last night. You're not under any obligation to purchase my breakfast." She looked at the floor to keep from meeting his gaze.

"My cousin was teasing." David stepped into the breach. "I apologize if he embarrassed or offended you. Reese is always ill-tempered before breakfast."

"I'm not offended," Faith admitted. "And I would appreciate breakfast."

"Well, that's settled," David pronounced. "Think nothing of it. Come in and join us in the wait. Allow me to introduce myself. I'm David Alexander, Reese's attorney, business partner, friend, and first cousin." He offered Faith his hand as Reese ushered her into the room, then closed the door behind them.

"I'm Faith Collins," she said. "It's a pleasure to meet you, Mr. Alexander, but I really shouldn't intrude on your breakfast." She headed for the safety of the bedroom.

"Nonsense." Reese took her elbow and led her to the sofa. "Sit down, Mrs. Collins. You aren't intruding."

"But I'm not properly dressed," she protested.

"You look fine. Besides, it's early. You don't have to be completely dressed to eat breakfast." He smiled.

Faith wanted to point out the impropriety of dining alone with two men, but found herself unable to utter the words. Something about Reese Jordan's devastating smile affected her sensibilities. Her logical protests vanished. She smiled back at him as she graciously accepted the cup of coffee he placed in her hand. "Thank you, Mr. Jordan."

"You're very welcome, Mrs. Collins." The teasing light in his dark eyes matched the warmth of his smile. Reese looked as if he might elaborate, but a single sharp rap on the door interrupted him. "That must be breakfast."

"I'll get the door." David walked to the door to admit the waiter.

"Mr. Alexander, I must speak to Mr. Jordan about the impropriety of this situation immediately." Howard Clegg, manager of the Madison Hotel, shoved his way past David and into the Presidential Suite. The waiter, pushing a cart laden with breakfast, followed in Clegg's wake as a small crowd of curious job applicants filled the doorway.

"I knew something unsavory was going on up here!" the hotel manager crowed triumphantly. "I knew it as soon as the night clerk reported seeing you, Mr. Jordan"—he pointed his index finger in the direction of Reese's nose—"carrying this . . . this woman up here late last night." Clegg spat out his last sentence and directed his accusing finger at Faith.

Faith gasped and stepped back to avoid Mr.

Clegg's pointing finger and the malicious gleam in
his tiny eyes. David made a move in Faith's direction as the meddlesome onlookers pushed farther
into the room, but his cousin was quicker. Reese
stepped between Faith and the hotel manager, using
his body to shield her from the accusatory faces of
the crowd.

Reese Jordan stared disdainfully down at the thin,
insistent finger jabbing him in the chest, then looked
the loathsome little ferret in the eye.

"I suggest you remove your finger from my chest
before I take the liberty of removing it for you."
Reese spoke quietly, smoothly, as if he had casually
suggested opening a window or hanging up a hat,
but that deliberately soft voice carried a definite
warning.

"Are you threatening me, sir?" Howard Clegg's
face reddened, and his voice rose in pitch, but he
was wise enough or wary enough to remove his
finger from the middle of Reese's broad chest.

"I assure you, Mr. Clegg, that I would never
threaten you," Reese said as he made a show of
polishing the onyx stud in the center of his shirt.

Clegg smiled suddenly and straightened his
shoulders to make himself appear taller.

"I will, however, warn you against making further accusations or maligning the lady's character,"
Reese continued softly, watching the expression on
the manager's face change from exultation to fury.

"Why, you—" Clegg stepped forward, but was
brought up short by David Alexander's firm grasp
on his arm. "You can't waltz in here under the
guise of business and proceed to interview these . . .
these . . . soiled doves . . . these whores!" He flung

out his arm to indicate the crowd of women.

"Who're you callin' whores, mister?" came a shout from the angry women.

"Gentlemen! Ladies!" David stepped in to soothe the tempers of the antagonists and prevent a full-blown brawl. "Calm yourselves."

"Calm ourselves?" another woman shouted. "How can we be calm when that little weasel stands there bold as brass and calls us whores?"

"Yeah," agreed the woman standing closest to Reese and Faith. "We ain't the whores around here. She is. He's the one tryin' out the candidates, and she's the one that let him. Look at her standing there in nothing more than a dressing gown. A man's dressing gown." She eyed Faith jealously as she spat her vile insults in Reese's direction.

"Ladies." Reese spoke through clenched teeth. "You misunderstand the situation. Mrs. Collins is the woman I selected yesterday for the job. She has graciously accepted the position."

"I'll bet," someone in the group said with a sneer.

"You didn't select her yesterday," someone else said accusingly. "I was in line way ahead of her, and I didn't even get to talk to Mr. Alexander. You might've done some selecting, but you didn't do it yesterday afternoon."

The woman standing closest to Reese stepped around him and grabbed Faith by the lapels of the velvet robe. "You might say she slept her way into this job ahead of time."

"Well, since sleepin' with the boss *is* the job, who can blame the tart for usin' her talent to get it?" The accusation hung in the air before a series of malicious chuckles filled the room.

Faith stared with contempt and pity at the woman holding on to her, then grasped the woman's wrists and pushed them away.

The women turned their attention to Faith, waiting for an explosion, but Faith Collins surprised them. She turned with great dignity and walked away from the crowd and into the bedroom. They tensed, waiting for her to slam the door, but again she surprised them by quietly closing it behind her.

"Out!" Reese's shout echoed through the stillness. "All of you—out! Except you." Suspending the hotel manager's retreat with a dark, angry stare, Reese uttered a soft promise. "I'll deal with you on a personal level later. David, will you show Mr. Clegg to his office and keep him there?" Reese issued his orders, then followed Faith's path to the bedroom door, his long legs rapidly closing the distance.

Chapter Five

REESE TAPPED AT the door. Silence answered him. He turned the doorknob and stepped inside the room. The sight of Faith Collins standing beside the bed stopped him in his tracks.

She was wearing only a threadbare cotton chemise and pantalets as she struggled with the long laces of her corset. His brown velvet robe lay in a puddle around her bare feet. She turned at the sound.

Reese's heart thumped hard in his chest. He drew in a breath. She was crying. She didn't utter a sound, but huge tears fell from her gray eyes and rolled down her cheeks. The pain and humiliation in those tears was so evident that Reese could almost smell the salt and taste the bitterness.

Faith looked away in embarrassment and resumed her fumbling efforts with the corset strings.

Reese moved up behind her and took the laces from her hands. Faith sucked in her breath as he approached her. She shivered when his fingers grazed the sensitive flesh of her inner arm as he reached for the stray laces. He pulled her corset closed and began to tie the strings.

Reese's hands lingered at her back after he finished tying her undergarment. The scent of French milled soap, the kind supplied by the hotel, and the tangy salt of tears assailed his nostrils. His hands moved from the laces at her back to caress her upper arms. Long strands of ebony hair had escaped from her hastily arranged bun and clung to the nape of her neck. He experienced an unexpected, unwanted urge. Reese longed to nuzzle the strands of hair aside and plant his lips in their place.

Faith moved. She bowed her head to look down at the floor, exposing the slim column of her neck. Her movement was almost Reese's undoing. He reacted instinctively, bending his head to press his lips against her neck. Her voice, husky and thick with tears, stopped him.

"I'm terribly sorry for the scandal I've caused."

Reese turned her around to face him, but kept his hands on her bare shoulders. "You haven't caused a scandal—yet." He smiled down into her solemn eyes.

"I fell asleep in your carriage," Faith protested.

"Falling asleep in my vehicle wasn't a crime, nor did it cause a scandal."

"How can I explain this situation?" Faith wanted to know. "You heard those women out there. They think that I—"

"Who gives a damn what they think?" Reese demanded. "You know what happened and what didn't happen. We both do."

"But you can't possibly hire someone with a damaged reputation."

So that was the problem, Reese thought. She was worried about losing the job. "Do you want this job?"

"Yes, I do."

"Enough to forget about those women out there and others like them?" Reese needed to know before he made his choice because he wasn't about to cosset her all the way to Wyoming.

"But the scandal . . ." Faith began.

"Honey," Reese said bluntly, "if you take this job, you're going to cause a hell of a scandal, and you won't be able to do a thing about it." He watched her intently as her tongue moistened her lips before she opened her mouth to speak. "If you agree to my terms of employment, there's going to be plenty of talk, whether we like it or not, and there'll be a scandal, too. Are you woman enough to face it, Faith Collins, or will you run away, back to Richmond? Because, whether I like it or not, you seem to be the best woman for this job." He bent his head and captured her lips.

It began as an angry kiss, something Reese couldn't prevent, but it turned into something more. Fire erupted throughout Reese's body as he took her lips and felt her sway against him. He pulled her closer as he deepened his kiss, tangling his hands in her hair before running them down the curve of her spine. The stiff boning of her corset frustrated him, but his hands continued their avid exploration until they reached the bottom of her cotton cage. Reese cupped his large hands around the curve of her derriere, pulling her up against his groin. He groaned in sublime agony.

Faith was overwhelmed by her response to his kiss. She wrapped her arms around his neck and parted her lips to allow his silken tongue to slip through and sample the warm recesses of her mouth. She was surrounded by his arms, his mouth, his hard masculine body, and the taste and touch and smell of him. She melted against him, enjoying the coffee-flavored taste of his kiss and the hot, tangy scent that permeated the air around them. She breathed in that scent and nuzzled closer to its source. Reese groaned again. Faith pulled her mouth away from his, gasping for breath. Her senses swam, her knees threatened to give way at any moment. She tilted her head back as Reese brushed his lips against her closed eyelids before trailing them down her neck to place hot, wet kisses against the tattered lace covering the swells of her breasts. He dipped his tongue into the crevice between the soft mounds and tasted the tart droplets beading her flesh. Faith gasped in reaction, tightening her grip around his neck when her legs suddenly refused to support her weight.

The sound of her sigh and the slamming of a door somewhere outside the bedroom brought Reese to his senses. He opened his eyes and found himself confronted by the loveliness framed by her tight corset. He raised his head and, grinding his teeth against the agony in his loins, forced his arms to relax their hold on Faith Collins.

"Faith."

Faith smiled up at him, the deep gray of her eyes soft and luminous. "Hmm?"

"We're about to cause that scandal," Reese said.

His words instantly sobered Faith. She practically bolted out of his arms and across the room. "I'm sorry."

Reese quirked an eyebrow. "Not as sorry as I am." He walked to the armoir and removed her black dress. He handed it to her, then turned his back while she slipped it on.

"You can turn around now," Faith told him when she had her dress in place and had fastened the numerous jet buttons on the bodice. "Thank you." Her voice wavered.

"Don't thank me! Hell, I doubt very much if I'm doing you a favor by offering you this job." He paced the confines of the bedroom, impatiently raking his fingers through his hair. "I know for a fact I'm not doing myself one."

"I'm a grown woman, Mr. Jordan, and I know exactly what I'm doing."

"I'm not so sure," Reese mused aloud.

"Of course I understand," Faith said. "You explained the position to me last night."

"I lied."

"You what?"

"I lied," Reese repeated. "I lied to you by omitting a few pertinent facts."

"I don't believe it." Faith shook her head. "You wouldn't."

"I did," he affirmed. "Faith, exactly what do you think you'll be expected to do if you decide to take this job?"

"I'm to do as the ad in the paper says. I'm to be a sort of governess to your baby. I'm to provide for your child." Faith walked to where her cloak lay across a chair and removed a battered newspaper. It was folded open to the page containing Reese's advertisement. She looked him in the eye as she placed it in his hand. "See for yourself."

Reese shook his head in disbelief as he read the ad in the Richmond newspaper. The irony of the situation struck him like a blow. He smiled grimly. The best laid plans . . .

"Faith," he said, "I'm not looking for a governess. I'm looking for a mother. I don't want you to provide *for* my child. I want you to *provide* the child. To conceive him, carry him, deliver him, give him to me, and walk away. Forever."

Faith's knees weakened again. She sat down abruptly on the edge of the bed. "I don't believe it."

Reese crossed to the desk and removed a copy of the Washington newspaper ad from the top drawer. He looked her in the eye as he placed it in her hand.

"Oh, my!"

" 'Oh, my'? Is that all you've got to say?" Reese asked.

"You lied to me," she accused.

"I didn't exactly lie to you."

"You just said you did."

"I said I omitted a few pertinent facts," Reese corrected.

"It's the same as lying. You admitted it!"

"So? I just told you the truth," Reese reminded her. "I could have left you in ignorance, let you take the position, and simply . . ." Reese stopped in mid-sentence, suddenly realizing what he was about to reveal and to whom.

"What?" Faith goaded. "What could you simply have done?"

"Nothing."

"Nothing? Nothing? It must have been something. You started to say something. Go ahead,

Mr. Jordan, finish it. Tell me. What could you have
done so simply?" Faith stood up and faced him,
daring him to answer her.

"Seduced you," Reese said softly.

"What?"

"Seduced you, Mrs. Collins. I was going to say
I could have simply seduced you into having my
baby without telling you the truth. Believe me, that
probably would have been easier than this," Reese
said bluntly.

"Oh." Faith opened her mouth to say more, but
words failed her. What could she say? Everything
he said was true. He had proved it only moments
ago when he kissed her and made her forget everything except the feel of his mouth on hers. She
walked to the chair, sat down, and covered her
red face with shaking hands.

He moved away from her chair and began to
pace the room once more. "I don't have to explain
myself to you. The difference in the wording of
the ad in the Richmond paper was a mistake. I
didn't know about it until you showed me your
copy, but I could tell from our conversation that
you had a mistaken notion about the job. Hell!"
He realized he'd spent the past minute explaining
himself to her. "How was I supposed to know you
didn't know? All the others knew."

"You mean all those women in line knew you
wanted one of them to have a baby for you?" Faith
was shocked. "For money?"

"Of course they knew. It was in the ad. And it's
not completely unheard of. There are references to
such contracts in the Bible."

"That doesn't excuse you."

"I'm not asking to be excused. I know what I'm doing, and I have my reasons for doing it this way," Reese told her.

"But to buy a baby . . ." Faith stood up and walked around Reese to stare out the window at the street below.

"I'm not buying a baby," he said. "I'm renting a woman. The same way I would pay someone to clean my house or cook my dinner or—"

"Tend to your other needs?" Faith asked sweetly, suddenly flushed and as angry as he was.

"Exactly," Reese told her. "When you pay for something, you can make sure you get what you want out of the deal. Believe me, honey, if I could do this by myself, I would. I don't like being dependent on anyone for anything, but unfortunately this is something I can't do alone. I don't have a choice."

"Surely you have lady friends," Faith suggested. "You did imply that you excelled in seduction. Surely a lady or two would be more than happy to—"

"I don't sleep with ladies."

"Really?" Faith spat the question at him. "Then I don't think we have a problem."

"Oh, I'm willing to make an exception in your case." He hadn't meant to say that. "For business purposes."

"I see." Faith's cheeks stained with color. "I had no idea I was so irresistible."

"Look, lady"—Reese emphasized the courtesy title—"this deal will benefit both of us. You need money. A southern lady wouldn't dream of leaving her home to become a governess, unless the job paid well. Very well. And I don't know a southern family that doesn't need money."

"I have my reasons for applying for this job." Faith looked him in the eye, daring him to question her.

"Then let's leave it at that. You have your reasons, and I have mine." Reese met her gaze. "It's only business."

"I'm not even sure I like you," Faith told him honestly.

Reese smiled once again, a real smile this time, one that reached his eyes. "You don't have to like a man to do business with him."

"This is rather intimate business."

"All the better. There will be no emotional ties, no entanglements. Nothing permanent. I hire you to do the job, and once it's done you never have to see me again. And because you'll be in Wyoming, no one in Richmond will ever have to know. But you'll be thousands of dollars richer."

"I'll have to think about it."

"Fair enough. But don't take too long. I'm rather pressed for time. The sooner we get started, the sooner we can get it over with."

"How much time do I have?"

"I can spare a few days," Reese grudgingly admitted. "Go home for Christmas. Think about it. You can wire me your answer after the holiday." Reese walked to the bedroom door and opened it. "I'll have David escort you to Richmond."

Faith nodded in acknowledgment as he disappeared through the doorway. She didn't understand how it had happened, but suddenly she was thinking about accepting his bizarre offer. She told herself it was the money. She desperately needed the money.

Faith knew she shouldn't even consider taking the job, for money, for her ladies, or for any other reason, but she was thinking it over. And though she hated to admit it, even to herself, only part of the reason was money.

Chapter Six

"ARE WE APPROACHING Richmond already?" David Alexander looked up from the stack of paperwork in his lap and spoke to Faith for the first time since they'd boarded the train.

Faith stared at him. "Yes."

David removed his watch from its pocket and snapped open the lid. "Only a half hour off schedule. We made very good time." He placed his papers in the satchel on the floor beside his feet. He looked up and caught Faith still staring. "You get used to it," he said.

"What?"

"Traveling by train. If you spend any length of time in Reese's company, you get used to the trains. I always catch up on my paperwork. The ride is so monotonous."

"I apologize for my dull company," Faith said in a small, tight voice.

"Oh, no, Mrs. Collins, I didn't mean to imply you were a dull companion. Far from it. I only meant the journey. Any journey in a public coach is tedious when one is accustomed to traveling in a private car. There isn't anything to do in a public coach except read, sleep, or do needlework. And I

69

didn't bring my mending." He smiled at her, and Faith noticed for the first time his resemblance to Reese.

Faith laughed in spite of herself. "Surely you don't do your own mending."

David pretended to be affronted. "I'll have you know I'm very handy with a needle and thread."

Faith cocked her head to one side, her gray eyes sparkling with mirth. "Then you should fit right in." As soon as the train stopped, she picked up her cape and, bunching her skirts in one hand, stepped into the crowded aisle.

David followed close behind.

"Did you leave your buggy at the livery?" David asked as they stepped from the train to the busy platform.

"No." Faith shook her head.

"I'll hire a hack."

"It isn't very far to my house. We could walk," Faith suggested.

David pointed up to the gray overcast sky. "Looks like more rain. Do you want to chance it?"

Faith shivered. "No."

"I'll hire a hack."

Less than twenty minutes later the hired buggy pulled up beside the dilapidated picket fence surrounding Collins House.

Faith watched as the curtain in the window of the front parlor moved back into place. The door flew open, and a small red-haired woman hurried down the porch steps, carefully avoiding the loose boards.

David Alexander helped Faith out of the buggy.

"Aunt Tempy!" Faith cried as the bundle of energy ran up and embraced her.

"Faith, oh, Faith." Temperance Hamilton hugged her niece as if she had spent years away from home instead of one night. "I missed you so much."

Faith smiled. "I haven't been away that long, Aunt Tempy."

"Well, it seemed like forever. You know I can't tolerate Virt, Agnes, and Hannah for long on my own. Their empty-headed chatter drives me crazy. I'm sure I don't know why the good Lord didn't see fit to give them brains instead of looks. . . . Oh, pardon me for running on like that." Tempy turned to study Faith's escort. "I'll have you thinking I'm no smarter than the others. You must be Mr. Jordan. We got your telegram last night. Bert Winthrop made a special trip out after midnight just to deliver it. And it's a good thing, too. I was beginning to worry about Faith being gone so long."

"Aunt Tempy," Faith interrupted, "you're chattering."

"Good Lord!" Tempy looked mortified at the idea. "Where are my manners? Do come in, Mr. Jordan."

"Actually . . ." David began as Tempy took her niece by the elbow and ushered her toward the house.

"Aunt Tempy, this isn't Mr. Jordan. This is Mr. David Alexander, Mr. Jordan's attorney." Faith stopped on the porch to perform the introductions. "Mr. David Alexander, meet my aunt, Temperance Hamilton."

"You're David Alexander? But we thought . . ." Tempy began.

"Mr. Jordan asked me to see Mrs. Collins home," David explained. "He thought she might need some time to get ready for the journey, and since Christmas is just days away, he thought she would prefer to spend the holiday in the company of her family rather than with strangers." David opened the front door and allowed the women to precede him.

"Oh, Faith!" Tempy was practically jumping up and down with glee. "That means you got the job! How wonderful!" Tempy stepped inside the house and turned toward the front parlor. "Virt! Hannah! Agnes! Joy! He hired her! Our Faith is going to work in Wyoming!"

The other women crowded into the hallway, each trying to hug Faith and to get a better look at the attractive gentleman escorting her.

David studied the women crowded around him. He couldn't believe his eyes. They were all considerably older than Faith, except the little girl, who looked to be no more than five or six. David smiled to himself, enormously pleased to discover that Collins House, while big and full of women, was not some sordid Richmond bordello. David was certain Reese would be even more pleased and relieved. He couldn't wait to tell him.

"Do have a seat, Mr. Alexander." Hannah and Agnes led David to the horsehair sofa, then quickly seated themselves on either side of him. Faith noticed they spread their skirts as they sat down to hide the bayonet holes in the cushions. And, bless them, they had also made certain David sat in the most comfortable spot in the room.

"Would you care for some refreshment?" Tempy asked, politely.

"Tea," Hannah said. "We have some very nice tea. Tempy, you know where I keep it. Would you care for a cup of hot tea, Mr. Alexander?"

When she returned, a few minutes later, Tempy set the tray on the table in front of Hannah. "Will you pour, Hannah?"

"I'd be delighted." Hannah smiled, pleased at the opportunity to preside over a tea table once again.

David Alexander shifted uncomfortably on the sofa between Hannah Colson and Agnes Everett and accepted the cup of tea Mrs. Colson placed in his hands. He waited patiently while she finished pouring tea for the ladies, then took a drink from his cup. He accepted a gingersnap from the plate Tempy offered.

"Oh, please, Mr. Alexander, take another. It's been so long since we've had a gentleman in for tea." Hannah smiled prettily.

"It's time for Joy's nap," Tempy commented. "I'll just take her to bed." She took Joy by the hand. "Say your good-byes."

Joy smiled shyly at the stranger, then hugged each of the older women around the waist. When she reached her sister, she threw her arms around Faith's neck and squeezed her tightly. "I missed you, Faith."

"I missed you, too." Faith brushed a kiss on Joy's brow.

"You're not going away again, are you?"

"Not without you, pumpkin."

"Promise?"

"Cross my heart." Faith solemnly traced a cross above her heart.

"Good." Joy hugged Faith a second time. "Night-night, Faith."

"Good night, angel." She blew kisses at Joy until Tempy led the little girl down the hall to the bedroom the three of them shared.

Hannah, Agnes, and Virt took their cue from Tempy and left the room, leaving Faith alone with David Alexander for the first time since their arrival.

"She calls you Faith," David said.

"What?"

"Your little girl calls you by your given name. It's unusual."

Faith had forgotten about the fiction she had woven for David Alexander and Reese Jordan.

She thought quickly, scrambling for a plausible reason before she answered. "Joy has always been around adults. My aunts and the other ladies call me by my given name. Joy learned to do the same." Faith shrugged. "She's never known anything different." Faith clenched and unclenched her fists while her top teeth worried her bottom lip. She should have thought of this. She should have had Tempy explain the situation to Joy.

"I suppose you're right," David agreed. "Well, I'm going back to Washington. You can give me your answer now if you've made up your mind, or you can telegraph Reese at the Madison after Christmas."

Faith relaxed. Joy hadn't given them away. "I haven't made up my mind yet. I need to think about it."

David studied his surroundings closely. The house had once been elegant, but was now falling down around their heads. Light patches marked the walls where paintings had once hung, the windows were boarded up, and telltale water stains marred the plaster ceiling. The house was in desperate need of repair from roof to basement. David didn't have to be a banker to know the cost of repair was way beyond Faith's present means.

David stood up and retrieved his hat. "I really must be on my way." He bowed and moved toward the front door.

"WELL, WHAT DID you find out about her?" Reese demanded as soon as David stepped inside the door of the Presidential Suite at the Madison Hotel.

"I had a miserable journey, Reese. I'm dying to deliver my report to you, but do you think I could grab a cup of coffee first?" David joked.

"Anything. Just give me the verdict." Reese stalked to the silver coffee pot sitting on a tray beside his desk.

"You're in a generous mood today. How about a pay raise and your share of the Union Pacific stock along with the coffee?"

"How about a twisted arm and unemployment?" Reese shot back as he handed David a cup of coffee and took the damp overcoat his cousin offered in return. "What did you learn?"

"I learned that Faith Collins is a very proud woman."

"Tell me something I haven't learned on my own."

"Well, she lives on Clary Street in Richmond in a house that's falling down around her head. She shares it with her daughter and four other women—two aunts and two relatives by marriage."

"Her side or his?" Reese wanted to know.

"Hers. They're sisters-in-law of one of her aunts. Her daughter, Joy, is an adorable little girl of five or six, judging from her missing front teeth."

"Five," Reese remarked absently, remembering Faith's description of her family. "Any men?"

David couldn't control his grin at the innocent-sounding question. "While I was there I saw an army lieutenant."

"I was afraid of that. She made everything sound too good to be true. I knew there had to be men in the picture. How else are five women going to earn enough money to live on?" Reese began to pace the length of the room.

"They take in sewing."

"What?" Reese stopped in his tracks and stared at his cousin.

"I said they take in sewing. The lieutenant was there because he'd ripped his jacket." David finished his coffee and sat down on the sofa to watch Reese resume his nervous pacing. "Give me a hand with these. My feet are frozen." He lifted one booted foot in Reese's direction.

Reese yanked the wet boot from David's foot and dropped it beside the sofa. "Sewing? Making dresses, that sort of thing?" Reese searched his memory. She was dressed in rags. "Can she earn a living like that?" With the exception of his maternal grandmother and a few other women at the ranch, all the women of Reese's acquaintance were outfitted in the latest fashions from London or Paris.

"No," David told him. "They call themselves the Richmond Ladies Sewing Circle. They don't make ladies' fashions. They make quilts, embroider, and take in mending, mostly from the soldiers stationed in Richmond."

"Union soldiers?"

"Apparently."

"Like the army lieutenant." Reese resumed his pacing.

David nodded. "He came to the front door bearing a basket of fruit. A Christmas present for the ladies for treating him decent, he said. They refused to take it. Said that it wouldn't be proper for a household of unmarried women to accept a gift from a gentleman. The lieutenant turned right around, walked to his buggy, and proceeded to mutilate his jacket."

"What?"

"He ripped off every button, every insignia, and slit the sleeves. Then he went back to the front porch and asked them to mend it. He told them he'd spent his pay on Christmas, but he would trade them the basket in exchange for repairs. Faith graciously accepted the jacket and the fruit."

"Just like that?" Reese stopped, then turned to look at David.

"Just like that."

Reese shook his head in disbelief, then raked his fingers through his hair in an attempt to restore some order to the thick black strands. "She wouldn't take a basket of fruit from a soldier she'd met before, but she'll consider having my baby for money?"

"Yep," David confirmed. "Unless she changes her mind."

"Is there a chance of that?"

"Of course. There's always a chance."

"She won't change her mind," Reese said confidently. "She needs the money too badly." But he decided to sweeten the deal.

For the next half hour, Reese asked David very specific questions about the house in Richmond and about each member of the household.

Chapter Seven

"DO YOU WANT to talk about it?" Tempy asked suddenly.

"Talk? About what?" Faith turned to face her aunt. They were sitting at the kitchen table, relaxing after clearing away the remains of the Christmas feast.

It was quiet. Hannah and Virt were napping, and Agnes was busy knitting a scarf in a corner of the parlor. Joy was pretending to serve tea from a miniature tea set to the dolls seated in tiny chairs at a tiny table in another corner of the parlor.

Faith observed the procedure from a distance, carefully noting the differences in the two dolls seated at the table. On Joy's right sat a baby doll with real blond hair and an exquisitely painted bisque face. Her arms and legs were made of the same bisque. She was dressed in a beautiful nightie made of white eyelet. On the left sat Faith's offering, a small cloth doll with brown embroidery floss for hair and a carefully embroidered face. She was dressed in a blue gown made from scraps of uniforms and a white pinafore made from one of Aunt Tempy's petticoats.

Faith had spent many hours lovingly crafting the doll long after Joy had been put to bed. She was the

best Faith had had to offer, and she would probably still be under the Christmas tree if Aunt Virt
hadn't pointed her out. In her excitement over all
her wonderful brightly wrapped packages, Joy had
completely overlooked the plain brown-wrapped
packages at the back of the tree.

Faith wished now that she had put them away.
They couldn't compete with all the wonderful things
Augustus Jenkins had delivered.

Tempy studied Faith's face as she watched Joy
at play. "She's a little girl, Faith. It's her first real
Christmas and she's thrilled with all her new toys.
Just as you were thrilled with your first doll."

"I know, Aunt Tempy. It's just that I wanted to
give it to her. I wanted to be the one to provide all
these gifts."

"Didn't you?" Tempy's gray eyes were demanding an answer.

"He did," Faith said resentfully. "I had nothing
to do with it."

"Really? I'd say you had a lot to do with it. I
presume these gifts are from David Alexander. He
seemed quite taken with you."

"No," Faith told her. "They're from Reese Jordan.
David Alexander might have suggested them, but
they all came from Reese."

"Reese?" Temperance probed a little deeper. "You
didn't tell me you were on a first-name basis with
your future employer."

Faith saw the concern in Tempy's face. "There's
a lot I didn't tell you, Aunt Tempy. I didn't know
how."

"I'm listening now, if you want to talk about
it."

"Reese Jordan wants me to have his child." Faith dropped the news quietly and carefully, as if to muffle an explosion.

Tempy's mouth formed a perfect O, and her command of the English language momentarily failed her. When she finally recovered her power of speech, her voice was an astonished whisper. "He *what?*"

"He wants me to have his child. The Richmond ad contained a mistake. He isn't hiring someone to provide *for* his heir. He's hiring someone to provide the child. In his words, to conceive it, carry it, deliver it, and hand it over to him—forever. And he's willing to pay me very well for the service." Faith stood up and began to pace around the kitchen, stopping every now and then to straighten the cups in the cupboard or to restack a dish. "When I arrived at the Madison Hotel, his suite was full of women applying for the job. I stood in line half the day before I saw Reese Jordan from a distance, but I never got a chance to speak to him. And I never would've had a chance at all if fate hadn't intervened."

"What happened?"

Faith took a deep breath and began to relate the chain of events that had led to her first meeting with Reese Jordan. She held nothing back except the uncontrollable mix of emotions she had experienced when Reese Jordan kissed her. The memory of his kiss and the feel of his hands intimately tying the strings of her corset still had the power to make her blush.

"He saved you from a thief, took you to dinner, and offered you a job as his . . . his companion, all in one evening," Tempy observed sarcastically when Faith finished talking. "He sounds like a scoundrel."

"Oh, he's very charming and very persuasive when he wants to be."

"Most scoundrels are."

"And yet there is something about him," Faith murmured. "He showed me the ad in the Washington paper. He chose to tell me the truth when he could very easily have set out to seduce me."

"He was probably afraid you would find out from one of the other applicants. He chose to tell you his version before someone else told you hers." Tempy patted the bench next to her.

"Maybe, but he didn't seem to be afraid. He seemed to challenge me. Can you understand that?" Faith sat down.

"I don't know," Tempy admitted, "but what I understand or don't understand doesn't matter. The question is whether you understand. Can you go along with this business arrangement?"

"He wanted me, Tempy," Faith whispered. "I felt it."

"Other men have wanted you," Tempy reminded her. "Despite what your Aunt Virtuous says, I know that at least three men have approached you since the end of the war."

"A drunk, a man old enough to be my grandfather, and a married captain with a wife and two grown children in Wisconsin," Faith said. "All of them offered to take me away from all this"—she waved her arm toward the parlor—"and set me up in a little place of my own. Their offers were not flattering."

"Did you find Reese Jordan's offer flattering?"

Faith thought for a moment. "Yes, strangely enough, I did. I didn't feel dirty or that he was offering me a sordid 'arrangement.' I felt he was offering me an opportunity. Have I shocked you terribly, Aunt Tempy?" A pink tinge colored her cheeks as Faith turned to face her beloved aunt.

Tempy smiled at Faith. "I'm surprised, but far from shocked. Your face lights up when you talk about him."

Faith turned a deeper shade of pink and, lowering her eyes, contemplated the folds in her apron as she spoke. "Aunt Tempy, we desperately need that money, but I don't know what to do. I should be appalled at Reese Jordan's offer, but I'm not. The idea of having his baby—" Faith stopped suddenly and met her aunt's eyes. "What would people here in Richmond think if they found out? Can you imagine the scandal if any of our friends even suspected?"

"Better than you," Tempy confided. "Don't you think I know what you're feeling, Faith? I wasn't always your aunt Tempy. I was young once and very much in love."

"I never knew . . ." Faith began.

"Of course not. It happened before you were born, and it isn't the sort of thing I would normally talk about. But, Faith darling, I do understand some of what you feel. I was sixteen, younger than you are now. All my sisters were married and away from home, and I was left behind with a sick mother and a house to oversee. I thought life was passing me by until the day Kevin O'Malley rode up to the house, fresh off the boat from Ireland. Papa hired him as a horse trainer. He was the most beautiful man I had ever seen and far better educated than any horse trainer I'd ever met. We fell in love. Kevin wanted to marry me, but Papa refused to consider his proposal." Tempy stopped and blinked back tears, then rose from the table, walked to the stove, and poured two steaming cups of coffee. She carried both cups back to the table, placed one in front of Faith, and sat back down at the scarred pine table.

"What happened?"

"I ran away with Kevin. We went to Baltimore, married, and planned to take a ship to the West Indies. My father tracked us down. He had Kevin beaten, then signed him on as a crewman aboard a ship. I never saw him again. Our marriage was annulled. The family thought they could forget it. Thought I'd forget it, but I didn't. And neither could they. I had a part of Kevin with me. I was carrying his child." Tempy paused, remembering. "When Father found out, he sent me to stay with a distant cousin in Philadelphia until the baby was born." She smiled at Faith. "I couldn't keep my child. Circumstances and my father prevented it."

"Oh, Aunt Tempy, I'm so sorry." Faith got up from the table and embraced her aunt.

"Don't be sorry, Faith. A few weeks after I returned to Richmond, your mother gave birth. She was ill for long months afterward. I stayed here to help with the other children and to take care of you. I've always been here for you. I couldn't keep my child, but I've always been here when you needed me."

"You never married."

"I would have liked to marry, but not without love, and I loved only Kevin. After the scandal I caused, I never had another opportunity to marry. Oh, I received lots of offers, but none of them were marriage proposals," Tempy concluded.

"It's such a shame, Aunt Tempy. You've missed so much," Faith told her.

"Have I missed any more than you?" Tempy asked. "I've loved a man, Faith, and had that love returned, and I've experienced the joy and the heartbreak of bearing a child. I don't want you to miss that, but I don't want you to sacrifice yourself just to provide money for the rest of us. Do you understand the difference?"

"Have you any regrets, Tempy?"

Tempy smiled sadly. "I don't allow any. And if you choose to accept Reese Jordan's offer, do so because you feel it's the right thing for you to do. Don't look back, and don't regret your decision. If you choose to reject his offer, do so for the same reason. I love you, Faith. I'll support your decision. We all make the best choice at the time. It's all any of us can do. You can't live your life regretting the past. Life is too short and too precious for that. Think about what you want, my dear. Don't think about us or about the money."

"But the money is important, Tempy," Faith reminded her. "It's important to all of us, to our well-being and livelihood. I didn't realize how important until today." Faith looked around at all the food and gifts. "Reese's money was responsible for all this." She waved her right arm to indicate the Christmas bounty.

"These are just things, Faith. Can you carry a child and then give it up for money? Ask yourself that question before you decide. Ask yourself why you would even consider doing it. Why? That's what's important."

Faith kissed her aunt on the cheek. "What made you so wise, Aunt Tempy?"

Tempy smiled at Faith. "Experience." She watched as Faith walked into the parlor to take tea with Joy and her dolls. "And love," she whispered.

FAITH SPENT A sleepless night tossing from side to side, turning first one way and then another, bumping Joy in her futile attempt to find a comfortable position.

No matter which way she turned, slumber eluded her. She could not escape the workings of her mind, which was busy replaying the afternoon's conversation with Aunt Tempy and Tempy's revelations about her own life.

"Can you carry a child and then give it up for money? Ask yourself why.... Why?" Over and over Aunt Tempy's voice echoed through her mind.

And then another voice was taunting her. A deep, husky voice—fierce, yet strangely tender. Reese's. "I want you to provide the child. To conceive him, carry him, deliver him, give him to me, and walk away. Forever." Forever. And his voice: "If I could do this by myself, I would."

"Ask yourself why."

"I have my reasons...."

On and on through the long night Faith heard the voices—Aunt Tempy's full of love and concern,

Reese's husky, with a very different emotion.

She asked herself why she wanted to have Reese Jordan's child. Because he was willing to pay her a great deal of money? The mercenary part of Faith told her she should do it for the money. But the other, womanly, side of Faith insisted she should do it for love. While it was unthinkable for her to do such a thing for herself, there were other people—dearly beloved ladies—to consider. What was unthinkable became acceptable when the lives of her ladies were at stake. And while Faith told herself she would do anything for her family, the womanly part of her, the deeply hidden, yearning part of her, urged her to do this for herself. Miracles did happen when one worked for them and maybe, just maybe . . .

Faith finally gave up all pretense of trying to sleep. She rose, bathed hastily, dressed for church, and went to the kitchen to prepare breakfast.

The wonderful smell of bacon frying roused the others from their beds and they began to file into the kitchen to help. Hannah was the first to enter and found there was very little to do. Faith had everything prepared.

Hannah smiled. "It isn't fair, Faith. You've been up early two days in a row, making breakfast for all of us."

"I don't mind," Faith said. "I couldn't sleep, and I enjoy making breakfast, but you can brew some tea if you like."

Hannah was pleased with the chore. It was the thing she did best. "It's so nice to have real breakfasts again, with bacon and ham and biscuits and eggs. You've become a cook, Faith. Imagine that.

Before the war you would never . . ." Hannah put the kettle on to boil and spooned tea leaves into the china pot. "Never mind. You spoil us so. We'll all miss it."

"Miss what?" Tempy stood in the doorway.

"Faith," Hannah told her. "When she leaves us to go to Wyoming."

"Has she decided to go?" Tempy asked, watching Faith closely and waiting for an answer.

"Of course she's going," Virt answered from behind Tempy. "She'll lose the job if she doesn't. She has to go."

Tempy took the platter of bacon from Faith and set it on the table. "Are you going, Faith?"

"Yes, Faith, are you going?" Agnes chimed in.

"Well," Faith said, teasing, "after breakfast I'm going to church, but that's as far as I plan to travel—for today, anyway. Isn't that right, pumpkin?" She reached down and lifted Joy, who was pressed against Tempy's skirts, into her arms.

Joy nodded, and Faith successfully diverted the conversation. Agnes's question was forgotten, for the moment.

But it wasn't forgotten for long. Faith was abruptly reminded of it in the churchyard after the Sunday service.

"Faith? Faith!" A large woman, dressed in bright red wool, waved her handkerchief in Faith's direction.

Faith turned at the sound of her name and groaned aloud at the sight of Aunt Virtuous in conversation with Lydia Abbott.

What now? Faith wondered as Aunt Virt and Mrs. Abbott made a beeline in her direction. Lydia

Abbott was a notorious busybody and the biggest gossip in Richmond.

"Faith." Mrs. Abbott managed to breathe Faith's name once again, though she was winded from the trek. "What's this Virt tells me about your going to Wyoming? Your aunt has been bragging that you've landed a job as governess for the child of a very rich man. And Myrtle Jenkins told me all about Augustus's trip out to your house with a wagonload of Christmas presents. Your new employer must be paying you quite well if you spent money on Christmas"—she looked at Faith slyly—"when everyone in town knows you need money for your taxes and that tumbledown house. It's so exciting. Imagine little Faith Collins going out west alone to work for a rich gentleman. Why don't you stop by the house for Sunday dinner and tell us all about your job? I just can't get over it—Faith Collins actually working for a living."

"I don't think there is anything left to tell, Mrs. Abbott. Everyone else seems to have filled you in quite thoroughly." Faith glared at Virtuous. She didn't begrudge her aunt a little boasting . . . but to Lydia Abbott of all people. "Thank you for your offer, but we have Sunday dinner waiting for us at home." Faith put her arm under Aunt Virt's elbow and steered her away from Lydia. "Good day, Mrs. Abbott."

"Virt told me everything except when you're leaving. When are you going to Wyoming?"

"I don't know." Faith ground out her reply through clenched teeth.

"You mean your employer hasn't told you yet?" Lydia prodded.

"Oh, she's leaving soon," Virt announced loudly. "Real soon."

Faith nudged her aunt with an elbow to the ribs. "Ssh."

"Well, if you don't hear from your . . . employer soon, Faith, let me know. Rich men have been known to change their minds, and governesses are expendable. My own children have had several, and I might be able to use you at my house."

"When pigs fly," Faith muttered.

"What was that?" Lydia asked.

"I said good-bye, Mrs. Abbott." Faith walked away with Virtuous in tow.

"How could you, Aunt Virt?" Faith fumed, when they were out of Lydia's hearing.

"I had to say something," Virt said defensively. "She came up to me and started talking about all the Christmas gifts Augustus had delivered to our house."

"You could have ignored her, but no, you had to brag."

"Well, why not?" Virtuous wanted to know. "It's nice that we finally have something to brag about."

"But now everyone will expect me to go."

"Well, why not?" Virt studied her niece. "You *are* going to Wyoming, aren't you, Faith?"

Faith avoided her aunt's eyes and hurried to catch up to Tempy, Joy, and the others who were walking ahead. Virt trotted after her, determined to get an answer.

"You didn't answer my question," Virt accused as soon as she caught up with Faith.

Tempy turned to Virt. "What question was that, Virt?"

"I simply asked Faith if she was going to Wyoming."

"I saw you talking to that big mouth, Lydia Abbott," Tempy said. "Did you tell her Faith was going to work in Wyoming?" Tempy grabbed her sister's arm.

"What if I did? She's going, isn't she?" Virtuous jerked free of Tempy's grasp. "You are, aren't you, Faith?"

Faith opened her mouth to speak, but Hannah jumped in to heal the family breach. "Of course she is, but the idea of leaving all of us is so new, Faith just needs a little time."

Chapter Eight

FAITH DID NEED a little time. More than a little time. But she didn't have it.

The second bill soliciting payment of delinquent taxes arrived on Monday morning, two days after Christmas. Payment was due by December 31. Failure to pay would result in forfeiture of the Richmond and Petersburg properties. Time had run out.

Faith pulled on her worn black traveling cape and gloves, then headed for the front door, the envelope containing the property tax bill clutched in one fist.

Tempy followed close on her niece's heels. "Faith, where are you going?" Tempy asked.

"To take care of this."

"Faith?"

"Don't worry, Tempy, I know what I'm doing." Faith smiled at her aunt, then opened the door. "I'll be back shortly."

She walked quickly down the street, not daring to slow her steps until she reached the telegraph office.

"What can I do for you, Miss Collins?" Bert Winthrop stood behind the counter.

"I need to send a telegram, Mr. Winthrop, right away."

"Who to?" Winthrop grabbed a blank sheet of paper and a pencil.

"Mr. Reese Jordan, the Presidential Suite, Madison Hotel, Washington City."

"What's the message?"

"I'll write it out for you." Faith took the paper and wrote out her request. "I'll wait for a reply." She handed him the message along with payment.

"The reply might take a while," Bert warned.

"That's all right, Mr. Winthrop. I'll wait." She sat on the hard wooden bench in front of the iron stove and waited while Bert Winthrop telegraphed the message.

REESE JORDAN LOUNGED in a leather wing chair in the smoking room of the Madison Hotel, a thin cigar clenched between his teeth. He sat upright when a messenger called his name.

"Here." Reese folded his newspaper and tossed it aside.

"Telegram for you, Mr. Jordan." The boy handed Reese a folded slip of paper.

Reese flipped him a coin. He unfolded the paper, then decided against reading it in the lounge. He refolded the note and, grasping it firmly, hurried up the stairs to the privacy of his suite.

His fingers shook slightly as he leaned against the door of his suite and unfolded the paper. The message was brief and to the point.

I ACCEPT. REQUEST IMMEDIATE ADVANCE ON SALARY. SEND $3,086.34 TO THE BANK OF

VIRGINIA. THANK YOU. FAITH ELIZABETH COLLINS.

Reese's triumphant shout brought David running from the other room. "She accepted. Start packing, cousin. You're going to Richmond."

"I thought you would want to go," David said.

"It will be better if you go," Reese told him. "More businesslike."

"What about the arrangements?" David wanted to know.

"I'll take care of everything. Are the contracts ready?"

David nodded. "Everything except the amounts."

"We'll go over those when she gets here. Here, take this." Reese walked to his desk and began writing. "It's a bank draft. See that it's deposited in Faith's bank account. Oh, and make sure the older ladies have access to the account."

David glanced at the bank draft. "Have you lost your mind, Reese? This draft is for ten thousand dollars. You haven't signed the contracts yet or settled on a fee. This is too much."

"Not for this. Don't you see, David? The money is my guarantee. She can't possibly pay this back. She'll have to stay as long as I need her."

"I have a better way to guarantee she'll stay," David said. "You don't know how much this plan of yours is going to cost. She could ask for an exorbitant amount."

Reese looked down at the telegram in his hand and smiled. "The woman who wouldn't accept a fruit basket? I don't think so."

"Why not make sure?" David said. "Marry her."

"I'm not interested in standing up with her in front of a preacher."

"You won't have to. You can marry her by proxy. I'll stand up for you," David explained. "It's all very legal. Quicker and easier than arranging an adoption. And quieter. Once she leaves Wyoming, you'll be guaranteed a divorce on grounds of desertion."

"If she leaves," Reese pointed out.

"She'll leave."

Reese thought it over. "A proxy marriage is risky."

"No riskier than the other plan."

"All right, David, but don't quibble about the amount. She's worth any amount. And, David . . ."

"Yes?"

"If she asks, tell her you deposited the requested amount in her account."

"She requested that much money?"

"She requested much, much less than I'm sending," Reese explained. "It's the end of the year. Think, David, why would she need a specific amount of money?"

"Taxes. Of course. She owns a house and possibly other property."

"And when those crooks in office find out she can pay the amount she owes, they'll probably raise the tax. They want land, not money. I'm sending enough to allow her to keep her house and to pay back whatever else she owes. She's got to have a place to go to when our arrangement ends. She can't stay in Wyoming."

"Anything else?" David wanted to know.

"If you need it, there is more money where that

came from, but don't tell her that. And, David, hurry back."

"Are you sure you don't want to go to Richmond yourself?"

"I'm positive." It was safer for Reese to stay in Washington and have a vague picture of Faith somewhere in Richmond than to be able to visualize the tiniest details of her surroundings. He intended to follow his plan and keep the relationship purely business. Their arrangement was temporary. He would never forget that.

Reese's eyes narrowed and his face darkened at the thought. He carefully folded the telegram and placed it in the breast pocket of his jacket next to his heart. He snatched his coat from the hall tree and thrust his arms into the sleeves, then put on his hat and gloves.

"Where are you going?" David looked at his cousin. Reese's lighthearted, triumphant mood had vanished.

"To the telegraph office and the train station. You change and pack. You'll be traveling most of the night. I'll take care of the other details."

Forty-five minutes later the key on the telegraph handset in Bert Winthrop's Richmond office began to jangle. Bert grabbed a pencil stub and began to write.

"It's for you, Miss Collins."

Faith jumped as if she'd been shot. She stood up and walked hesitantly to the counter, her body stiff from the long wait on the hard wooden bench. "What does it say?" Her soft voice quavered with suppressed excitement.

Bert Winthrop looked down at her. She was

standing on tiptoe, attempting to read the words
scrawled on the paper from across the width of the
high counter. Her face was flushed with excitement
or from the heat of the stove; he couldn't tell which.
Her big gray eyes sparkled. He realized for the first
time that Faith Collins was a beautiful woman. He
had always thought of her as Miss Collins. Efficient,
quiet, hardworking, dull Miss Collins. A diligent
gray sparrow in a houseful of flighty hens. The
transformation was amazing. This Miss Collins took
his breath away.

"What does it say, Mr. Winthrop?" Faith asked
again.

Bert read the hastily scribbled words. "It says,
'Delighted by your acceptance. David will arrive
early morning. Waiting anxiously for your arrival.
R. Jordan.' "

"May I see it?" Faith asked.

"You can keep it." Bert handed over the paper.

Faith clutched the piece of paper to her bosom.
She shifted her weight from one leg to the other,
bobbing up and down in front of the counter.

"I guess this means you'll be goin' out west."
Bert's observation brought Faith to her senses.

She tucked the note into her new black silk
purse and carefully walked back to the bench.
She smoothed the strands of hair that had escaped
from her tidy bun and took a deep breath to calm
her nerves.

Faith thought for a moment and then gave Bert
Winthrop a hesitant little smile. "Yes, Mr. Winthrop,
I suppose it does."

Chapter Nine

DAVID ALEXANDER ARRIVED in Richmond early the next morning. He hired a hack at the livery and drove to Collins House.

Faith answered the door when he knocked. "Do you have it?" she whispered urgently.

David nodded. He reached inside his overcoat and patted the breast pocket of his jacket. "It's safe and sound."

"May I see it?"

David shook his head. "I'm sorry, Mrs. Collins, but I have very explicit instructions from Reese. It's better if no one knows I have this on me." David tried to soften her disappointment.

Faith looked up at him with understanding in her eyes. She had been the victim of a robbery. "The bank opens at eight-thirty."

"Good. We have three hours before our train leaves. Are you ready?" She looked tired, as if she'd slept very little the night before.

"Yes, we're all packed, but Joy is still sleeping." Faith stared at David Alexander. He looked tired. There were dark circles under his eyes, his suit was wrinkled, and he still stood on the front porch, his hat in one hand, his satchel in the other. "Goodness, where are my manners? Come in, Mr. Alexander.

99

Make yourself comfortable while I get you a cup of strong black coffee." Faith stepped aside and allowed David to enter the house.

He started in the direction of the parlor, but she led him past it to the kitchen. A fire burned in the big cast-iron stove in the corner of the room. A pot of coffee simmered on top.

"Aunt Tempy, you remember Mr. Alexander?"

Tempy turned from the stove. "Of course I do. Sit down, Mr. Alexander. Let me take your hat and coat while Faith pours you a cup of coffee."

David handed his coat and hat to Temperance, but kept his satchel full of documents by his side. Faith poured the coffee and placed a cup in front of him. David took a sip of the hot liquid before he spoke. "You," he said to Faith, "and one of the other ladies will need to come with me to the bank and to the courthouse."

"Why?" Faith asked.

"I have to transfer some money into your aunts' account." David placed his cup back in its saucer. "And we need to accomplish the marriage."

Faith nearly dropped the coffee pot. "Marriage? Mr. Jordan didn't say anything about a wedding."

"I'll go," Tempy volunteered.

"Fine. You can be our witness." David continued, "We'll go to the courthouse as soon as it opens, then to the bank. Miss Hamilton, we'll also need you in Washington. To witness the contracts. It will mean an overnight stay, but Reese will pay your expenses." David took another sip of coffee, then reached for the plate of biscuits Tempy put before him.

"What time will Mr. Jordan arrive?" Tempy was

nearly bursting with excitement.

"He's not coming. I'll be standing in for him," David said.

"I'll be marrying you?" Faith gestured toward David.

Temperance prudently took the coffee pot from her niece's hand and placed it on the stove.

"You'll be marrying Reese," David assured her, "by legal proxy."

"He's not coming to our wedding?"

"He has business in Washington," David said gently.

"It doesn't matter, darling." Tempy rushed to soothe Faith's wounds. "You'll still be married to him."

Faith looked David Alexander in the eye. "For how long?"

"Until the baby's born."

"And then what? Annulment?"

David shook his head. "Divorce."

Faith took a deep breath, straightened her shoulders, and pulled herself up to her full five feet. "At least I know where I stand."

THE FOUR OF them—Faith, Joy, Temperance, and David Alexander—boarded the ten-fifteen train.

Faith sighed with relief. They had somehow managed to take care of everything. David Alexander had safely deposited the bank draft in an account at the Bank of Virginia. The taxes were paid. And Faith was married to a man who hadn't even come to the ceremony. A man who sent her thousands of dollars but forgot to send a plain gold band.

Faith and Joy had said loving good-byes to Hannah, Agnes, and Aunt Virt. Faith had pressed ten dollar gold pieces into each of their hands as she hugged them.

Tempy also said good-bye to the others. She left Virt in charge of the family until she returned, then handed her older sister a list of things to do while she was gone, hoping the chores would keep them too busy to worry.

Faith smiled at Joy, bouncing on the seat opposite her own, her little nose pressed against the window in her eagerness to see everything, her warm breath fogging the glass.

"Look, Faith." Joy pointed down the tracks.

Faith turned to look out the window and watched as the train station grew smaller and smaller in the distance. She bit her lip as a mixture of excitement and apprehension tore at her insides. It was comforting to look across the seat and find Tempy seated firmly next to Joy. The deal had been made. Soon she would leave for Wyoming, but for a little while longer she had Temperance with her.

The train ride to Washington seemed uncomfortably long. It was cold in the passenger car. Faith changed seats so that she, Tempy, and Joy could huddle together for warmth. David sat alone, wrapped in his greatcoat. The first burst of excited conversation died with the passage of time. The four of them dozed, succumbing to the hypnotic rhythm of the train and the boredom of confinement.

IN WASHINGTON, REESE Jordan spent his hours working. He had made all of the arrangements for the trip to Wyoming and was clearing his desk in preparation for Faith's arrival. His other business ventures could wait until the details of his agreement with Mrs. Collins were outlined on paper. Every detail had to be clear, concise, and legally binding. Reese Jordan believed in contracts, and he was about to affix his signature to the most important contract of his life. He glanced impatiently at the clock, then thumbed through the morning newspaper to the page announcing the train schedules. By now she should be Faith Jordan and well on her way to Washington. But Reese refused to think about the marriage. It was a mere technicality. Just another way of guaranteeing the deal. He wasn't going to acknowledge her as his wife. She would remain Faith Collins as far as he was concerned.

He looked at the clock once again. Two more hours to wait. He began sorting his mail, determined to complete the task without interruption.

A cream-colored vellum envelope caught his eye. He studied the handwriting and the return address: Senator Darcy's office. The senator was head of the Appropriations Committee and was sponsoring several bills regulating the uses of the open range in the Wyoming Territory.

Reese ripped open the envelope. How long had it been buried under the pile of paperwork on his desk? Damn, he thought, of all the times for this to happen. Inside the envelope was an invitation to a New Year's Eve reception and dance at the senator's residence. He glanced at the date on the invitation and then checked the desk calendar. Tonight. And Faith Collins was arriving in two hours.

Reese paced between the desk and the window

for several minutes, thinking, planning, calculating. He smiled as he thought of a way to turn the situation to his advantage. The reception started at nine. That should give him adequate time to get her ready.

He grabbed his hat and coat, pulled on his gloves, and hurried out of the suite.

THE TRAIN WHISTLE sounded shrilly as the iron monster pulled into the Union Station.

David Alexander rose from his seat, stretched his arms, and reached for the sleeping child lying across the laps of the two women in the seat across from him. "I'll carry her," he told them. "You ladies have held her for hours. You must be tired."

Tempy lifted Joy from across Faith's lap and handed her to David. She was stiff and numb from the weight of Joy's legs, and she knew Faith was just as stiff. Joy's head had rested across Faith's arm and in her lap for the better part of the journey. "Thank you, Mr. Alexander," Tempy said gratefully.

Faith nodded in agreement. "My limbs are numb," she said, stretching her legs out in front of her. She bit her lip against the painful tingling in her arm and legs.

"Take your time, ladies. Reese is supposed to meet us. I'll take Joy out to the carriage and come back for you." David made his way down the aisle, five-year-old Joy Collins following sleepily behind him.

Reese spotted David as soon as he exited the train. He jumped down from the carriage and hurried to meet him. "Where is she?"

"Still on the train," David told him. "I took Joy to

give them a minute to stretch their legs in privacy. She's been sleeping in their laps for over half the trip." David smiled down at the little girl.

"Ladies? How many did you bring with you?" Reese knew a moment of panic. Suppose the others couldn't bear to be parted from Faith? What would he do with all those women in tow?

"Just one of her aunts. Relax, Reese. We need someone to witness the agreement, and I thought Mrs. Collins would be more comfortable with one of her relatives. And one of her trusted aunts is less likely to talk to strangers about this scheme," David explained.

Reese sighed in relief and held his arms out to take the child. "Give her to me. I'll hold her while you go back for the ladies."

David handed Joy over to Reese and went back to the train to help Faith and Tempy with their belongings.

Reese studied the child he held. Her hair was different from her mother's. It was blond and curly, almost white. Her nose was smaller, too, turned up at the end where Faith's was slim and elegant. But the bone structure was essentially the same. One was pale, one was dark, like a photograph and its negative, but anyone could see the likeness.

Joy squirmed in his arms and yawned. Reese stared at her eyes. They were gray. Identical in color and shape to Faith Collins's eyes.

Joy looked up at the stranger. She struggled to sit up and Reese shifted his arms to accommodate her wiggling. Her legs locked around his waist, and she anchored her arms around his neck. A brush of moisture touched his neck. A red mitten covered her right hand, but its mate dangled across Reese's chest from a cord sewn to the right mitten. Reese reached up and pulled her right hand from around his neck. Her thumb was red and swollen and wet. Something tightened in his chest as he smiled at Faith Collins's little girl. "You must be Joy."

Joy nodded shyly. "Who are you?"

"My name is Reese."

"Weese," Joy repeated, then looked up at him with those solemn gray eyes. "Where's Faith? Where's Aunt Tempy?"

Faith stepped down from the train and searched the crowd for several seconds before she spotted Reese Jordan holding Joy. Her heart pounded painfully in her chest, and her breath seemed to catch in her throat as she hurried across the platform. She stopped in her tracks and stared at the sight.

Tempy halted behind her niece. "Faith, what is it?" She was alarmed. Faith had stopped so suddenly.

Faith didn't answer. She stood rooted to the spot, unable or unwilling to move. She caught her breath as Reese held a tiny red mitten by its cuff while Joy slipped her hand inside.

Tempy followed her niece's gaze. A tall, handsome man in a black overcoat stood next to a carriage. He held Joy in his arms.

David Alexander moved to stand next to Temperance. He was followed by a porter. "Oh, there's Reese," he said, waving his hat to catch the other man's attention.

"So that's Reese Jordan," Tempy murmured.

"Come along, Faith." Tempy grabbed her niece's elbow and propelled her forward along the sidewalk. "I want to meet this Mr. Jordan." She glanced at Faith. Her niece's cheeks were a very becoming shade of pink. Tempy frowned. Her own heart raced a tiny bit faster at the sight of him. The man was definitely a handsome scoundrel. She picked up the pace, taking longer steps, until they stood directly in front of Reese Jordan.

"There she is," Joy announced to the man holding her. "There's Faith and my aunt Tempy."

Reese looked down.

Faith looked up.

Their eyes met.

She was pale, her black dress was crushed, the front of it hopelessly wrinkled, several locks of hair hung down to her shoulders, and a doll was pressed against her breast. There were purple shadows beneath her eyes, but her cheeks were a lively shade of pink, and her mouth, where she had bitten her bottom lip, was a swollen, pouting red.

Reese cleared his throat and quickly turned his attention to the other woman. She was short and slim, like her niece. There was a definite family resemblance; even her eyes were gray, like Faith's and Joy's, but the hair peeking out from beneath her black bonnet was a lively shade of red. He smiled at her and relaxed.

David made the introductions. "Miss Temperance Hamilton, may I present my cousin and employer, Mr. Reese Jordan."

Reese shifted Joy onto his left arm and extended his right hand. "It's a pleasure, ma'am." Reese was surprised when the warm greeting sprang from his lips. He had been prepared to dislike Faith Collins's aunt on sight.

"Yes," Tempy told him, taking his hand. "I think it just might be, Mr. Jordan." Her gray eyes were completely candid, and Reese knew instinctively that she had been equally prepared to dislike him. Tempy smiled back, but unlike Faith, who stood stiff and tense at her side, Tempy relaxed.

"Let's get out of the cold," David suggested, taking control of the situation. He ushered Temperance and Faith into the carriage, then climbed in after them. He took Joy from Reese's arms and waited while his cousin sat down on the seat next to him. Joy wriggled her way between the two men. She leaned her head against Reese's arm.

"Back to the hotel, Murray!" Reese shouted to his driver as the carriage rolled away from the station and onto the busy street.

They arrived at the Madison Hotel thirty minutes later. Reese had reserved the two-bedroom Vice Presidential Suite for Faith and Joy. Their dinner sat waiting to be eaten.

He had also ordered a bath for Faith. A brass tub filled with water stood in the center of the dressing room. Steam danced along the surface of the water, then drifted toward the high plaster ceiling. A hotel maid waited next to the tub. She told Faith and Temperance she had been hired for the evening. She was to help Faith dress.

"Dress?" Faith was astonished. "For what?"

"We're going to a New Year's ball," Reese Jordan said. He stood just inside the dressing room door. His back rested against the door frame, his long legs crossed at the ankles, his arms folded over his chest.

Faith and Temperance turned in unison to stare at him. Faith sucked in her breath at his intrusion while Tempy gasped at the sheer audacity of the man.

"What did you say?" Faith demanded as soon as she was able to speak.

"I said you and I are going to a New Year's Eve ball at Senator Darcy's residence." He walked over to Faith and lifted her chin with the tip of his finger. His chocolate-brown eyes bored into hers.

Faith thought he was going to kiss her right there in front of Tempy, Joy, and the maid. Her eyes closed of their own volition while her face tilted up a bit more.

"Your bathwater is getting cold." He let go of her chin and stepped back. "Hurry up. I don't like to be late."

Reese turned and walked back to the door.

"I don't care what you like," Faith shot back at him, angry at herself for thinking he had feelings. "I haven't signed any contract. You don't own me."

He stopped in his tracks.

Faith stood her ground.

The tension was so thick she could feel it. It hung like a storm cloud in the air, energy crackling. Joy bit her lip and started to cry at the sound of Faith's angry voice. Tempy took Joy's hand and beat a hasty retreat into the bedroom. The maid followed close behind her.

Reese turned to face Faith, his right eyebrow raised in disbelief. "You've signed one. And in addition to that, there is the tiny matter of Christmas and a bank draft."

"I didn't ask you to send Christmas gifts."

"But you did ask me to send money to the Bank of Virginia in your name, if I recall correctly. I have your telegram on my desk." His normally husky voice was clipped and cutting. He was every inch an aristocrat. As aristocratic as any Virginia planter. "How long do you think it will take you to pay back a salary advance of three thousand dollars? Nine months? A year?"

Faith's eyes widened with shock at his words. He would be cruel enough to remind her of the job she'd been hired to do.

"Unless you have three thousand dollars to spare, Mrs. Collins, I suggest you hop into the bath."

Faith hated him for forcing her to face her obligation. She glared up at him, her clear gray eyes as sharp as steel.

Reese gave her his most charming, endearing, smile. The smile guaranteed to melt the hearts of any number of hostile women. "It's a party, Faith. We'll enjoy ourselves." He felt like a heel for forcing her to attend the ball with him, but how was he going to get someone else at this late date? He wasn't about to change his plans. "How long has it been since you've attended a party?" He opened the door, then checked his watch. "You have exactly one hour."

Chapter Ten

ONE HOUR. SHE cursed him under her breath as she stepped into the hot water. She cursed him as she quickly bathed when she would rather have soaked out the aches and pains of the long train ride. And she cursed him for making her attend a New Year's Eve party when she had only one night left to spend with Tempy. Faith rubbed the sponge over her body with vicious force. He wanted her to attend a party in Washington—a Yankee party in the home of a Yankee senator.

She would stick out like a sore thumb, and she wasn't in the mood for further embarrassment and humiliation. She didn't have anything to wear except the black dress she'd just taken off. Was he planning on conjuring up a dress out of thin air? She rinsed the soap from her skin. Leave it to a man like Reese Jordan to overlook such important details.

"Have the fireworks ended?" Tempy peeked inside the dressing room in time to catch her niece wrapping a towel around her damp body.

Faith nodded but didn't answer, nor did she look at Temperance.

"I gave Joy her supper and left her playing in our bedroom. I thought I would take a hot bath when you finish dressing, then crawl into bed. Such luxury!" Tempy sighed dramatically. "I'd forgotten how good it felt to have a maid do things for me. I could get used to it. I guess it's a good thing I'm going home tomorrow."

Faith raised her head and met Tempy's smiling gray eyes. Her own eyes shimmered with unshed tears. She felt very fragile all of a sudden, very alone. "I wanted to spend this evening with you, Aunt Tempy. Our last evening together."

"I know you did, my dear, but perhaps it's better this way. I don't want you to go to Wyoming with swollen eyes because we sat up all night crying. Go to this party and tell me all about it in the morning."

"I don't want to be humiliated. What am I supposed to wear, Aunt Tempy, my shift?" The words rushed to her lips.

"Oh, no, Faith." Tempy's soft voice quavered with excitement. "Wait until you see it. It's beautiful! You'll look just like a princess. I'll be able to keep the girls entertained for months by telling them about it."

"About what, Aunt Tempy?"

"Your ball gown. Faith darling, Mr. Jordan bought you a ball gown. It's lying across the bed in your room and it's perfect for you. The dressmaker had one made up. The dressmaker is in the sitting room waiting for alterations. I couldn't stand it any longer. I had to come in and get you!" Tempy couldn't contain her enthusiasm. She handed Faith a cotton robe. "Hurry."

Faith shivered in the cool air as she followed her aunt into the sitting room.

"Come here, my dear." The seamstress motioned to Faith. "It's warmer next to the fire." She held out her hand. "I'm Madame LeClerc. Here are your underthings. Let's get you dressed. Monsieur Jordan is not a patient man."

Faith started to protest, but Tempy gave her a warning glance.

A mound of underclothing was stacked on the sofa next to the dressmaker. The maid took the top garment from the pile and held it out for Faith. She stepped into pantalets that were shorter than the ones she usually wore. The silk, smooth and soft against her legs and buttocks, was decorated with French lace. Faith sighed reverently. "I've never worn anything like this." She slipped her arms into a low-cut camisole. A dozen tiny pearl buttons ran down the front of the undergarment, and it, too, was made of silk so sheer that Faith could see through it.

Madame LeClerc nodded approvingly. "Monsieur Jordan has excellent taste. He likes soft, beautiful undergarments."

"He selected these things?" Faith asked.

"Who else?" The dressmaker shrugged and handed several more garments to the maid. "Breathe in."

Faith did as she was told while Tempy laced her corset. It was cut very low in the front, and Faith instinctively tugged at the top.

"Leave it alone," Tempy admonished. "If you tug at it, your dress won't fit properly."

Faith sat on the sofa and smoothed a pair of sheer silk stockings over her legs. She slid the satin garters into place and rose from the sofa in corset, camisole, pantalets, and stockings waiting for the next layer of clothing and the inevitable hoops. But she waited in vain for hoops that weren't necessary.

"Now for the gown." Madame LeClerc motioned the women forward.

Tempy helped the maid guide the dress over Faith's head, then stood back to admire her niece.

The bright burgundy silk shimmered in the light from the fire. The skirt was too narrow to be worn with hoops. The fabric was pulled tight across the front and allowed to fall in elegant folds from a small bustle in the back. A two-foot train trailed behind.

The neckline was wide and scooped to frame Faith's collarbones and breasts. The sleeves were wisps of silk trimmed with silver embroidery. It was a masterpiece of elegance, designed to entice without revealing.

Madame LeClerc adjusted the folds and straightened the train. She whipped out a needle and thread and adjusted the seams along the sides to make the dress fit more snugly across Faith's petite frame.

A knock sounded at the door to the suite. "Ten minutes," Reese warned.

"Hurry," Faith urged.

"Let him wait," Madame suggested. "It does a man good to wait."

Tempy nodded in agreement with the dressmaker and went to work brushing Faith's hair.

They took their time, ignoring the unmistakable sound of Reese's footsteps measuring the length of the hall.

Faith relaxed. She was tired of being rushed. He could leave without her or he could wait like a gentleman.

Reese waited impatiently for twenty more minutes before Faith opened the door.

He noticed her hair first. The straight black mane was plaited into one long, fat braid and coiled around the top of her head like a coronet. The style was simple yet elegant, and it suited her.

Reese's brown eyes darkened. He would have liked to see more of her, but she was enveloped from shoulders to shoes in a burgundy velvet cape.

"We're late," Faith reminded him, brushing past him as she stepped through the doorway.

He pulled his gold watch from the pocket of his evening clothes. "So we are," he commented as he followed in her wake.

David was waiting for them in the carriage. His satchel was open on his lap, and papers were spread across the seat. The oil lamp beside his head was lit, the wick glowing brightly. He looked up when they entered and nodded a greeting in Faith's direction. "You look lovely, Mrs. Collins."

"Thank you." Faith smiled at him.

Reese glared at his cousin. He sat next to Faith and stretched out his legs, trying hard to disregard the soft lavender scent that emanated from the burgundy velvet. He shifted his weight away from her and noisily cleared his throat. "What do I need to know?" He directed his question at David, then settled back against his seat and proceeded to ignore the woman next to him. He focused his gaze on his cousin and seemed to listen intently to David's summary of the Darcy bill, but his mind

was not on politics. Reese Jordan's sole concern
was keeping his body under control while the tantalizing scent of lavender soap conjured up erotic
visions of bathtubs and wet, slippery skin.

The journey to Senator Darcy's home was mer-
cifully brief. Reese wasn't sure he could have han-
dled an additional mile. He alighted from the coach
before it had rolled to a stop and stood waiting
for David to assist Faith. He was just about to ask
David to escort her inside when his cousin took
the matter out of his hands. With one stern look
at Reese, David excused himself to join a fellow
attorney and his wife.

Reese reluctantly offered Faith his elbow. "Shall
we?" he said from behind clenched teeth.

Faith placed her gloved hand on his arm and
allowed him to lead her up the steps and into the
house.

The senator's butler met them at the door.

Reese deposited the engraved invitation in the
butler's hand. "Mr. Reese Jordan," the man announced, "and . . ."

"What was your husband's name?" Reese hissed,
waiting impatiently for Faith to answer.

Faith didn't hear him. She was too busy absorb-
ing the sights and sounds in the mansion. She was
enchanted by the presence of uniformed maids and
waiters carrying trays of drinks. "Champagne," she
whispered, in awe.

Reese turned to look at her. "Champagne?"

"Yes." She nodded for emphasis. She'd never had
champagne and couldn't wait to try it.

Reese whispered a reply to the butler.

"Mr. Reese Jordan and Mrs. Champ Collins."

Faith frowned at him, puzzled. Mrs. Champ Collins?

They moved forward. Faith turned her back to Reese, unfastened her cape, and handed it to a waiting maid. Reese had relinquished his hat and coat. He turned to Faith and touched her elbow.

She turned to face him.

The burgundy silk dress fit her like a second skin, molding the curves of her body, thrusting her hips and breasts into prominence. He liked it because it had none of the flounces, bows, and jet beads currently in vogue. It had been simply made—simply made to torture him, he thought, as he attempted to focus his gaze on something other than her silver-edged décolletage. The neckline was modest compared to some he'd seen, but his height gave him a unique vantage point. It was almost impossible for him to look down at her and not feast on an enticing display.

Reese swallowed hard. Perspiration dotted his upper lip. His body was suddenly hot. He needed a drink. Hell, he needed several!

He gripped her elbow and led her farther into the room, where he promptly lifted two glasses of champagne from a passing tray.

"How thoughtful—" Faith began.

He drank them both, then placed the empty glasses on a table. He made the mistake of looking down at his companion when she spoke. He quickly acquired two more glasses of champagne, but this time he downed his in one gulp and handed her the second glass.

"You must be thirsty." She followed his lead and gulped some of the wine, choking when the bubbles tickled in her throat.

He grunted a reply.

She managed another swallow of champagne before he removed her glass from her hand. He placed it on a tray beside his own, then led her across the room to where David stood conversing with another couple.

Reese released her with a terse "I'm going to talk to the senator."

"But . . ." she sputtered, embarrassed and bewildered by his rudeness.

Reese left her standing next to his cousin and hurriedly stalked away.

David introduced Faith to his friends. They exchanged pleasantries until the orchestra began to play. "Would you care to dance?" David asked.

Faith nodded, then allowed him to lead her onto the dance floor.

"I haven't danced in years," she confided, as they moved in time to the music. "I was afraid I had forgotten how. I must warn you to watch your toes, Mr. Alexander."

David smiled. "I think they're safe." She was hesitant in some of her steps, but her natural grace kept her from stumbling. "May I say, Mrs. Collins, that you dance beautifully, despite your understandable lack of practice?"

"You may." Her lilting laughter drifted across the room.

Reese glowered at the couple on the dance floor. He hadn't heard a word the senator had said. No matter how hard he tried to ignore them, he couldn't keep his eyes off Faith. His gaze was continually drawn to the surprisingly

lovely woman in burgundy silk. Reese wanted
to hold her in his arms. He wanted to whirl
her around the room. He wanted to hear her
laugh and bask in the warmth of her smiles.
And he was furious with himself for wanting
that.

"Don't you agree, Mr. Jordan?"

Reese forced himself to concentrate on the senator's words. "Sir?"

"I was explaining the points of the bill," Senator
Marcus Darcy said. "Don't you think—"

"Excuse me, Senator," Reese left his host as
abruptly as he'd joined him. "I've promised this
dance." He pushed his way through the crowd of
dancers until he stood behind his cousin. He tapped
David on the shoulder.

"I believe this is my dance." Reese's words were
clipped and curt.

David looked at Reese and then at Faith Collins.

"Well?" Reese demanded.

David smiled apologetically at Faith, then
stepped back, releasing his hold on her.

Reese placed one hand on her waist, then took
her hand. She was stiff, unyielding.

"I don't remember promising you a dance," she
hissed at him as he guided her through the beginning of a waltz.

"I didn't ask." He winced as she deliberately
stepped on his foot. He tightened his hold around
her waist.

"You should have."

"So you could refuse?" He smiled down into her
stormy gray eyes.

"Yes," she told him.

"You're in no position to refuse."

She trod on his foot once again, then smiled sweetly. "Slavery has been abolished, Mr. Jordan. Or haven't you heard?"

"As long as there are rich people and poor people, Mrs. Collins"—he pulled her closer to him—"slavery will continue to exist." He smiled back at her. "In some form."

Faith's wide, full mouth tightened into a firm, straight line. Her brows knitted together above her gray eyes. She gritted her teeth and waited for her chance.

They whirled around to the three-quarter rhythm. "If you step on my foot one more time," Reese warned, anticipating her next move, "I'll be forced to take retribution."

"I'm not afraid of you." Faith knew she was playing with fire, but she couldn't resist the urge to taunt him.

He pretended to miss a step and jerked her up against the hard length of his body. "You should be."

"You wouldn't hurt me," she said with more conviction than she felt.

"Who said anything about hurting you?" he queried softly, pressing his body intimately against hers, his eyes devouring the sight of the alabaster mounds framed by silver lace. The warm, musky scent of lavender drifted up from the bodice of her gown to tease him.

She was pressed against him. She could feel the heat of his body through his clothing and hers. She could smell the clean, woodsy fragrance he wore and could feel his warm breath against her temple. And she could feel that hard male part of him pressing into her stomach. Her blood seemed to race through her veins. Her heart hammered in her chest. She forgot the steps of the dance, lost all sense of rhythm. She stumbled, lurching against him, trampling his feet in the process.

Reese's arms gripped her, his fingers biting into her waist as he struggled to keep his balance. He muttered an obscenity under his breath. The woman was a menace on the dance floor.

He tilted his head slightly, and Faith noticed a tiny, pale crescent marring the underside of his chin. His sun-baked skin and the faint shadow of his beard seemed to highlight the imperfection. It was a normal, everyday scar, the kind gleaned from a childhood fall, not a by-product of war. It drew Faith like a magnet. She wanted to touch it, to caress it with the tip of her finger, press her lips to it, pay homage to that tiny, almost imperceptible flaw.

"Pay attention to your steps," he ordered, dragging her thoughts back to the dance as he dragged her feet back into the rhythm of the waltz.

Faith focused her attention on her feet. Her face colored in embarrassment. "I'm sorry. It was—"

"Forget it."

The music ended. They whirled to a stop.

"But—"

Reese grasped her elbow. "Just forget it." He looked around and spotted a waiter. "I need a drink." Tiny dots of perspiration marked his upper lip. His breathing was ragged. His body throbbed in frustration.

"So do I." She licked her lips.

Reese stared at her, his right eyebrow quirked at an angle. Her breathing was shallow and rapid. Her chest rose and fell so quickly her breasts threatened to spill over the embroidered neckline of her gown. A trickle of moisture slid over the rounded slopes, then down the valley, disappearing into the silk of her undergarments. His taste buds itched to sample the salty droplets. He leaned toward her, intent on capturing her lips beneath his own.

Her eyes widened, softened to a warm pewter color, then slowly closed.

"Sorry. Excuse me." A man's sharp elbow caught Reese in the rib cage. Reese turned to find the culprit and was instantly reminded of his surroundings.

He stood at the edge of the dance floor, Faith Collins scant inches away from him. A dozen or so couples pushed past them on their way to dinner.

"Reese! Reese Jordan!"

Faith's eyes snapped open at the sound of his name.

Reese turned to his left.

Senator Darcy motioned to him. "Over here, my boy. There's someone I want you to meet. He'd like your opinion on something."

Reese nearly groaned aloud. He offered Faith his arm, and she tucked her hand into the crook of his elbow.

He realized his mistake immediately. He clamped his mouth shut in an effort to gain control over his body. A muscle in his jaw began to twitch under the strain, and Reese wondered how in the hell he was going to talk with his mouth closed. But he suffered in silence as he led Faith over to the senator with about as much enthusiasm as a man marching to the gallows.

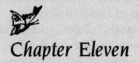

Chapter Eleven

NEGOTIATING THE CONTRACT was hell. The two parties faced each other across a cherry dining table brought in for the occasion. Faith Collins and Temperance Hamilton sat on one side, Reese Jordan and David Alexander on the other. A stack of legal contracts was centered between them, occupying neutral territory.

The silver coffee pot was considered neutral territory by necessity. It was in great demand that early in the morning. The participants tended to monopolize it, especially since two of the four negotiators were nursing headaches of monstrous proportions.

The battle lines had been drawn, the parties stalemated on either side. David looked at Reese, then at Faith. "Let's go over the terms of the contract once again."

"We've been over the contract," Reese interrupted. "What's the point of going over it again?"

"The point," David said firmly, "is to sign it. Neither of you has agreed to do that yet."

"She has to sign it. I've already paid an advance on her salary," Reese stated.

"I've already spent that money. I can't give it back," Faith reminded him.

125

"The least you can do is sign the damned contract." Reese glared at her. He hadn't slept, and he had a bitch of a headache. He was in no mood to negotiate every point of the contract.

"Not the way it stands." Faith gritted her teeth and rubbed her forehead. Her head ached, probably from all the champagne she'd consumed. Why hadn't Reese warned her about the effects of too much champagne?

"What's wrong with it?" Reese was spoiling for a fight and it was all Faith's fault. If she hadn't worn that damn red dress, he wouldn't have been in this condition.

"Everything." Faith crossed her arms over her chest. The man reeked like a saloon of cigar smoke, alcohol, and expensive perfume. How dare he show up looking and smelling this way? It was insulting. As insulting as being ignored all evening while he talked politics with Yankee robber barons, and then being dropped off at the front desk of a hotel at two o'clock in the morning without so much as a good-night kiss! He had some nerve!

She had nerve, he thought, sitting there refusing to sign. Who did she think she was, looking at him as if he'd crawled out of the gutter, when she was the one who'd gotten tipsy on champagne? What right did she have to glower at him? He was the one who'd kept his wits about him. If he hadn't dropped her off at the hotel, he'd have made love to her in the carriage—without a contract. How would she have felt about that?

Reese reached for the coffee pot. She beat him to it, her hand already on the silver handle. He seized the pot and pulled it in his direction. Faith stubbornly refused to let go.

"Children, children," Tempy chided, taking the pot from their hands and pouring each of them a cup. "You're behaving like spoiled, pigheaded little brats." She looked to David for confirmation.

David agreed. "We aren't getting anywhere. Why don't we call the whole thing off?"

"No!" Reese and Faith shouted simultaneously.

"Then stop this nonsense and let's get down to business." David's voice was firm. His patience was stretched to the limits by their stubbornness. It was time to compromise or quit. "First of all . . ."

He explained the contract thoroughly, then went over the sticking points. "The fee is twenty thousand dollars." He looked to Reese.

Reese nodded in agreement.

Tempy gasped at the enormous amount of money.

Faith shook her head.

"Oh, hell!" Reese muttered in disgust. "What's wrong with that? Not enough?"

"Too much," Faith said firmly.

"Too much?" Reese sputtered, surprised. "What the devil . . . ?" For a minute he had forgotten he was dealing with a woman of principle. "How much do you want?"

"Half that amount," she told him. "I'll accept ten thousand."

Reese looked at David. "All right. I agree to pay you ten thousand. Half now and half at delivery. Agreed?" He stared at Faith, willing her to agree.

"Minus the advance of three thousand eighty-six dollars and thirty-four cents, of course."

"Minus the advance," Reese agreed. She didn't know about the extra six thousand that David had deposited in her bank. And by the time she found out, the contract would be signed, witnessed, and recorded. He wanted to be sure she couldn't come back after the divorce, begging for more money or claiming he'd cheated her. She'd get twenty thousand whether she wanted it or not.

"Mr. Jordan agrees to provide food, clothing, and shelter for both Mrs. Collins and her daughter, Joy. He will also pay any additional living expenses for the duration of the pregnancy," David continued. "Mrs. Collins agrees to reside at Mr. Jordan's ranch in Wyoming for up to one year. She agrees to leave as soon as she is able to travel following the birth of the child." He looked at Faith.

She started to agree when Temperance whispered in her ear. "I agree to leave as soon as my health permits, provided a suitable wet nurse is in residence. My aunt pointed out that finding a wet nurse might take some time. I won't deprive my child of nourishment." Faith blushed profusely as she met Reese's gaze. "Is that acceptable to you, Mr. Jordan?"

"Acceptable and reasonable," he told her. "I appreciate your concern for my child as long as you understand that you are forfeiting your rights to him. You must leave Wyoming and never attempt to contact him."

Faith shifted in her chair. Her eyes brimmed with tears and her stomach lurched convulsively, but she didn't speak.

"Do you understand?" Reese asked bluntly, running his fingers through his hair.

Faith nodded.

"Do you agree to forfeit all rights of motherhood?" Reese met her gaze. "Permanently?"

"Even if you die?" Faith asked. "Or get killed?" She pulled a handkerchief from her pocket and began twisting it. She pinned him with those solemn gray eyes.

"Even then." He flinched when he met her gaze, but he refused to look away.

Faith hesitated. "What would happen to him if you died?"

"Mr. Jordan will be the legal father of the infant, and the baby will be his legal and rightful heir. A guardian is to be named in Mr. Jordan's will and appointed to take care of the child until its majority," David explained.

Faith looked at the attorney. "David, I want you to be the baby's guardian. If something should happen to Mr. Jordan, I want you to agree to raise my child."

"I'll decide what's best for my heir," Reese told her. He had already signed a new will naming David guardian of any offspring, but that was beside the point. He couldn't allow Faith Collins to dictate terms.

"Then I'm afraid you'll have to find someone else," Faith said quietly. She rose and leaned over the table. "This point is not negotiable. The guardian must be David Alexander." She was aware that only David would know her whereabouts if something happened to Reese. He would be her only link to her child.

She held her breath. She thought he might refuse. He certainly looked as if he wanted to. His eyes were dark and stormy and narrowed to mere slits in his face. He clenched his teeth. The muscles in his right cheek quivered under the strain.

She leaned down to whisper something in her aunt's ear. Tempy pushed her chair away from the table.

Reese remained seated. He wanted to call her bluff. He wanted to challenge her, but he didn't. He sat in impotent fury, knowing he had to agree to her condition. He could tell from the deliberately impassive look on her face that she would not concede.

"All right, dammit!" He did not lose graciously. "I agree to your terms." He waited for her to gloat over her victory, but again he had misjudged her.

Her softly spoken thank-you sounded grateful and sincere.

And so it continued throughout the morning as they examined, discussed, and decided upon every minute detail of the contract until they reached the stickiest point of all.

Uncomfortable with the final item, David cleared his throat and reached for the last sheet of paper. "All that's left to settle is the actual . . . uh . . . number . . ." He cleared his throat once more, louder this time, and tried again. "The . . . uh . . . actual number of . . . attempts at conception."

"*What?*" Tempy couldn't believe her ears. She blushed to the roots of her red hair at the idea of setting an actual number.

"We must establish a time frame. If the child is not delivered within one year, the contract is null and void." David struggled to maintain his professional demeanor.

Reese grinned.

Tempy and Faith huddled together, discussing the ramifications of the scheme. They whispered together for several minutes before they arrived at a number.

"Do you think three will be sufficient?" Faith asked.

Reese grinned again, this time with smug satisfaction. "I think three will be fine."

David scribbled in the number without allowing time for further debate.

In their haste to settle on a number, neither Reese nor Faith thought to ask if "three" referred to the number of times they would share a bed or if it meant three minutes, three hours, three days, weeks, or months. That should have been spelled out. But it wasn't. And the two of them had very different ideas about what it meant.

David handed Reese and Faith a copy of the agreement, then held out his pen.

"There is one other thing," Reese said casually. "From the moment you sign this paper, Mrs. Collins, you will live with me. Only me. If I even suspect you've been with another man, the contract will be declared invalid and the money forfeited."

"How dare you?" Tempy leaped to her feet.

"I dare, Miss Hamilton," Reese answered silkily, "because there must be no question about my son's paternity. I want him to have impeccable bloodlines and an untarnished reputation." He fixed his chocolate-brown eyes on Faith. "I may not choose to announce it publicly, but we

are legally bound until the end of your pregnancy. The proxy marriage is real. We are temporarily husband and wife. In Wyoming we will
live as husband and wife. I'll expect you to
behave circumspectly. There will be no other
men in your life for the duration of the contract."

Faith recoiled as if he'd slapped her. Her cheeks
turned a brilliant red. Her chest heaved in indignation. Her gray eyes flashed angrily. "Is that your
final condition?" Her words were frosty.

"It is."

"Good." Faith continued to face him. "I, too, have
a final condition. You see, Mr. Jordan, I am very
fastidious. If you ever come to me in your present state—reeking of alcohol, tobacco, and someone else's perfume—I will consider the contract
null and void whether I carry your child or not.
I'll gladly forfeit the remainder of the money, but
you will forfeit all rights to my child." She swallowed quickly to discourage the bile churning in
her throat. "I agreed to that farcical ceremony, and
I, at least, had the courage to utter the words. In
person. Understand this, Mr. Jordan: There will
be no other women in your life for the duration
of the contract." She flung his words back in his
face.

Reese said nothing. He jerked the pen from
David's hand and scrawled his signature on one
copy of the agreement, then the other, before
shoving the instrument at Faith.

She took the pen and without even glancing his
way, signed her name to both documents. She
passed the papers to Tempy to witness.

Once that was done, Faith quickly stalked out the door. She walked down the hall, past the door to the Vice Presidential Suite, and into the water closet where she violently expelled the contents of her stomach.

"SHE DRIVES A hard bargain," Reese admitted. He was up to his chest in hot, soapy water, eliminating the odor, easing away the excesses of the night before, and nursing a snifter of brandy. The hair of the dog that had bitten him. "Hell of a way to start off the New Year."

David threw back his head and laughed. He sat on a chair inside the folding screen, a few feet away from the bathtub. "I'll say. Your plan almost blew up in your face."

"She almost blew up in my face. I've never seen a woman get quite that angry or turn so green." He knew it was cruel, but he couldn't help chuckling at the memory. "I hope she made it to the basin."

"Get used to it," David warned. "Pregnant women are often nauseated. I'm told morning sickness is a force to be reckoned with."

Reese took another sip of his brandy. "I should have ordered some champagne along with the coffee this morning, but I was too busy suffering to worry about her."

"Well, you'd better get used to worrying about her." David chuckled at Reese's puzzled expression. "She's your responsibility for the rest of the year."

"And Joy," Reese said thoughtfully. "Don't forget about Joy."

"Or the baby," David reminded him. "The whole purpose of this unorthodox scheme is to produce a baby." He smiled at Reese, a dimple creasing his left cheek. "Looks like you're about to have the family you've always craved, Reese."

Reese frowned, his eyebrows knitting his forehead. He hadn't realized his needs were that transparent. "It's time. Most men already have families by the time they reach my age. I'm not getting any younger. I don't want to be too old to enjoy my son."

"Ancient at thirty-one," David teased. "I hope you enjoyed yourself last night and sowed all your wild oats." David was well aware of how Reese had passed his time after leaving Faith Collins at the hotel.

"I played cards," Reese told him, "and I drank. I didn't indulge the ladies."

"Very circumspect behavior." David grinned at his cousin. "And good practice. Because it looks as if you're going to be on a very tight rein from now on." His eyes sparkled with mischief as he opened his mouth to add further insult.

But Reese was quicker. He raised his arm, and the wet, soapy sponge went flying through the air, leaving a trail of bathwater in its wake. It sailed the length of the tub to collide with David Alexander's big mouth.

"You were saying?" Reese taunted.

"I ought to keep my damn mouth shut." David accepted Reese's taunt good-naturedly. He tossed the sponge back, then dried his face with a towel, got up from the chair, and walked to the door. "I think I'll check on the ladies."

"I'm going to take a short nap," Reese told him. "Why don't you tactfully suggest Faith do the same?"

"With you? Or alone?" David couldn't resist.

"Alone." Reese laughed. "I'm not a complete fool. I do know when to retreat."

"I'm relieved to hear it," David commented dryly, "because the lady in question is likely to make mincemeat of you if you cross her path before sundown."

"I'll have to take my chances. Our train leaves at five-ten this afternoon. What about yours?"

"A couple of hours later. I thought I'd take Miss Hamilton out to dinner before we head back to Richmond. It's the least I can do after forcing her to witness this morning's battle." David dreaded the long trip to Richmond and back, but he was committed to escorting Temperance Hamilton home.

Reese stood up in the tub. He wrapped a towel around his narrow hips. "Wake me up in a couple of hours. Oh, and David . . ."

"Yeah?"

"I left a name on my desk."

"So?"

"See what you can dig up on him while you're in Richmond."

"Do you want me to ask the aunts?"

"No," Reese answered. "Keep this quiet. Be discreet."

David smiled. He was an expert at nosing around. He'd learned the ropes from Pinkerton himself. They both had.

He walked into the next room and retrieved the slip of paper from Reese's desk. He smiled when he read the name. Reese might pretend a casual curiosity, but David wasn't fooled. He glanced at the paper a second time, then flipped it into the fireplace.

Champ Collins.

Chapter Twelve

REESE JORDAN SNEAKED a glance at the woman sharing the carriage seat with him. She sat still, her back impossibly straight, her shoulders held back, her head tilted at a haughty, regal angle.

Her nap hadn't seemed to improve her disposition. She was still angry. Her face was chalk white. Her beautiful wide mouth had flattened into a thin, disapproving line. She hadn't said a word since leaving the hotel, and her hands were clenched into fists in her lap.

It was not a promising beginning.

Faith gritted her teeth in an effort to keep them from chattering. Her emotions were in turmoil, her nerves stretched to the breaking point. She hadn't the faintest idea how she would get through the next twenty-four hours. And she couldn't begin to think about the coming days, weeks, and months in the company of Reese Jordan. But she would have to manage—somehow. She had signed her name to that contract. It lingered in her mind, in bold black ink, mocking her each time she thought about it.

She glanced at the man sitting beside her. She shivered each time she thought about the intimate nature of their agreement. She wondered if he expected her to sleep with him tonight on the train. She shivered again, but whether from apprehension or anticipation she couldn't tell. She swallowed hard to keep the churning of her stomach at bay. She hoped she would make it to the station before she disgraced herself in the carriage.

It was not a promising beginning.

The carriage rolled to a stop at the station. David leaped down from his seat and assisted Temperance. Reese lifted Joy into his arms and held out a hand for Faith.

Reese took one look at her face and handed Joy to David. Swinging Faith into his arms, he sprinted for the platform and the private railroad car he'd had brought from Chicago for the journey.

David set Joy on the ground, then took her hand and followed behind, but at a much slower pace. Temperance kept step by his side.

"Welcome aboard, sir." A porter tipped his hat and stepped forward to open the door for Reese.

Reese hurried to the water closet. He lowered Faith to her feet. She wavered like a colt on wobbly legs, clutched her stomach, and vomited into the basin. Reese dipped a washcloth into the pitcher. He untied the bonnet ribbons under her chin, pulled the hat off, and tossed it aside. He smoothed the cool cloth over her hot face.

"Better?" he asked, handing her the cloth.

Feeling horribly embarrassed, Faith nodded.

He tilted her face up to look at him. Some of the chalky whiteness had left her features. The healthy color was beginning to return. "There's no need to feel embarrassed, Faith. All of us get sick once in a while."

Her eyes were questioning.

He smiled. "Even me." He moved away from her. "Stay here for a moment. I'll get you something to drink."

Her eyes shot up.

"No champagne." He held up his hands in a gesture of surrender. "I promise." He backed out of the washroom and closed the door.

"Where is she?" someone said.

He turned around to face Temperance. "In there." He pointed to the door. "I was about to get her something to drink." Reese moved toward the bar in the far corner of the room. He poured a glass of water and handed it to Temperance.

Tempy knocked on the door. "Faith? It's me, Tempy. May I come in?" She didn't wait for Faith's muffled reply. She opened the door and walked in.

Faith threw her arms around her aunt, seeking comfort. "Oh, Aunt Tempy, I feel like a fool!"

"Nonsense." Tempy's voice was brisk and firm. "You're entitled to a fit of nerves."

"Is that what it was?"

"Of course, and the effects of a little too much champagne last night. It happens to everyone." Tempy brushed the damp hair away from her niece's face.

"That's what he said."

"Really?" Tempy's opinion of Reese Jordan rose a few notches. She handed Faith the glass of water. "Here, take a sip. Rinse your mouth out. You'll feel better."

Faith did as she was told, then turned back to Tempy. "I've never . . ."

Tempy wanted to remind her niece that she was about to do many things she'd never done before, but thought better of it. She didn't want Faith to be ill again. "It will be all right, my dear." She patted Faith's cheek with her gloved hand. "Everything will turn out fine." Tempy smiled at Faith.

The train whistle sounded. Tempy pulled away from Faith. "I wish I could stay aboard," she admitted. "I wish I were going with you." Tears brimmed in the corners of her gray eyes.

Reese tapped at the washroom door. "The train will be pulling out in a few minutes."

Tempy opened the door. Faith looked past Reese and suddenly recalled where she was. Her gaze darted around the interior of the railroad car, without focusing on the furnishings. She was looking for something. "Where's Joy?" She stepped into the room and headed for the outer door, intent on finding her sister.

Reese blocked her path. "Easy now." His voice was gentle. "She's outside with David. She wanted to watch them loading the horses. They'll be here in a minute."

Seconds later the door of the car opened and Joy rushed in, full of exciting news. She ran toward Faith, but Reese intercepted her.

"Easy, Joy, your mother isn't feeling well. She's still shaky on her feet." He took Joy's hand and led her to the sofa. "Why don't we sit here where you can keep an eye on her while you tell me all your news. Say good-bye to your aunt Temperance." He gave the instruction to Joy, but meant it for Faith as well.

Joy ran to Tempy and hugged her around the

waist. Tempy leaned down and Joy planted a sloppy kiss on her aunt's cheek before turning back to Reese. "Where is Aunt Tempy goin', Weese?"

"She's going home to Richmond. But we're going on a long train ride," Reese explained.

"You and me?" Joy was torn between excitement and hesitation.

Reese nodded.

"Is Faith goin', too?"

"Yes, sprite, your mother is going with us." The pet name rolled off his tongue. He had awarded the tag to Joy the instant he heard her call Faith by her given name. He knew it was an unusual form of address for a child, especially in the South. Reese had never heard southern mothers called anything except Mother or Mama, and to his way of thinking, Joy was unique. A child with an independent spirit, like an elf or a fairy. A sprite.

Joy looked down at him, a puzzled expression on her face. She opened her mouth to say something.

Faith drew in her breath and held it.

"Well, good-bye, Faith," Tempy said, a little too loud. She hugged Faith quickly, then hurried over to Reese and Joy, determined to save the day. "Joy, be a good girl for Faith and Mr. Jordan, and remember what we talked about." She waited for Joy to blurt out the truth, but Joy surprised her.

"Yes, ma'am, Aunt Tempy. I won't forget." She smiled at Tempy, proud of herself.

The careful coaching of the night before had paid off. Joy would keep their secret a little while longer.

Faith let out a sigh of relief.

The train whistle blasted a second time, and David came to the doorway. "We have to go, Miss

Hamilton. They won't hold the train any longer."

"Yes, I understand." Tempy inclined her head in David's direction before turning back to Reese. "Take care of my girls," she ordered.

"I will."

Temperance was taken aback by his quick promise. "If Faith gets ill again . . ."

"I'll take care of her," Reese said firmly.

"But—"

"I'll wire you from the next stop and let you know how she's feeling." The telegram would probably arrive in Richmond before Temperance did but it was the least he could do to allay the woman's fears.

Temperance looked up at Reese, her gray eyes locked with his brown ones. "I expect to be kept informed of . . . things."

"Fine." Reese didn't flinch from the look in her eyes, but he didn't commit himself further.

"Well, fine." Temperance knew he had promised all he intended to promise. "Good-bye." She blew kisses to Faith and Joy, then preceded David out the door and down the steps to the platform, where she stood waving, tears rolling down her cheeks, as the train chugged away.

Moments later Faith pulled away from the window. Temperance was a tiny speck in the distance, almost completely obscured by the thick black smoke billowing from the stack on the engine. She turned back to the room.

They were alone.

She panicked. "What did you do with Joy?"

"I murdered her and threw her tiny body off the train while you were waving good-bye to your

aunt." He shrugged tiredly. "What do you think
I did with her? She wanted to see her bedroom."
He opened the door.

Faith inched closer to him and peeked inside.
Joy sat in the middle of the child-sized bed. She
had shed her traveling coat, gloves, and bonnet
and scattered them across a pink rug in a path
from the door to the bed. Joy looked up from her
doll and waved to Faith. "Look, Faith! Weese said
it was my very own room on the train, and he
brought all my dolls and my table and chairs and
everything. See?"

Joy's enthusiastic grin was infectious. Faith
smiled in spite of herself. She had forgotten the
pleasure of having her own room. Before the war
she had taken it for granted. After the war necessity
had demanded she forget it.

She walked over to the bed and sat down next to
Joy. Faith took one small foot in her hand and began
to untie the laces. She removed the other shoe as
well, leaving Joy in her thick wool stockings. "We
don't want to ruin the pretty pink bedspread with
dirty old shoes, do we, sweetie?"

Joy shook her head. "My room is pretty, isn't it,
Faith?"

Faith glanced around the room, noting the panel-
ing stenciled with pink dolls, the miniature chest,
the table and chairs, toys and books. She looked
toward the doorway. Her eyes met Reese's. "It's
the prettiest room I've ever seen."

His shoulders seemed to widen before Faith's
eyes.

"Honest?" Joy's gray eyes were huge. "Prettier
than yours, before the war?"

"Cross my heart." Faith did just that.

Joy scooted closer and hugged Faith tightly. "Oh, thank you, Faith." She bounded off the bed, ran to Reese, and clasped him around the knees. "Oh, thank you, Weese!"

Reese gently ruffled her hair with his hand, but his eyes were focused on Faith. "You're welcome, sprite."

Joy returned to her bed, her attention on her dolls.

Faith stood up and walked toward the man in the doorway. "Yes, thank you, Reese."

"She had to have a room." He shrugged off her thanks. He didn't want her gratitude.

"What was it before you had it turned into a little girl's dream?"

"My office."

She opened her mouth to speak, but he interrupted her. "I can work just as easily out here." He closed the door to Joy's room and motioned toward the living area.

Faith looked at the sitting room, studying the details for the first time.

It was a large room, paneled in light oak. The floors were covered by woven carpets, but instead of the usual patterns found in Turkey rugs, these rugs were a bright orange decorated with stylized designs. A large Duncan Phyfe desk and matching chair occupied one corner of the room. A leather sofa and two leather wing chairs were grouped around a big cast-iron stove. Several low tables of oak and pine were scattered about holding books, lamps, and carved figures of animals. The walls were hung with paintings, mostly landscapes, and a grouping of pastel sketches and pen-and-ink drawings. A large, detailed map of the western territories hung behind Reese's desk. Faith moved closer to get a better look at one of the pen-and-ink drawings.

The subject of the drawing was a huge flat rock rising out of the ground. It towered over the line of trees at its base. But the most amazing feature of the drawing was the attention to detail. Faith could see that the sides of the rock were grooved, fluted, like Doric columns. Faith had never seen anything like it.

"The white men call it Devils Tower." Reese had moved to stand beside her. "The Sioux call it Grizzly Bear's Lodge because the grooves look like the marks made by giant bears attempting to climb to the top."

Faith laughed softly. "I think I prefer the Sioux name. Have you ever seen it?"

Reese nodded. "It's in the northeastern part of the territory."

"Wyoming?"

"Yes."

"How fascinating! Will we live close enough to see it?" She traced the ridges with the tip of her fingernail.

"No," he told her, watching as her face crumpled in disappointment. "We live about five miles outside of Cheyenne, in the southeastern part of the state." Reese touched her shoulder. "Why don't you take off your coat and gloves? We'll be traveling for four or five days. You might as well make yourself at home." He strolled over to the bar and produced a kettle from beneath it. He filled it with water, then walked over and set it on the stove. "I'll show you the rest of my home on wheels while the water is heating."

Faith unbuttoned her coat and pulled off her gloves. Her hands automatically went under her chin to untie her bonnet strings. She was surprised to find her hat gone.

Reese grinned. "I think it landed in the bathtub."

"I don't remember removing it," Faith admitted.

"I'm not surprised." He smiled again. "You were busy over the basin. I took it off. You can get it later." He threw her coat over his arm. "Come, I'll show you the bedroom."

"The bedroom?" She looked at him as if he had sprouted horns.

"Yes, Mrs. Collins, the room with the bed in it. The one we'll sleep in."

"Together?" That one word transformed her slightly husky contralto into a squeak.

"How else are we going to make a baby?" He asked the question so casually, it took a moment for the words to penetrate.

"What about Joy?" She clung to the only legitimate excuse she could think of.

"Joy has her own room and her own bed." Reese stared at Faith. For a woman who had been married and had borne a child, she seemed unreasonably nervous. "She won't be sharing ours. Why do you think I turned my office into a bedroom for her? She needs her privacy, and we will need ours." He sounded so patient, but in truth his patience was rapidly running out. He'd already paid ten thousand dollars for the right to put his seed in her, and he was eager to get on with it. He took her hand and led her to the door next to the washroom.

"Well, here it is." He turned the cut-glass doorknob, then let the door swing open.

Faith gasped in surprise.

A huge bed made of carved oak dominated the room. The massive headboard was shaped like an arch. A bouquet of intricately carved roses was centered beneath the arch. The ribbons holding the bouquet together trailed down either side of the wood and wrapped themselves around the posts. The feather mattresses were piled high, the goose-down pillows, fluffy and plump. The bedcovers were made of gold satin. And the footboard of the enormous bed was a smaller version of the headboard.

It was the most beautiful bed Faith had ever seen. It looked warm, comfortable, inviting, and sinfully opulent. The room looked the way she imagined a king's bedroom might look, with a bed all decked out in gold and walls covered with forest-green satin. Large pillows in matching gold and green lay scattered about the floor. A small oak table stood on either side of the headboard, each holding a brass lamp. One table was stacked with leather-bound books while the other held a vase of red roses. Their lovely scent filled the room, almost overpowering it.

Reese walked to an oak armoire and opened one of the doors. He hung Faith's coat inside, then placed her gloves on the shelf. Her burgundy silk ball gown was hanging inside. He must have had the baggage sent ahead.

"You can have the right side. I'll take the left."

Her gaze was riveted on the bed before she realized he was talking about the armoire.

His brown-eyed stare followed her gaze to the bed. "We'll decide on that later," he teased, his body hardening at the thought.

Faith whirled around and started for the door, determined to escape his presence. She slammed into Reese's unyielding chest.

His arms went around her waist to steady her.

She braced her hands against his forearms and felt the electricity that arced between them. Her flesh tingled in anticipation. Her mouth went dry, and her skin grew hot. She wet her lips with the tip of her tongue.

Reese watched in fascination as her lips parted. His head dipped toward hers.

Faith looked up at him. His eyes were dark, smoldering, almost black. She watched his face move closer to hers. She thought he would kiss her. She waited, hoping. But his lips bypassed hers. She sighed in disappointment until she felt his cool lips against her neck. His mouth nibbled at her ear, sucking ever so slowly on the lobe. She sagged in his arms, her legs refusing to support her weight.

Reese ran his hands up her rib cage and under her arms, silently urging her to move them upward, around his neck. She tried to loop her arms around his neck, but couldn't. She settled for grasping handfuls of the wool covering his shoulderblades. Faith pulled herself against him, turning her head just enough to offer him her other earlobe. His exploring hands inched forward, cupping the undersides of her breasts. He grazed the tips with the sides of his thumbs. Faith's whole body seemed to jerk at the contact.

His warm, wet tongue traced the line of her neck from her earlobe to the fabric of her collar. He palmed her breasts again. Her heart pounded beneath his right hand. Her breathing was rapid, ragged, almost matching his.

He bent his knees and swung her up into his arms, his attention focused on the massive bed—his parents' marriage bed, the bed in which he'd been conceived, the bed where his son would be given life. He started toward it with Faith cradled against him.

"Weese?"

He almost dropped Faith. The sound of his name spoken from the doorway was sobering. He turned around and lowered Faith to her feet. Joy stood watching them, her eyes wide with wonder. "The kettle is singing."

"What?"

"The kettle you put on the stove," Faith whispered. "It's boiling."

"So am I," Reese whispered back, although Joy's intrusion had cooled his ardor considerably.

Faith straightened her dress and patted several strands of hair back into place. She walked to Joy and took her by the hand. "Let's go rescue the singing kettle." She turned back and looked at Reese. "Are you coming?"

Reese muttered an obscenity and ground his teeth together at her poor choice of words.

Chapter Thirteen

HE HAD WATCHED her all evening, his dark eyes following her every movement, every gesture, like a predator about to pounce on his prey. Faith had been so nervous she could hardly swallow the food the chef at the Madison Hotel had packed for them. She blushed each time she looked up from her plate and felt his eyes on her. He undressed her with those eyes, and she knew that if Joy hadn't been sitting beside them, filling the heated silence with her childish chatter, his hands would have completed the task his eyes had begun. Her body heated at the thought. She was filled with conflicting emotions—tension, anticipation, and fear. Fear not of Reese but of the unknown. After tonight there would be no turning back, no escaping her fate. She had bargained with the devil, and it was time to give him his due.

She closed the door to the pink bedroom. Joy slept soundly, curled up on her side, her dolls close by. She would sleep until morning. Faith could not procrastinate any longer.

She glanced around the sitting room. Reese had been seated in front of the wood stove sipping a glass of brandy when she left to put Joy to bed. But

now the room was empty. He was gone. She wondered if he was curled up in bed waiting for her.

Faith took a deep breath to steady her nerves.
A glass of white wine sat on the table beside his
empty brandy snifter. She picked it up and drained
the contents in three swallows. She put the empty
glass back on the table, then walked around the
room methodically extinguishing the lamps on her
way to the bedroom.

Reese sat outside on the tiny rear porch of the
railroad car, one booted foot propped against the
rail. The night air was crisp and cold, but the sky
was clear. He studied the constellations, searching his brain for the English and Cherokee names.
The tip of his thin cigar glowed bright red in the
dark as he inhaled the soothing taste of tobacco,
then exhaled, blowing smoke rings in the dark.
He listened to the rhythmic clacking of the train
against the tracks and watched the shower of cin-
ders sparkle in the night before they cooled to ash
and dissipated on the wind. And he tried to count
the minutes. He was killing time, waiting until
he could go back inside the car. He thought he
heard the splash of water. She might be bathing.
He pulled the lapels of his heavy wool coat a little
tighter against the biting chill. His mind conjured
up the image of Faith Collins in the bath, slick
and wet and warm. . . . He shifted uncomfortably
to accommodate the predictable hardening in his
groin. He'd give her five more minutes.

The five minutes expired. Reese made his way
inside the car. His booted toe kicked a table leg,
and his knee bumped the sharp corner. "Ouch,
dammit!" He squinted into the darkness, trying

to make out the shapes of the furniture. Outside there had been some moonlight. In here there was nothing. Why the hell hadn't she left on a lamp? "Shit!" His unprotected hip slammed into one of the wing chairs.

The sound of the bedroom door banging against the wall woke Faith. She sat up, instantly alert. Reese Jordan stood beside the bed. "Ssh!" she warned.

"Ssh, hell!" Reese grumbled, lowering his voice. "I cracked my knee, not to mention my hipbone. Why didn't you leave a lamp burning?"

"It's dark," she said, with bizarre logic.

"I know it's dark. That's why you should have left a lamp on. I can't see the damn furniture in the dark." Reese wrenched off his coat and tossed it in the direction of a chair. He sat down.

The side of the bed dipped beneath his weight. Faith grabbed at the other side to keep from rolling against him. "There's no need to be offensive," she told him primly. "I was on my way to bed. Why should I have left a lamp on? I didn't know where you were."

"You knew I'd be coming to bed," he accused.

"I knew no such thing!" Faith lied. "You were gone when I came out of Joy's room."

"I was outside freezing my ass off," he informed her as he yanked off his boots and let them fall to the floor. "Giving you time to do . . . whatever. I was acting like a gentleman." He sneered at the last word. "The least you could have done was leave a light on."

"But I always blow the lamps out," she protested stupidly. "I never leave them on." It was all she could think to say when she felt the slight stir of

cool air, the whisper of fabric as he pulled off . . .
Good Lord, he was taking off his clothes!

"Did Champ blow the lamps out?" The bed
righted itself as Reese stood up to remove his
pants.

"What?"

"I asked if your sainted husband blew the lamps
out before he came to your bed?"

Faith thought for a second. "Well, of course he
did! He wouldn't have been much of a gentleman
if he hadn't."

Reese's hands brushed the surface of the bedside
table, searching for something.

Faith heard the scratching sound a second before
she smelled the unmistakable odor of sulfur.

"You can't . . ." She struggled to sit up, the covers
clutched to her chest. She squeezed her eyes shut.

"There is a hell of a lot to be said for not being a
gentleman." Reese replaced the globe on the lamp
and turned up the wick.

The room took on a golden glow. "I don't much
care for fumbling around in the dark. I like to see
what I'm getting." He walked around to her side
of the bed and lit that lamp as well. He touched
the side of her face, then chuckled. "Don't you?"

Her eyes flew open, then widened at the sight
of him.

He was naked.

She closed her eyes once again, tighter than before.
But it was too late. The image of his nude body,
bronzed by the glow of the lamps, was indelibly
etched on her brain. His skin was golden, much
darker than hers, his chest wide and bare with finely
sculpted muscles. She was surprised to find he had

two round brown patches on his chest, each with a hard little nub in the center. She hadn't realized men had nipples.

"Shy?" Reese asked sardonically. He yanked the covers from her clenched fists, flipped them back, and slipped into bed beside her.

Faith jerked the covers back into place and attempted to roll away. He was too close. She could feel the heat of his body.

He reached out to grab her. "What's this?" he asked when his fingers encountered a handful of flannel nightgown. It had been a long time since he'd slept with a woman who owned a flannel nightgown, and he had never had to fight his way through one, flannel or otherwise. "Don't tell me," he muttered. "Let me guess. You always wear a flannel nightgown to bed."

"Only in the winter." Faith blushed at his blunt statement. "In the summer I wear cotton."

"And your sainted husband never asked you to take it off?"

"No!" She pinned him with her wide gray gaze. "Did *he* ever take one off you?"

"Certainly not!" Faith was shocked at the suggestion.

"There's a first time for everything. Don't expect me to wade through yards of fabric to get to you." He turned on his side and pulled her close against his hard body.

"I don't expect you to do anything," Faith told him, holding herself still, afraid to relax into his inviting warmth.

She lay rigid in his arms, her spine unyielding. Reese sighed aloud. He hadn't thought she would require wooing. She had agreed to this. She had even signed a contract giving him the right, but apparently she expected a little effort on his part. It shouldn't take too much, he reasoned. Old Champ hadn't put too much effort into it himself, and he had fathered Joy. Reese shifted his weight onto one shoulder and maneuvered his arm beneath her. He caressed her, moving his hand from her waist up the column of her back and down again while his other hand exerted subtle pressure against the small of her back, kneading her stiff muscles, silently urging her closer.

A moan of pleasure escaped Faith's lips as his hands worked their magic.

"Open your eyes, Faith," he ordered. "Look at me. I won't hurt you."

She did as he asked. She looked at his face.

Reese sucked in his breath. Her eyes were an unguarded smoky gray, her mouth soft and inviting. She looked as if she wanted to be kissed. "Did your husband ever do this?" he asked as one hand moved from the small of her back up her spine while the other hand moved down to caress her firm bottom.

Faith shook her head. Reese watched as the long black braid moved against her pillow. "Did he kiss you?"

This time she nodded.

"Like this?" His lips claimed hers, gently at first, then more forcefully. He pulled her to him. Her breasts flattened against his chest. He could feel the twin points pressing into him. His hands fondled the flesh of her buttocks through the flannel. He deepened his kiss. He wanted to feel her skin. The flannel nightgown frustrated him. He pulled away, placing a light kiss on the tip of her nose. "Well?"

She didn't pretend not to understand. Again she shook her head.

"It's a miracle Joy was ever conceived," Reese muttered into the hollow of her neck.

It *was* a miracle, Faith thought. She couldn't imagine her mother and father ever doing anything like this. She clenched her fists. Her fingers ached with the need to tangle themselves in his dark hair and pull him closer. She wanted him to touch her, but more than that, she wanted to touch him, to explore the magnificent body he'd shown her.

"Is this your only nightgown?" Reese's question brought her attention back to him.

"No," she whispered.

"Is it new?" He nuzzled her neck.

"No."

"Good." His hands moved from her back to her front. He traced a line from her neck to the embroidered edge of her nightgown. He anchored his fingers in the flannel, then ripped the offending garment from neckline to hem. "We won't be needing this."

Faith gasped in shock. He had ripped away her nightgown and exposed her nakedness. Her gaze shot up, and she opened her mouth to speak, to tell him what she thought of his barbarous behavior. The expression of total admiration on his face stopped her. His eyes smoldered. He looked her over from head to toe. She reddened under his scrutiny, but she was warmed and encouraged by it as well. Reese Jordan was seeing what she had to offer, and he did not find her lacking. The expression in his eyes gave her confidence, made her bold. He had ripped away her nightgown and uncovered her secret self. There was no reason to hide.

She placed her palms against his chest.

He froze. He hadn't expected that.

His skin was hot. Incredibly hot. She smoothed her hands lightly over his flesh, searching for those beguiling nipples. The muscles of his chest contracted under her touch, rippling beneath her fingers. Faith found what she had been searching for. She touched them, grazing the buds with her fingertips. The tiny nubs hardened instantly.

Reese bit back a groan. He hadn't expected that, either. His hands began an exploration of their own, leaving her neck, moving lower, mimicking her hands until they found what they sought. He cupped the satiny globes, feeling their weight and shape. He smoothed his palms over them, teasing the tips with his thumbs. Her nipples hardened in response.

She closed her eyes. Her teeth caught at her bottom lip. She sucked in a ragged breath.

"Look at me," he urged. "Look at us."

Faith forced her eyes to open, forced herself to look.

The sight was shocking yet titillating. Her hands, white against his bronzed chest, teased and toyed with his nipples. His hands, dark against her fair skin, caressed her breasts. The color rose in her cheeks, stained them a vivid scarlet, but she didn't pull away. Her hands continued to explore as she copied his movements.

Reese caught both of her hands in his. He dipped his head and trailed his tongue along the crevice between her breasts. She smelled of lavender, perspiration, and woman. The scent of her teased him, taunted him, until the swelling in his groin became almost unbearable. He pushed at one breast, then the other. He touched one nipple with his tongue.

Faith jerked her hands from his grasp and tangled them in his thick black hair, holding his head against her breasts. Her whole body leaped in response as myriad sensations, like tiny electrical charges, raced through her, igniting every nerve ending.

Reese felt the response and concentrated on his task. His fingers touched, his tongue tasted, his teeth nipped, his mouth sucked one roseate peak and then the other. He worshiped the lovely white globes, lavishing attention on the hard little points, leaving them moist and gleaming in the lamplight.

His hands snaked down her rib cage, over the slight concave of her belly to the profusion of curls at the juncture of her thighs. His fingers massaged the curls, then probed the soft folds, seeking admission to the moist recesses.

Faith clamped her thighs together. The white heat of passion pooled beneath his questing fingers. She was afraid. No one had ever touched her where he was touching. One of his fingers slipped through her defense. It probed the soft, sensitive folds.

She was tight. God, she was so tight. His mind reeled at the thought of entering her. His burgeoning length was rock hard and painful. He wasn't sure he could wait much longer. He wanted to bury himself in her wonderful depths, to plant his seed in fertile ground. "How long has it been?" he breathed.

"How long?" she parroted dumbly, unable to comprehend the meaning of his words when his hands were doing such wonderful things to her. She opened her legs wider, allowing him access. She moved restlessly, seeking . . . something.

"Have you . . . slept . . . with a man lately?" He ground out the words.

She shook her head, but in answer or in passion, he couldn't tell. And he wanted, needed, to know.

"Have you been with a man since your husband died?" Perspiration beaded on his lip with the effort to control his raging desire. He moved his fingers inside her, willing her to answer.

"No!" She gasped at the pleasure-pain his fingers wrought. "Never!"

He had his answer. He withdrew his fingers. His mouth crushed hers. His tongue skimmed her teeth and explored her mouth, teasing, tasting.

She kissed him back, eagerly, feverishly following his tongue with her own, learning the rhythm of desire. Her hands fluttered over him, lightly touching, tracing his shoulders, his hair, his rib cage, before resting on his lean hips. She could feel that hard male part of him pressing against her, arrogantly demanding entrance. A raw, aching need burned where he touched her and spread through her stomach to her breasts. She urged him forward.

The feel of her hands on his sensitive flesh ignited Reese. He moved between her thighs. His hands fastened on her waist and pulled her to him. He groaned as she cuddled closer, her body cradling his arousal. His arms and legs quaked with the need for release. There was no reason to delay. She squirmed against him. She was ready.

His mouth left hers. He dipped his head and caught one distended nipple in his mouth. He nipped at it gently, carefully, as he moved his hips closer. Tremors shook his arms as he braced himself above her. He let go of her nipple and rested his forehead against her breast. "Now," he rasped, "put your legs around me. Now!"

Instinctively Faith obeyed him, locking her legs around his waist. He surged forward into her moist sheath. "God!" He groaned in ecstasy.

She screamed.

He felt the barrier. "Damn you, damn you, damn you." Reese repeated the litany of curses as he withdrew slightly, then thrust into her again, harder this time. He filled her completely, shattering the stubborn barrier and all his foolish illusions.

Faith cried out a second time. He captured her mouth with his, smothering her protests. She unlocked her legs from around him and tried to pull away. He pushed closer, immobilizing her with his greater weight. "Be still, dammit," he whispered harshly against her mouth. "Your squirming is making it worse! Be still!" Reese fought to maintain control.

His body strained with the effort. He tried to stop, but that control was beyond him. He had waited too long, wanted too much, and dammit, she had brought this on herself.

Her arms went around his neck. Her legs tightened around his hips. She gritted her teeth, squeezed her eyes shut, and pressed her face against his shoulder. Her tears dampened his skin. Her nails carved tiny crescents in the back of his neck, but she held on as he lifted her hips with his hands and began to move. Slowly at first, then faster.

The pain subsided to a dull ache, then disappeared completely as a new, different ache took its place. She moved instinctively, matching his thrusts with thrusts of her own. She listened as they matched the sound and motion of the train, the blood roaring in her ears as loud as the train rumbling down the track. She clung to Reese, straining to grasp something just beyond her reach. She pressed closer to him, her mouth seeking his. She licked the salt from his lips, then thrust her tongue through the seam. Her mouth began to imitate the motion of their bodies. The roaring was louder in her ears. She began to shiver uncontrollably, her muscles contracting painfully. Then suddenly she was surrounded by pleasure. She called out his name. In surprise. In wonder. In glorious, heart-stopping release.

Reese felt the trembling of her body, heard her call his name and sigh in blissful surrender. He paused, then allowed his body to have its way, moving in and out, faster and faster, until . . .

Her name was a guttural cry, wrung from the very depths of his body. He shuddered in her arms and spilled himself inside her warm, welcoming body.

Chapter Fourteen

FAITH SMILED SHYLY up at Reese. She had never dreamed that what went on between a man and a woman could be so magnificent, so unbelievably beautiful. The wonder of it took her breath away.

They lay sprawled across the big bed. She stretched, luxuriating in the aftermath of their lovemaking. Her toes touched the calf of his leg. She was brimming over with emotions, and she wanted to share them with the man who had taken her to the stars. Faith wiggled her toes against his leg to get his attention.

Reese jumped as if she'd burned him, then moved away. He looked down at her, but he didn't smile back. His eyes were harsh, their depths burning with an angry light.

He studied her. She looked like a wanton. Her eyes were soft. Her lips were red and pouty, bruised from his kisses. The tender skin on her neck and breasts showed signs of abrasion from his beard. Her black hair fanned out over her pillow. It had been braided. When had he unbraided it? She smiled at him, stretching sinuously, like a sated kitten. Well fed, contented, well loved. He could almost hear her purr. And why shouldn't she purr with satisfaction? Why shouldn't she be content? She'd used him. Played him for a fool. Lied. Damn her for the deceptive little bitch she was! He had been duped!

"Unless there's been another virgin birth I haven't heard about, you owe me an explanation. And, lady, it had better be good." His voice sliced through her veil of rosy contentment like an Arctic wind.

"I don't understand," she said warily as she reached for the sheets.

"You don't? Well, let me explain it." He pinned her to the mattress with his frosty gaze. "Joy is not your daughter! You are not a widow! There was no Champ Collins! And that wedding ring you're wearing is a fake! *You* are a fake, *Mrs*. Collins." He sneered as he spoke the words. "Is that clear enough for you to understand?"

"How did you find out?" Faith's eyes widened, and the color drained from her face. "How long have you known?" She clutched the covers to her chin as she whispered the questions.

"Oh, that's rich!" He got up from the bed and began to pace, unfazed by his lack of clothing. "I may have been taken in by your saintly widow act, but I know enough about women to know a virgin when I bed one."

"Oh." Her reply was barely audible, but Reese heard it and it added fuel to the fire of his anger.

"Yes. *Oh*." He stopped pacing and whipped around to face her. "Did you think I'd be too inexperienced to know the difference?" That idea made him almost as angry as her deception. "Dammit, woman"—he refused to say her name—

"if I had wanted an untalented, untutored, green, inexperienced, wide-eyed virgin, I'd have advertised for one!"

She seemed to disappear before his eyes, to blend right into the bed. She pulled the covers tighter.

That irritated him. "Don't bother." He flung the words at her. "I've seen all you've got to offer."

He should have slapped her. That would have been kinder than the words he threw at her. Tears welled up in her eyes. He had spoiled the most beautiful experience of her entire life. He had ruined it.

Reese saw the glimmer of tears in her eyes and the stricken expression on her face. "Damn!" he said. "Don't start with the tears. It's too late for that."

She wrapped the sheet around her and swung her legs off the bed.

"Where the hell do you think you're going?"

"I thought I heard Joy," came the timid reply.

"Get back in bed." He reached for his trousers. "I'll go." He slipped on his clothes and boots and stalked out the door.

Faith rolled over in the huge empty bed. She curled up into a ball and let the tears roll down her face. She cried hot, burning, silent tears. She cried until there were no tears left, then lay awake, waiting, listening for Reese's return.

At dawn she climbed out of bed and tiptoed into the washroom. There was no sign of Reese. She bathed quickly with cold water, hastily washing away the traces of his lovemaking. She finished bathing and tiptoed back to the bedroom. After buttoning herself into her old black silk, she began to pack her meager belongings.

From the rear porch of the railroad car, Reese watched the first pink streaks lighten the sky. He had sat outside in the freezing cold for hours, watching the landscape roll by, hoping the chill wind would cool his burning anger.

God, he dreaded facing her this morning. His head ached, and his throat burned from the biting cold wind, the lack of sleep, too much bourbon, and too many cigars. And damn, he was still angry. Angry at her, but mostly angry at himself because he had allowed this to happen. He had been taken in by a pair of big innocent gray eyes. She had told him she was a widow, and he'd believed her. Simple as that. Why would she lie to him? Why? For money? She needed money. Badly. Desperately. Why else would a virgin sign a contract like the one he'd offered her? Until tonight she had been a virgin. A nest-building, ring-wanting, let's-get-married-in-a-church virgin. He had spent his entire adult life avoiding such women, and now he had allowed himself to be caught. Trapped. Betrayed. Tricked. By a virgin with a pedigree a mile long. Why hadn't he learned his lesson about ladies with pedigrees? Hadn't Gwendolyn taught him anything?

Gwendolyn. Reese closed his eyes and pictured her in his mind. Her features had blurred a bit over the years, but he didn't need to see them to know what they were. Long blond hair, china-blue eyes, porcelain complexion, perfect hourglass figure, and a mouth that could do wonderful things to a man. He should know. She'd had many hours to practice on him. And then she had that Boston Brahmin pedigree. He had wanted her. And he had

wanted that pedigree and the respect and stability
that went with it.

And she had wanted him. Gwendolyn Terrill
had been enchanted with the idea of toying with
the forbidden. And he, Reese Jordan, had been the
forbidden. He could see it so clearly now. But then
he had been blinded by pride and lust. Mostly lust,
he admitted but he had also wanted to enter the
superior bastion of Boston society. The society that
had allowed him admittance to Harvard on the
strength of his father's name and money but had
denied him the respectability he craved because of
his heritage.

Reese had never made a secret of his background.
There had never been any reason to hide it. His
mother was part Cherokee. All the Alexanders were
a mix of Cherokee and Scots blood. Reese's father
was English. Reese was all three. The mixed blood
running through his veins had always been a source
of pride for Reese. He'd always been accepted by his
society.

But he hadn't been accepted at Harvard. Not
until his father bought his admittance. Bloodlines
mattered in Boston society where a good pedigree
meant the difference between acceptance and rejection, success and failure. Money might buy his way
into Harvard, might even open a few doors, but it
couldn't guarantee acceptance in a society dominated by narrow minds. Only an impeccable pedigree, a blue-blooded lineage, or an advantageous
marriage could do that.

Reese reached into his jacket pocket and withdrew
another thin cheroot. He struck a match and lit it,
enjoying the taste of the tobacco. He had thought

himself in love with Gwendolyn. The moment he saw her, he wanted her. And he was young enough, rich enough, arrogant enough, to think he could have her.

Reese remembered his wedding day as clearly as if it were yesterday. The church was filled to capacity. Boston society had turned out to see one of its own wed an outsider. Reese's own family had journeyed from the territory. His father, his mother's father, his mother's mother, her brothers and sisters, the family he loved, had traveled to Boston to share his happiness, to welcome his bride into the family. They waited eagerly to meet the woman Reese had chosen. They waited in the hot, stuffy church all afternoon.

Gwendolyn hadn't walked down the aisle on her father's arm. She sent a note instead, saying she had never intended things to go so far. Certainly she'd never intended to marry him.

It was just a game.

Half of the wedding guests laughed at the setdown Gwendolyn Terrill had given Reese Jordan. The rest shared his pain, his humiliation, his shame, because it was their shame as well. Boston society had played a cruel joke on Reese Jordan. It would serve as a lesson to other young upstarts.

He had tried to let it go, tried to forget her, but he couldn't. His love for her hadn't died that easily. Weeks later he'd found himself on her doorstep asking to see her, begging for an audience.

Gwendolyn had kept him waiting on the stoop for nearly an hour before she breezed past him on the arm of her tall, blond, entirely suitable escort. Reese turned away. They'd never spoken again.

Why the hell hadn't he learned from that mistake? He could have prevented this fiasco with more careful planning. Why had he changed his mind about the doctor? He should have had Faith examined. He had planned so carefully, so meticulously, for all possibilities except one. A virgin. A damned virgin. They seemed destined to be his Achilles' heel. His ultimate downfall.

He ought to put her pretty little ass on a train back to Richmond. He ought to stop payment on his bank draft and send her packing. He ought to . . .

Reese sighed. It was too late for all that. He had paid good money for her services, and he'd be damned if he would let her get away with cheating him! Besides, he might already have achieved his goal.

He flipped down the collar of his coat, then made his way back into the railroad car. He needed to wash before breakfast. The train had a scheduled forty-five-minute stop at the next station for water, fuel, mail, and passengers.

Reese was familiar with the schedule. He'd made the trip a half dozen times since the joining of the Union Pacific and Central Pacific tracks in Promontory, Utah, back in May.

He would have to face her sometime. He'd already made arrangements for breakfast for the three of them.

Reese stepped out of the washroom just as Faith closed the door to Joy's room. She was holding the little girl in her arms. A carpetbag and a small trunk sat next to the door. Faith's eyes were bloodshot and swollen. Her nose was red. She looked as if she'd spent the night drinking—or crying. She looked like hell.

"Where do you think you're going?" He nodded his head in the direction of the trunk.

"We're getting off at the next stop." Faith looked at him. His hair was wet. Drops of water ran down the inky strands and dotted the white shirt that hung open halfway down his chest. A linen towel was draped over one shoulder. He smelled of soap and spice. He had obviously just finished shaving. There was a speck of lather below his ear. He'd never looked more handsome to Faith.

"Yes," he agreed, "you are getting off at the next stop. For breakfast. And then you're getting right back on." He calmly began to button his shirt.

He didn't sound very angry, but his words still had an edge to them.

Faith pulled herself up to her full height, squared her shoulders, and raised her head to meet his steady scrutiny. "No, Mr. Jordan," she said firmly. "Joy and I are going back to Richmond."

His fingers stopped. He'd managed only half his buttons. "You aren't going anywhere with my child, except to breakfast."

"Joy is not your child," Faith reminded him.

"Nor is she yours," he countered. "What is she? Your kid sister?" It was a guess on his part, but a lucky one. He could tell by the expression in her red-rimmed eyes that he'd hit the mark.

"That's beside the point."

"I wasn't talking about Joy," Reese told her. "I was referring to the child you may be carrying inside you at this very moment."

Faith tried to step back away from him, but the

door to the pink bedroom stopped her. "I'm not carrying your child."

"How do you know that?" Reese asked.

"I just know," Faith insisted stubbornly.

"Did you do something to prevent conception?" His face was taut, his eyes narrowed dangerously. "Did you do something this morning?" He wanted to shake her. He moved forward but caught himself before he touched her.

"No, I—" she began.

"Then how do you know? Answer me."

"Because she's carrying me," Joy piped up, staring at her hero with big silvery gray eyes almost identical to Faith's. "Faith's not big enough to carry two little girls."

Joy's innocent remark dissolved some of the tension gripping them. Though he tried hard to maintain his anger, the corners of Reese's mouth turned up slightly. He and Faith had been so caught up in their battle, they had forgotten Joy.

She was a perceptive five-year-old, equipped with sharp eyes and ears. He would remember that in the future. He touched the tip of Joy's turned-up nose. "You're absolutely right, sprite." He reached for her and Joy held out her arms. He took her from Faith and set her on her feet. "Why don't we walk to breakfast? You're getting a little too big for Faith to carry."

"Because she's carrying your child?" Joy asked, solemnly repeating the phrase she'd heard Reese use.

"Something like that." His brown-eyed gaze met Faith's. His eyes held a silent warning, as if he dared her to open her mouth and protest.

She took her chances. "I don't want to go to breakfast with you." Her voice was soft, yet firm. She was prepared to stand her ground.

"But you will." Reese's full lips were pulled into a tight, disapproving line.

"No, Mr. Jordan, I won't." Faith refused to budge.

"Suit yourself." He sounded nonchalant, but his unyielding stance indicated otherwise. "Stay here if you like, but Joy and I are going to breakfast."

"Joy is not going with you."

He looked down at the child in his arms. "Are you hungry, sprite?"

Joy nodded.

Faith extended her arms in Joy's direction. "Come on, Joy, we're getting off. We're going back to Richmond."

Joy stayed where she was. "I'm hungry."

"We can eat on the train to Richmond," Faith explained.

"Is Weese going with us?"

"No, Mr. Jordan is staying on this train."

"Will I have my woom on the train to Wichmond?"

"No, sweetie, we'll sit on benches, as we did the first time." She stepped closer to take Joy out of his arms.

Joy shook her head and clung to Reese. "I want to stay with Weese."

"You can't, sweetie." Faith was getting a little desperate. "You must come with me."

"You can stay with me if you want, sprite," Reese promised as Joy tightened her arms around his neck and buried her face in his jacket.

"No, she can't!" Faith glared at him. "She's my responsibility."

"The contract you signed gave me the responsibility for Joy and for you," Reese corrected her smugly, reminding her of her legal obligation. "You may return to Richmond if you want to, but you relinquish all rights to Joy for a year."

"I would never do that!" Angry tears sparkled in Faith's eyes.

His voice was firm. "If you return to Richmond, Joy will stay with me."

"That's not fair! You can't—"

"I will." He shifted Joy to one arm and reached out to touch Faith's cheek. She jerked away from his fingers. "You lose, *Miss* Collins."

"It's *Mrs.* Jordan." Faith did not concede defeat graciously. She was angry with him for using Joy against her. And angry with Joy for betraying her. "I hate you."

"Fine." Reese's expression was closed, unreadable. "Hate me all you want. After breakfast." He took her elbow and guided her toward the door. He was furious with her for her stubborn refusal as well as for her deception and for reminding him that he'd agreed to marry her. And he was furious with himself for ruthlessly coercing her into submission.

He hated using Joy against her, but he would do whatever was necessary to keep Faith Collins within his reach. He refused to acknowledge the painful expression on her face or the way her angry words ripped at his insides.

Chapter Fifteen

"ALL RIGHT, DAMMIT, you win," Reese exploded as the train slowly chugged its way out of Chicago.

He had endured yet another silent breakfast—the third—and that was enough.

Faith ignored him.

"Did you hear me?" Reese asked. "I said you win."

"I wasn't aware we were competing." The chill in her voice was unmistakable.

"The hell you weren't!" Reese got up from his desk and began to pace along the length of the carpet right in front of where Faith sat embroidering. "You've given me the silent treatment for the past two days. I've had enough of it. I'm tired of sitting outside in the cold half the night. And I'm tired of picking you up off the sofa and putting you to bed every night." He was also tired of waking up each morning throbbing with unrequited desire. Oh, she was more than willing to curl up to him in her sleep, to share his body heat and plant her firm little fanny against his naked arousal. But the minute she opened her eyes she turned frosty. If he so much as touched her while she was conscious,

175

the air turned decidedly colder.

"I'm quite willing to sleep on the sofa," Faith reminded him. "I didn't ask to be carried to your bed each night. In fact, I would prefer to sleep alone."

"Too bad," Reese told her, "because that wasn't part of the deal." He pointed a finger in her direction. "You haven't lived up to your end of the bargain. According to our contract you owe me more time in the sack."

Faith stood up. His finger missed touching her nose by a mere fraction of an inch. She stared at his finger, then looked him over from top to bottom, refusing to be intimidated. "And you, Mr. Jordan, owe me an apology." She folded away her sewing and placed it in her basket.

"For what? Remember, you're the one who lied. You told me you were a widow and Joy was your little girl."

"I never said Joy was my child. You assumed—"

"So you lied by omission. What about your sainted husband, Champ?"

"Your assumption," Faith pointed out. "I never actually told you I'd been married."

"You're wearing a wedding band." He grabbed hold of her left hand and lifted it up in front of her face so she could see the thin gold band. His touch burned her flesh. Her body tingled with awareness.

Faith snatched her hand away.

"What was I supposed to think?" Reese asked.

"All right!" she yelled at him, losing control. "All right, I admit it. I lied to you. I deceived you. I betrayed your trust. I let you believe I was something I wasn't. Is that what you want to hear?"

Tears formed in her eyes then rolled down her cheeks. She ruthlessly wiped them away with the back of her hand.

Reese placed his hands on her shoulders and pulled her into the warmth of his wide chest. "What I want to hear," he said gently, "is why."

Faith pulled away from him. "The reason doesn't matter."

"It does to me."

"Why?" She turned on him. "Because you can't stand the thought of a liar and a cheat giving birth to your child? Isn't that all you really care about? Your contract? Your child? Your way?" She whirled around and raced into the safety of the bedroom. She slammed the door, then turned the key in the lock.

Reese stared at the bedroom door. "Faith, open the door."

There was no answer. He rattled the knob. The door was locked. He wanted to break it down. He longed to kick the damn door in, grab Faith, throw her down on the floor and make hot, sweet love to her. That was what he wanted to do, what he needed to do to ease the throbbing ache in his groin. So why the hell didn't he do it?

Because, he reminded himself, there was a better way to get her attention, an easier way. There was no need to break down a perfectly good door. He had Joy.

He walked to the open door of the pink bedroom. Joy was sitting on the floor playing with her dolls. She looked up at Reese and smiled.

"Hello. You wanna play dolls with me?" She looked so hopeful, he couldn't resist.

He smiled back. "Sure, sprite, why not?"

Faith, lured by the sound of their laughter, found them playing dolls several hours later.

Reese was sitting on the floor, his jacket discarded, his brocade vest unbuttoned, a licorice stick clamped in the corner of his mouth. Joy sat across from him at the little table. A black ring surrounded her pink mouth, and there were traces of the sticky black candy on her hands as well. Her two dolls occupied the other chairs.

At first glance they appeared to be having an afternoon tea party, but closer inspection revealed a very different kind of entertainment. A deck of cards lay in the center of the miniature table, and a pair of cards lay face up in front of each player— Reese, Joy, and the two dolls. A stack of copper pennies stood in front of Joy.

"Hit me again," Joy ordered, squealing with delight as Reese flipped another card in her direction. "Hit them, too!" She pointed to the dolls.

Reese threw back his head and roared with laughter, then dutifully tossed a card in front of each doll.

"Did we win? Do we get another penny?"

"Yep, you win again." Reese shook his head. "Dealer loses. The house pays a penny. You're quite a cardsharp, sprite."

"Pay us a penny." Joy bobbed up and down in her chair. "We won!"

Reese stuck his hand in his vest pocket and extracted three more shiny pennies. "Next time we play for licorice sticks, sprite. If I keep giving you pennies, I'll be broke."

"Are you actually teaching her to play cards?" Faith asked from the doorway. "To gamble?"

Reese removed the candy stick from his mouth, broke off a piece from the end, and offered it to Faith. He grinned unashamedly. She sounded so shocked, so outraged. "Well, actually, I'm teaching her how to cheat."

"Cheat?" Faith moved closer and snatched the licorice out of his hand. "Thank you."

"You're welcome," Reese answered. "She's quite good at cheating." He handed Joy a penny, then placed one in front of each doll. "She's greedy, too. Must be a family trait."

Faith narrowed her eyes at him and drew in a breath before she realized his brown eyes were sparkling with laughter. He was deliberately trying to make her lose her temper. "Joy can't read. How can she cheat?"

"She hasn't lost a hand yet." He raised one eyebrow. "Of course I've dealt all the cards."

"Of course," Faith agreed, fascinated by this side of Reese.

"And I stacked the deck," he added.

"Then how does she win?" Faith eased out of the doorway. She moved to the other side of Reese and sat down on the edge of the bed, absently licking the licorice with her tongue.

Reese bit back a groan at the sight of Faith's pink tongue circling the stick of candy. He muttered a curse under his breath, damning himself for being such a fool. He shrugged out of his vest and casually draped it across his lap. "By using her feminine wiles."

Faith laughed at him. "You can't be serious."

"Oh, but I am." The look in his brown eyes confirmed the truth of his statement. "When she looks

at me with those big gray eyes, I willingly part with
my money." His voice was low, husky, filled with
need. He stared at Faith's mouth. "Must be another
family trait."

The impact of his words slammed into her. She
began to tremble, too stunned by the desire etched
in his face to do anything. She simply stared back
at him and waited for him to kiss her.

"Weese!"

The moment was lost.

Reese turned to look at Joy. "What is it, sprite?"
He took deep breaths, hoping to restore some of his
control. God, that look in Faith's eyes! The invitation there was a look men dreamed of seeing.

"Are we gonna play?" Joy demanded his attention.

Reese removed his watch from his vest pocket,
flipped it open, stared at the dial, then looked at
Faith. "I think Faith came to tell us it's time to eat."
He winked at Faith.

"I came to apologize," Faith announced.

"And . . . ?" Reese encouraged, winking at her
again.

"And to tell you it's . . . time for Joy to wash up
for lunch."

"I don't want to!" Joy stood up and swept the pile
of cards and the pennies off the table. "I want to
play with Weese!" She glared up at Faith, a sullen
expression on her determined little face.

"Joy!" Faith was shocked at Joy's behavior. She
rushed to pick up the cards littering the floor.

"Leave them alone," Reese said softly. "Joy threw
them down. Joy will pick them up. Won't you,
sprite?"

"No!" She stamped her little foot for emphasis.

"Sprite, *you* will pick up the cards and the pennies, won't you?" Reese tried again. He spoke softly, as before, but there was a definite edge to his words.

"I won't!" Joy searched Reese's face for signs of anger. Finding none, she tried her hand at cajoling. "Faith will pick them up."

Faith gasped at the blatant manipulation.

"Faith didn't throw them down," Reese pointed out.

"Reese, she's—" Faith attempted to intervene.

"She's jealous," Reese announced, "of you. And the time I spend with you. She's having a temper tantrum because you came in and spoiled her fun." He looked at Faith, recognizing the anxiety on her face.

"Please, don't spank her."

"Trust me." He smiled. "I know how to handle jealous females." He ushered Faith out of the room, then turned his attention back to Joy.

Faith hovered anxiously near the door, listening for the first sounds of trouble. Minutes later Reese opened the door and stepped out.

"What happened?"

"I explained the terms. Joy will stay in her room until she picks up the cards and pennies and apologizes for her behavior. No lunch, no dolls"—he held up Joy's companions—"and no conversation."

"Well?"

"We're at a standoff," Reese admitted, tossing the dolls into a chair. "She's stubborn. She's thinking over my offer. She's cautious, too. Must be another—"

"Family trait," Faith confirmed. She smiled up at him, at the perfectly sculpted features, at the shining brown eyes. A sudden realization stunned her. Her heart, full to overflowing, pounded in her chest. Somewhere between Washington and Chicago she had fallen in love with Reese Jordan.

"About those family traits . . ." Reese took Faith's arm and led her toward the sofa. "I think we ought to discuss a few of them."

"What about lunch?" There was a funny little catch in her voice, an almost breathless quality. He noticed it right away.

He nudged her back onto the sofa. "Forget lunch," he ordered. "This is more important."

"What?"

Reese studied her face. That look was back in her eyes. And this time he wasn't going to lose his opportunity.

He bent his head.

She met him halfway.

She closed her eyes just seconds before she felt his mouth—cool, firm, demanding, tasting of desire.

Her lips parted easily, allowing his tongue access to explore.

Reese's mouth claimed hers hungrily. She was warm, welcoming, and impossibly sweet. Like licorice.

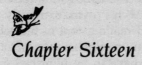

Chapter Sixteen

THE SUN COULDN'T set fast enough to suit Reese. Tension hung in the air like a stale odor, so thick he could smell it, taste it. But there was a subtle difference, because now it was spiced with anticipation, with the knowledge of what was to come. And if heated looks, smoldering eyes, moist lips, and pounding hearts were anything to go by, this promised to be an exciting night.

He turned his chair around to face the window. Was it his imagination, or was the sun a little lower on the horizon? He sighed, pulled out his watch, and glanced at it. There was still an hour or so of daylight left to endure. He turned back to his desk and the stack of work awaiting his attention.

Reese smiled when he found the telegram from David that had been waiting for him at the telegraph office in Chicago. David hadn't been able to ferret out any information on Champ Collins. Reese could just imagine David's frustration.

He wondered suddenly if he shouldn't delay sending a reply calling off the search. David had enjoyed himself tremendously during the contract negotiations. Maybe he should let his cousin suffer a little longer or, better yet, let David approach the aunts. It might be interesting to see what story they concocted.

Champ Collins, Reese thought, a product of Faith's evasions and his own extremely vivid imagination. He had made a fool of himself over a figment of his own imagination. And Faith had let him. She would have to be punished for that omission.

He pushed the paperwork aside and turned his chair back to the window. He listened to the splashing in the washroom as Faith supervised Joy's bath. The little tyrant had finally emerged from her room an hour or so ago with tears in her eyes and words of apology on her lips.

Faith had fed her an early supper and plopped her into the bathtub. It had been a long, tiring day for Joy, and as soon as she was clean and dry, he planned to tuck her into bed. He hoped to do the same to her older sister soon afterward.

The kissing session they'd shared before lunch hadn't done anything to ease the throbbing in his groin.

"Hello, Weese."

Reese turned his chair back around. Faith stood beside Joy in the doorway of the washroom. Joy's long blond hair was wrapped in a towel. She shivered in the cool air and huddled closer to Faith.

Reese got up from his chair and poured another scuttle of coal into the stove.

"She slipped in the tub and got her hair wet," Faith explained, "so I washed it." She wet her lips nervously and looked at Reese. "It shouldn't take too long to dry if I sit with her in front of the fire and brush it."

"Take your time." Reese smiled at Faith. He could tell she was as anxious as he was. "The sun hasn't gone down yet." He pulled a wing chair closer to the stove and sat down. "Come here, sprite. I'll tell you a bedtime story while Faith combs out your tangles."

Joy wiggled out of Faith's arms and ran to Reese. She settled herself into his lap, resting her head against his chest. "Are you still mad at me?"

Reese's expression was infinitely patient and tender.

Faith caught her breath at the serenity of the little domestic scene.

"I was never mad at you, sprite." He tilted Joy's face up to look at him so she could see for herself. "I was disappointed in you. There's a difference."

"Oh." Joy snuggled up against his hard frame.

Faith pulled the leather footstool up next to the chair. She removed the towel and painstakingly worked a wide-toothed comb through Joy's wet hair.

Reese's deep voice filled the silence as he related the story of how the grizzly bear lost his tail. Joy listened, awed by the legend. Faith, too, was entranced by the ancient story as she combed Joy's hair in front of the warm stove. Joy stuck her thumb in her mouth and toyed with a button on Reese's shirt.

Reese finished his story. He waited patiently for some reaction from his audience, but Joy's eyelids had closed. She slept peacefully, her small face pressed against his white linen shirt.

Faith put down the comb and quickly braided the shiny blond strands.

"It's so soft and silky." Reese touched Joy's hair. "It's a shame you have to braid it." He was touching Joy's blond hair, but his gaze was pinned on Faith's braided coronet.

She swallowed nervously. "It tangles so."

"It's still a shame." He held her gaze a second longer.

Faith reached for Joy. "I'll take her," she offered. "I've already turned back the covers."

"No." He maneuvered out of the chair, careful not to wake the sleeping child. "Let me." He smiled down at Joy. "I'd like to tuck her in."

Faith hesitated, withholding permission, reluctant to forfeit her right to the privilege. "If you really want to . . ."

"I do." He nodded and moved toward the pink bedroom. He paused in the doorway. "And then I want to tuck you in bed." His husky voice rumbled through the quiet room.

Faith blushed at the idea, but didn't try to dissuade him.

"And, Faith?"

"Yes?"

"I want to undress you. No nightgown and no braid."

"Anything else?" Her voice was a breathy whisper.

He grinned. "Leave a lamp burning. I want to be able to find you."

Faith paced the length of the bedroom. She wasn't sure quite what to do. He wanted to undress her. How was she supposed to occupy her time while she waited for him to tuck Joy into bed?

She walked to the bed and flipped the covers back. The sun had been down less than an hour. It seemed indecent to go to bed so early. She looked down at the bed, then quickly made it up again. She paced the room twice more, pulled out a couple of hairpins, then put them back again. He wanted to undress her. She wanted him to take down her hair. She turned her gaze back to the bed. It was hard to ignore it. It dominated the room. She turned the covers down once again, debated a minute or two, then started making it up—again.

"Leave it." Reese stood in the doorway. He was smiling at her. "I think we'll be able to make better use of it if it's turned down."

Faith dropped the corner of the blanket, then turned around. "How? Is . . . ?"

"Joy's sound asleep." He stepped into the room and closed the door. The click of the lock sounded abnormally loud to Faith's sensitive ears.

"I didn't know what to do," Faith admitted. "I'm not used to having idle hands." She gestured with her hands, waving them, palms upward, in the direction of the bed.

"I know what you mean," Reese replied solemnly.

"You do?" Her big gray eyes stared up at him.

He nodded once. "I'm not accustomed to having idle hands, either." He grinned suddenly, showing a flash of beautiful white teeth. "Come here. Let's put these idle hands to work." He reached for her, and Faith walked into his arms.

"What do I do?" Faith whispered.

Reese smiled. "Anything you want." He plunged his fingers into her hair and began searching for the pins while his mouth sought hers.

Faith reached up and pulled the silk tie away from the neck of his shirt.

Reese froze. His lips ceased their exploration of her mouth. His heart pounded loudly inside his chest. He waited.

Faith looked up and met his gaze. He seemed puzzled, unsure. She smiled shyly. "You said I could do anything I wanted."

He nodded once, without speaking.

"I wanted to take off your shirt. To undress you." She hid her face in the white linen. She could feel the hot flush of color staining her cheeks.

Reese began to breathe again, in quick erratic fashion. "Go right ahead," he instructed as Faith pulled his shirt from inside his trousers and began undoing the buttons one by one.

He found it hard to concentrate on unbraiding her hair. Faith pressed warm kisses against his chest as she released each button, exposing more flesh. He wondered what she would do when she ran out of buttons.

He was barely able to breathe when she went down on her knees in front of him to undo the last button.

She pressed a kiss against his navel, then boldly dipped her tongue inside, touching, tasting.

Reese's heart skipped a beat. He grabbed her arms and jerked her to her feet. There was no time for Faith to protest his rough handling of her, as his mouth found hers. He kissed her hungrily, demanding a response.

Faith kissed him back, as hungry as he, nipping at his bottom lip with her teeth, invading his mouth with her tongue, tasting him, marking him, branding him with her flavor, as he branded her. Her knees buckled as her blood surged through her veins. She locked her arms around his waist, pressing her breasts against his naked chest. The jet buttons on her bodice bit into him, leaving a row of tiny indentations.

He pushed away, putting his hands between them in an effort to unfasten her dress and rid himself of those sharp little buttons.

Faith whimpered her displeasure as he moved away. Her legs wobbled unsteadily, hampering his attempts to unclothe her.

Cursing profusely, Reese made a grab for her before she slipped out of his reach. He turned and pressed Faith firmly against the hard wood of the bedroom door. He wedged his muscular leg between hers, using his thigh to keep her upright while his mouth continued its passionate assault. His hands busied themselves with the stubborn little buttons.

His groin throbbed, his thigh muscles quivered, and his hands shook as he struggled with the buttons. His precarious control was rapidly deserting him.

Faith pulled her mouth away from his. She kissed the side of his neck beneath his ear, then moved higher. Her hot, inquisitive tongue tasted his earlobe, then began an excursion into the circular maze of his ear.

His control shattered. He tugged at her bodice. Jet buttons dropped to the floor, scattering in all directions. He shoved the fabric off her shoulders, then down her arms, baring her chemise and the rounded tops of her breasts.

She pulled her arms out of the sleeves of her dress, then pushed his open shirt off his shoulders. It slid down his arms, coming to a halt at his wrists. Impatiently he jerked the cuffs over his hands without bothering to undo the cuff links, then tossed the garment in the direction of the chair. He turned his attention back to the battle at hand—the hook on her waistband.

Her busy tongue left his ear and began a trail of fire along his jaw toward his chin. The slight rasp of his beard teased her taste buds. Faith flicked her tongue along the corner of his mouth. He tasted tangy with sweat and a flavor that was recognizable only because it belonged to him. It was the essence of Reese.

Reese tilted his head slightly and caught her teasing tongue in his mouth. She tasted wonderful. He couldn't get enough of her. He was greedy. He wanted more. He drank in the intoxicating sweetness of her mouth as he ground his hips against her belly.

Faith moved against him, welcoming the feel of his firm length pressing into her.

"God, stop that!" he managed. "It feels too good!"

She snuggled closer, testing his limits.

His hands moved down to hold her hips steady. "Dammit, woman, stop!" he muttered, his breath fanning her lips and chin. "My hands are shaking so badly I can't get your skirt off! I feel like a callow schoolboy."

She slipped her hand between their bodies, grazing his thigh as she moved to press her palm against him. Her voice was deep, husky, triumphant. "You don't feel callow to me." She traced the hard shaft with her knuckles to illustrate her point.

Reese raised his head. He arched an eyebrow at her comment. He had heard similar remarks over the years, but somehow he'd never expected a woman like Faith to say such a thing. She was a lady. He studied her features. Her face was flushed with pleasure, her eyes sparkling with triumph, yet darkened to a smoky shade of gray. He was witnessing a transformation. A wonderful transformation. She had become a seductress right before his eyes, beneath his hands. She teased, she tantalized, she seduced. Reese chuckled softly. "How many callow boys have you felt?"

"None," she admitted, tangling her fingers in his dark hair.

"Then how do you know?" he teased, resisting her attempts to kiss him.

"No callow youth could feel like this," Faith told him with complete certainty, raising herself on tiptoe, bracing her back against the door, seeking his lips.

"You would be surprised." He allowed her a brief, unsatisfactory kiss. "Callow youths are just as hard. They have no control and no expertise, but they're just as hard."

"How do you know?" She nipped at his chin in frustration as he continued to evade her kisses.

This time he laughed. "I was one. Once."

"You? Never!" She tried another tack, brushing her half-bare breasts against his chest.

He sucked in his breath as the firm tips of her breasts inside their cotton cage brushed against him.

The whisper of the cotton was almost as erotic as her bare flesh. He ached with the need to lose himself inside her, but he was reluctant to end the game. God, she learned fast! Reese was thoroughly enchanted by the seductress she'd become. "Yes, me. Before I learned how to pleasure a woman." His words were harsh whispers, uttered through clenched teeth. "Before I learned control."

"Reese?" Her questing tongue left his lips and concentrated on his naked chest. She lapped at the points of his nipples.

"What?" He could barely think.

"Forget control. Pleasure me."

Reese pulled Faith away from the door, bent his knees, scooped her up into his arms, and carried her to the bed. She lay across the bed, looking up at him. He kicked off his shoes and socks, then fumbled with the buttons of his fly, his usually adept hands clumsy and shaking.

She sat up, then crawled on her knees to the edge of the bed. "Let me." Faith reached for him.

Reese moved closer.

She unbuttoned his trousers. His proud jutting length spilled out into her hands. She marveled at the soft-hard feel of him, the pulsating warmth. She ran her fingertips along his arousal, then closed her hand around him.

Reese sucked in a deep breath, then exhaled, groaning loudly as his breath rushed out. He caught her braid in his hand and tugged her toward him. "No more. I can't stand it!"

Faith released him, suddenly afraid she'd caused him pain. "Did I hurt you?" It was hard to tell from the expression on his face.

"No. But I can stand only so much." His breath came in gasps. "God, Faith, I have to feel you! Help me!" Reese pushed his pants down over his hips, then stepped out of them and kicked them aside.

She stared at him in wonder. He stood tall and proud, bronzed by the lamplight. A lump caught in her throat. Her first brief look at him had been burned in her memory, but now she realized her memory was faulty. She had thought him perfect, except for the small crescent-shaped scar under his chin. He was more handsome than she remembered; his legs were longer and more muscular, his thighs bulging with strength. But he was also flawed. Several scars, some round and puckered, another long and thin, marred his torso. Faith ached with the need to kiss those marks and soothe away the memory of his pain. She moved to kiss the puckered circle on his thigh.

His hands stopped her. He pulled her upward. His mouth tasted hers. He unfastened her skirt and the ribbons of her chemise, then gently, firmly, pushed her back on the bed and lifted her hips, tugging at her skirts until they came free and glided down over her legs.

When she was left in only her corset and stockings, Reese finished unbraiding her straight black hair. "Now you look the part," he whispered, nuzzling aside the long tresses to kiss the curve of one breast.

"What part?" Faith looped her arms around his neck.

"The seductress." He dipped his tongue into the moist crevice between her breasts.

"Am I your seductress?" She kissed the top of his dark head.

"You're learning." He encircled a hard bud with his mouth, leaving a wet ring on the white cotton. His breath fanned the damp fabric.

She shivered in reaction, arching toward him. "Teach me. Everything."

Reese rolled her to his side. He unlaced the strings of her corset and threw it aside. He left her cotton stockings and garters in place, then pulled her atop him. He forgot control. He forgot everything except her demands and his throbbing need to bury himself in her warm depths.

She whimpered with need as he lowered her onto his arousal. He taught her the rhythm, guiding her hips with his hands until he suddenly rolled her onto her back.

Faith urged him on, digging her fingernails into his shoulders, spurring him onward with the heels of her feet. She screamed his name, crying out her pleasure as she found her release.

Reese's control deserted him. He grasped her tightly, lifting her hips as he poured himself into her. "Faith!"

Sometime later Reese pulled the covers up over them, settled Faith closer against him, and blew out the lamp.

He closed his eyes and slept.

The stillness and the silence woke him in the gray predawn hours. The train had stopped. Reese sat up and leaned against the carved headboard.

Faith groaned sleepily, brushing her hair out of her eyes. She pushed herself up to lay her head against Reese's chest. "What is it?" she whispered.

"The train has stopped," he told her, absently planting a kiss against her dark hair.

"Why?"

"Listen."

She listened. At first she could barely make out the sound, but as it moved closer she could hear the faint tinkling sound. "It sounds like wind chimes." She leaned closer to the window, then turned to face Reese. "What is it?"

"A rare opportunity." He grinned at her, his face alight with boyish pleasure. "A sight you shouldn't miss. Come on." He got up from the bed, slipped on his trousers, then bent to put on his socks and shoes. He retrieved his shirt from the floor and handed it to Faith. "Here. Put this on."

She slipped her arms into his shirt while Reese pulled a quilt and the down comforter from the bed. He handed Faith her shoes and draped the quilt around her shoulders.

"Hold on to this. We'll need it," he instructed, handing her the comforter before scooping her up in his arms, quilt and all.

"Where are we going?" Faith asked as he carried her out of the bedroom toward the door of the railroad car.

"Open the door and you'll see."

Faith did as he asked. Reese carried her outside onto the porch, into the freezing cold. She burrowed deeper inside the quilt. He walked to the chair, lowered Faith to her feet, then bent to brush the thin crust of ice off the seat with a corner of the quilt. He took the comforter from Faith, spread it across the chair, and sat down. Reese pulled

Faith onto one thigh and wrapped the cover around them.

The musical sound of tiny bells grew louder. Closer.

"Look!" Reese whispered in her ear.

The sight took her breath away. The ground was covered with a foot or so of powdery white snow that glowed eerily in the gray sky. The steel rails of the track were passable, but the train couldn't move. It was surrounded by a herd of buffalo, hundreds of them lumbering slowly across the rail-road tracks. The shaggy fur covering their massive heads, withers, and backs was topped with a layer of snow, but the fur hanging from their bellies was a solid mass of icicles, which swayed with each step.

They were so close that Faith could see the misty clouds formed by their warm breath. She could hear the beasts' labored breathing as they moved through the knee-deep snow.

"Oh, Reese." She turned her head to kiss his jaw. "They're magnificent!" She shifted slightly in his arms so she could see his face. "You knew when you heard the bells!"

He nodded. "I suspected."

"You've seen this before?" She searched for his hand amid the folds of the quilt. She laced her fingers with his.

"Once, a long time ago." His black eyes sparkled at the incredible beauty of the scene spread before them. "Take a good look, sweetheart. The herds are disappearing. We'll probably never have this privilege again."

She shivered at the sadness in his voice.

"Cold?" He nuzzled her ear and tightened his hold around her.

"Not enough to miss this," Faith assured him.

They watched the slow migration of the herd until the last cow moved out of view. The train blew its whistle one last time, then lurched forward as the engine gathered steam. They got up from the chair and moved to the rail for a final glimpse of the bison. Then Reese lifted Faith into his arms and carried her back to bed.

He made slow, sweet love to her as the sun rose over the horizon.

Chapter Seventeen

FAITH HAD JUST finished her morning bath when the train rolled into the Cheyenne station. Reese knocked on the washroom door.

"Oh, no! I'm not dressed! I look . . ." Faith stood beside the bathtub, her face pink from the hot water, her black hair loosely piled atop her head. She had wrapped Reese's brown velvet robe around her frame, and it clung damply in places. Faith's gray eyes sparkled with happiness. Her beautiful wide mouth was bruised and swollen from his kisses.

"Wonderful." Reese stepped into the room and placed a light kiss on her nose. "Take your time. The train will back our car onto a side track before they uncouple. The kettle is boiling on the stove. Joy and I are going to watch the horses unload while we wait for Uncle Charlie, Sam, and a couple of hands from the ranch. They'll be here soon," Reese told her, running a finger down her chin and neck to the enticing opening of the robe.

Faith moved closer, wanting his warmth, his touch. "How did they know we'd be here?"

"I sent them a telegram from Chicago telling them when to expect us." Reese leaned down and captured her mouth in a hungry kiss. "Now I wish I hadn't." He nibbled at her mouth. "Good morning, Miss Collins." He stopped and thought about what he'd said. "Wait. Now that we're in Cheyenne, you're Mrs. Jordan."

"Just like that?" Faith stared at him. "We've been married for days, but you've mentioned it only once. At the negotiations. Never before."

"As far as my family and the people of Cheyenne are concerned, we were married in Richmond."

"We *were* married in Richmond," she protested. "At least I was. You weren't there."

"Does it matter?" He tried to kiss her again, but she turned her face away. "It was legal."

"Reese—" Faith began.

"Look, how hard can this be?" Reese asked. "You pretended to be a widow without any qualms. You shouldn't have any problems playing the part of a loving wife." He caressed her shoulder, a gesture meant to reassure her. "If last night was any indication, you'll do fine."

Faith shrugged away from his gentle touch. "Meaning I passed your test?" she asked coldly. "You must think I'm a wonderful actress."

"I didn't say that," he hedged.

"It's what you meant," she accused.

Reese shook his head and turned back to the door. "Dammit, Faith, I'm not going to fight with you about this. Get dressed. I'll be waiting on the platform." The door rattled in its frame for several seconds after Reese stalked out.

Faith leaned against the edge of the tub. Tears stung her eyelids. She had started a fight. She'd ruined the lovely morning. Why? Just because he wanted her to pretend to be a happy bride for his family? No. She dabbed at the tears. She wasn't crying because he wanted her to pretend. She was crying because she didn't have to pretend. She *was* his loving wife. But to Reese she was simply a means to an end. A mere legal technicality to protect his child from bastardy.

She dried her eyes, washed her face, and began to dress. Mechanically, without thinking.

Eighteen minutes later she exited the private car and stepped onto the platform. From there she was able to get her first glimpse of the town. She was not impressed.

Cheyenne was a collection of false-fronted wooden buildings, many of them partially built in Chicago and then shipped to Wyoming by rail. The streets were dirt. Wooden sidewalks fronted some businesses, while others opened onto the street. The new town boasted a business district, three churches, and a two-room schoolhouse, along with other less respectable establishments. It also boasted a population of around six thousand.

It was new, rowdy, raw, and bustling with energy. The saloons, brothels, and gaming houses operated twenty-four hours a day and the sound of gunfire could be heard at all hours. Richmond, even in the days before the occupation, had more law and order. But something about Cheyenne drew Faith, and that something was Reese.

This town was Reese's home.

"Faith!"

She turned around. Joy was running toward her followed closely by Reese and two men dressed in faded denim pants and gingham shirts.

"We were watching the horses, Faith." Joy flung herself into Faith's arms. "Weese says I can have a pony. I get to pick him out. We're going to take him to the wanch with us. Uncle Charlie said he'll teach me to wide him." Joy's words were coming at a breathless rate. It was all Faith could do to make sense of them.

"What's this about a pony?" Faith stooped down until she was eye level with Joy.

"Weese said I could have one. Please, Faith?"

Faith looked to Reese for confirmation.

He nodded. "Faith, it won't hurt her to know how to ride."

"Why can't she learn to ride on an old mare? Why buy her a pony?"

"I'd rather have her tumble off a Shetland pony than a fully grown horse. Besides, she'll learn responsibility by helping take care of a pony of her own," Reese explained.

Faith thought for a minute. "All right, but I think you're spoiling her dreadfully."

Joy squealed with excitement, slipped out of Faith's reach, and ran to Reese.

The man standing beside Reese spoke to Faith. "Our family believes in indulging its children. It gives them a measure of confidence to know we want them to be happy."

Faith straightened and stood to greet Reese's companions.

"Faith, I want you to meet my uncle, Charlie Alexander. Charlie, this is Faith." Reese performed the introduction, smiling fondly at his uncle.

The younger man cleared his throat.

Reese chuckled. "And this is my cousin Sam, David's younger brother." He clapped Sam on the back, pushing him forward a little.

Faith studied Reese's uncle and cousin. She looked at Reese, then back at his relatives. There was a strong family resemblance. But these men were Alexanders, not Jordans. Reese apparently favored his mother's side of the family. Faith glanced back at Charlie and Sam, noting that some of their features resembled Reese's. The Alexanders were handsome men, but there were subtle differences between them. Reese was taller than Sam and Charlie. His eyes were a lighter brown, his nose straighter, his shoulders a fraction wider, his skin a lighter bronze.

Reese watched Faith, his full, sensual mouth flattened into a tight, disapproving line, his cocoa-colored eyes narrowed angrily, warily. It wouldn't take long now. He braced himself for her reaction.

She smiled at Reese's uncle, her gray eyes clear and shining with friendship. She extended her gloved hand. "It's a pleasure to meet you, Mr. Alexander, and you"—she turned to Sam—"Mr. Alexander. I met your brother in Washington. I liked him very much."

Charlie stared at her gloved hand for a moment before he accepted it. "You're southern."

"Yes, sir. Joy and I are from Richmond," Faith said.

"I was born and raised in north Georgia, in the mountains," Charlie told her, patting her hand before releasing it.

"North Georgia? How in the world did you come to settle way out here?" She stopped suddenly, remembering the war. Lots of southern men had migrated west. She frowned at her thoughtlessness.

"We came overland in 'thirty-eight. It was a long, hard journey. We settled for a while in the Indian territory, then followed Reese's father here before the war," Charlie volunteered.

Faith turned to look at Reese. "You never mentioned your father. Is he still here?"

"He died during the war," Reese said flatly.

"I'm sorry," Faith whispered.

Reese shrugged. "Come on, sprite." He hoisted Joy onto his shoulders. "Let's get the wagon loaded and get some breakfast. I'm starving." He walked toward the railroad car. A wagon and a buggy were hitched nearby. Two men were busy loading the wagon with furniture from Reese's private car.

"What about my pony?" Joy asked.

"After breakfast. How about joining us for breakfast, Uncle Charlie? Sam?" Reese said.

Charlie smiled at Sam. When Reese complained of starving, it was a sure sign he'd spent a busy night.

"We ate before the train pulled in," Sam said.

"You take the ladies to breakfast, Reese," Charlie suggested. "We'll load your belongings and pick up the supplies. Then we can see about the little lady's pony."

"Goody!" Joy shrieked.

Reese turned to take Faith's elbow. "Come on, Faith, let's eat. It's an hour's ride to the ranch."

Three hours later Reese helped Faith and Joy into the buggy. He hitched a fat, shaggy-coated Shetland pony named Brutus to the back of the buggy and climbed up beside them. Charlie and

Sam occupied the wagon seat while the two ranch hands trotted on horseback alongside the wagon. The little convoy pulled out onto the street headed west, toward the Trail T ranch. The sturdy wooden vehicle was piled high with trunks, carpetbags, toys, supplies, and furniture. Faith was stunned when she saw everything the wagon held.

"Reese, they took the bed out of your railroad car and loaded it onto the wagon," she pointed out.

"I know," Reese answered. "I told them to."

"Why? Don't you need a bed on the train?" Faith was puzzled.

"We'll need it more at the ranch." Reese chuckled.

"Don't you have a bed at the ranch?" The idea was appalling. It made her wonder what sort of primitive conditions she might find at the ranch.

"Not at the moment. It's on the wagon."

"That's your bed? The one you sleep in at home?"

"Uh-huh," he grunted.

"You had it dismantled and put in the railroad car to use on your trip?" She couldn't comprehend the extravagance.

"Uh-huh."

"Couldn't you have simply purchased a bed for the train?"

"It has one. I had it taken off and my bed put on," Reese told her.

"Why, for heaven's sake?"

Charlie began to laugh. Reese's eyes narrowed. He shook his head in warning.

"That bed belonged to Reese's father and mother," Charlie explained to Faith. "It was their marriage bed. Reese was born in that bed. He wanted to share it with you on your wedding night."

Faith blushed.

Reese stared moodily at the reins laced between his gloved fingers.

"Is that true?" Faith asked him.

He refused to answer.

She tried again. "How did you know I would agree to . . . marry you?" She stumbled over the words.

"Ma'am," Sam chuckled, "we all knew Reese was going to Washington to find a mate. Once he decided he wanted you, you didn't stand a chance. Reese always gets what he wants. If he makes up his mind to get something, nothing is gonna stop him. Right, Reese?"

"Shut up, Sam," Reese ordered.

"Then it's true. You planned everything, from the beginning—Christmas, the railroad car, the bed, everything!" Faith's words were low, sharp with pain and a deep sense of betrayal. "You planned everything."

"Blast it, of course I planned! I don't do anything without a plan of attack."

"Really?" Her tone was enough to give him frostbite. "Did you plan the attack on my purse? Did you hire that thief so I'd have no alternative but to accept your terms?"

"Hell, no!" Reese was hurt by her accusation. "I did not hire a thief to steal your purse. Lady, I wasn't that desperate."

"But you took advantage of the situation." She focused her serious gray gaze on him.

"Yes," Reese said. "I used every means at my disposal to get you to agree to"—he quickly glanced at his cousin Sam and his uncle Charlie, who were avidly eavesdropping—"marry me."

"You used bribes—dinners, Christmas gifts, money."

"Yes."

"Well, you succeeded," Faith announced. "You should be very proud of yourself."

"You got what you wanted, too, sweetheart," Reese reminded her. "Don't forget that."

Joy tugged on Faith's coat sleeve. "Faith, are you mad at Weese for buying me a pony?"

Faith pulled her little sister into her lap. "No, angel," she assured her. "I'm mad at myself for letting him buy me." Her voice was too low for Charlie and Sam to overhear.

"I didn't buy you, sweetheart." The endearment stung. "I rented what I thought was a fertile womb. And you succeeded in convincing me that you'd borne a child. You should be very proud of yourself, too." He flung her words back at her.

"Are you mad at yourself, too, Weese?" Joy was concerned.

"No, sprite, just disappointed." Reese turned his attention back to the horses.

"Reese," Faith began, shaken by anger, realizing she had embarrassed him in front of his family. "I'm sorry."

"Forget it." He didn't look at her.

"But . . ."

Reese jerked back on the reins. The buggy jolted to a halt. The wagon slowed down behind them. Reese maneuvered the buggy to the side of the road, then motioned for the wagon to pass them. Charlie waved good-bye as the wagon pulled out in front of them. "Look, you've been spoiling for a fight since early this morning." Faith opened her mouth to protest, but he shook his head to forestall her. "If you really want to fight, I'll oblige you. But not now. And not in front of my family. Your complaint is with me, not them, and I won't have you embarrassing them again. Is that clear?"

Faith kept quiet.

"Is it?"

"Yes!"

"Then keep quiet about your complaints until we get to the house. We can fight in the privacy of our bedroom."

"You don't really think I'll sleep with you after this, do you?" Faith sat up very straight in the buggy seat, every line of her body tense, waiting for his answer.

"Why not?" Reese asked. "We enjoy each other."

"I don't—"

"Shut up, Faith." He hooked a hand around her neck and pulled her to him. She expected his kiss to be hard and angry. She was surprised to find his lips soft, tempting, persuasive. The blood sang through her veins. This was what she'd been fighting for all morning. This was what she wanted.

Chapter Eighteen

THE MAIN HOUSE of the Trail T ranch was situated five miles northwest of Cheyenne, just off the road to Laramie, but the ranch itself was spread out over a vast distance. It was bordered on the north by Lodgepole Creek, and on the south and west by the foothills of the Laramie Mountains. Reese's father had staked out land surrounding the main house and the outbuilding back in 1862. Under the Homestead Act each head of household was allowed 160 acres of free land if a man agreed to live on and cultivate it. Benjamin Jordan had used that law to establish title to the section of land adjacent to the creek. A year later he had purchased an additional nine hundred acres from the government at $1.25 an acre. Reese had filed claim for ownership of those original acres in 1867, just before the Union Pacific Railroad began buying choice lots around Cheyenne. Reese Jordan now owned close to one thousand acres of prime grassland, grazing land for cattle, but if he hoped to increase his herd, he would have to acquire more. He had spent the better part of the past year lobbying the government to issue leases and grazing rights to federal land to local ranchers.

Faith studied the ranch house as the buggy bounced over the ruts and potholes in the road leading up to it. After the disappointment of Cheyenne, the main house of the Trail T ranch was a pleasant surprise. The central portion of the two-story house was built of log and stone to withstand the harsh Wyoming winters. It was flanked by long, low one-story wings and fronted by a huge porch. The drive leading to the house circled in front of the porch steps, making it possible to drive up to the front door. Had the house been made of white clapboard or red brick, it could have belonged on any Virginia plantation. The arrangement of the house and the other buildings surrounding it reminded Faith of her grandfather Hamilton's plantation. She found the comparison comforting. From her place in the buggy she could see two barns, a smithy, the stables, a log cabin, the corral, a paddock, and the smokehouse. Yes, everything seemed very familiar.

She squinted against the sun as she looked out over the open range, hoping to see the livestock. She turned to Reese. "Where are all the cows?"

"The milk cows are in the barn. The cattle are out on the range," he answered.

"By themselves?"

"Oh, they're probably keeping company with the cattle from a couple of other ranches."

"Then how do you know which ones are yours?"

"Mine all have the Trail T brand on them. The herd roams free during the winter. In the spring we round up all the Trail T stock and brand the calves." He maneuvered the buggy around the circular drive and pulled it to a halt behind the wagon. Charlie and Sam were busy unloading the last of the supplies. Reese climbed down from the buggy and held his arms out for Faith. "Let's go in out of the cold. I'll show you around the house." He reached up for Joy and lowered her to the ground.

"What about my pony? Can he sleep in the house, too?" Joy wanted to know.

"Absolutely not, sprite. Ponies do not sleep in little girls' bedrooms. They sleep in cozy stalls in the barn with the other horses. Especially Shetland ponies like Brutus."

"Can I go with you to put Brutus in the barn?" Joy asked.

"It's awfully cold out, sprite. Why don't you go inside the house with Faith while I take Brutus to the barn?" Reese was cold, tired, hungry, and suffering from a lack of sleep. Not that he was complaining about the way he'd lost sleep. He simply wanted to relax. He was in no mood to contend with a little girl or a stubborn pony. His patience was not inexhaustible. At the moment it was paper thin.

"I want to go with you!" Joy stamped her foot. "I want to help you tuck Brutus in bed."

Reese looked to Faith for help. "Explain to Joy why she can't go with me to the barn."

"I can't," Faith told him. "I don't understand myself. You insisted on buying her a pony against my better judgment, so the least you can do is let her go with you."

Dammit, today it seemed everyone had decided to turn on him.

"I seem to recall you saying something like 'She'll take better care of a horse if she owns it,' " Faith reminded him, gray eyes sparkling with mischief.

"You promised you would teach me how to take care of him," Joy piped up. "I want to go with you!"

"Oh, all right!" Reese grabbed Joy's hand, then walked around to the back of the buggy to untie the shaggy black pony.

"Can I ride him to the barn? Please?" Joy danced from foot to foot.

"Absolutely not!"

Faith waved good-bye, then turned and started up the stone steps to the house.

A high-pitched childish squeal of delight halted her on the top step. She turned around.

Reese was leading the Shetland pony. He carried the lead rope in one hand while he pressed his other hand against Joy's back. She sat astride the short-legged pony, clinging to his black mane while her short legs bounced against the pony's round belly. As Faith watched, Brutus stuck his nose into Reese's coat pocket.

"I don't have any sugar," Reese informed him.

But the greedy pony persisted. He burrowed deeper into Reese's pocket. The fabric gave way with a loud tearing sound.

"Dammit!" Reese muttered, elbowing the pony's muzzle in a futile effort to dislodge him.

"Don't you hurt my pony, Weese!" Joy ordered, just as Brutus grabbed hold of the torn pocket and pulled it completely off Reese's coat.

Reese stopped in his tracks and faced the pony.

Brutus pricked up his ears in a show of equine innocence and, with a toss of his head, sent the pocket sailing. Joy squealed with delight at her pony's trick.

Reese shook his head and turned his back to the pony, unimpressed by the innocent display. He tugged on the lead. Brutus seized his opportunity. He twitched his tail, flattened his ears against his head, bared his strong teeth, and nipped Reese on the arm.

Faith thought she heard Reese mutter, "*Et tu, Brute?*" between the colorful curses, but she couldn't be sure.

He tugged on the lead rope once again, and this time Brutus plodded docilely at his side. Reese rubbed absently at his arm.

Faith opened the front door of the ranch house and stepped inside.

The interior of the house was as much a surprise as the exterior had been. She had expected the inside walls to be the same natural log as the exterior, but found they were paneled in light oak. She'd expected rough plank floors and discovered they were hardwood, polished and sanded to a high gloss and covered in places by Turkey carpets like the ones in the railroad car.

The room was, in fact, a larger version of Reese's private car. Only the stone fireplace and the paintings were different. Faith relaxed, suddenly very comfortable with her surroundings. She removed her coat and gloves and carefully laid them across the arm of the leather sofa. She pulled the hatpin from her hair and balanced her hat atop the pile. She moved to warm herself in front of the fire.

She took a deep breath. The delicious aroma of freshly baked bread wafted through the house. She sniffed the air. Someone was in the kitchen, cooking. Faith moved away from the fire. She followed the enticing smells through the house to the kitchen. "Hello? Is anybody home?" She peeked through the doorway of the kitchen.

A young woman labored over the huge black stove, stirring the contents of a large pot. An older woman emptied loaves of bread from the pans onto a worktable. They chatted to each other, in a tongue foreign to Faith. They jumped at the sound of her voice, turning to face her.

Faith froze in the doorway, staring at the women. She hadn't expected to find anyone in the kitchen when she arrived and certainly not these women who were obviously relatives, yet Indians. "I hope you don't mind. We just arrived. I was waiting in the front room, but I smelled your delicious cooking and followed my nose." She shrugged. "It led me here. I'm Faith Col . . . Jordan, Reese's wi . . ." She held up her left hand, displaying Hannah's wedding ring. She tried again: "Reese's wi . . ." Faith gave up. "Reese's . . . outside," she finished lamely.

The younger woman spoke. "I'm Mary Alexander, Reese's cous—"

"Cousin," Faith interrupted, smiling at the smaller, feminine version of the Alexander men. "I met David in Washington, and Mr. Alexander and Sam today." Faith knew she was babbling, but she couldn't seem to stop. "There's quite a family resemblance." She stepped closer to the stove.

Mary nodded. "This is my mother, Sarah." She shrugged in a gesture of apology. "She doesn't speak English." Mary studied Reese's bride. She was very different from the first woman Reese had chosen. She talked to cover her nervousness, but she didn't mean to be rude. Her smile was genuine. Her black dress was old and worn, even threadbare in places. Her hair was mussed, and she had dark circles under her eyes, but she didn't seem to mind. There wasn't a vain or malicious bone in her body. She was beautiful on the inside where it mattered, and pretty on the outside as well. But she wasn't even aware of the beauty shining out of her lovely gray eyes. She would do Reese proud.

"Oh, I see. The language I overheard you speaking was—"

"Cherokee."

Faith whirled around. "Goodness, Reese, you startled me!" Reese was standing inside the kitchen door. "I thought you were out in the barn with Joy and Brutus."

"Sam offered to tuck Brutus into his stall for the night. I let him." Reese rubbed at the bite on his arm. "Brutus seems to like Sam a helluva lot more than he likes me. Joy stayed to help. I came inside to see about you."

"Me, why?"

"I didn't realize it was this close to dinner until Charlie reminded me. I forgot that Mary and Sarah would be here. I was sure you would walk into the kitchen, find Red Indians cooking dinner, and run screaming for help." His words were sarcastic, cutting.

Faith recoiled from his verbal abuse. She stared at him coldly. "I don't have a problem with Red Indians in the kitchen or anywhere else, but you seem to." She pulled herself up to her full five-foot height, straightened her spine, and looked him in the eye. "Now, if you will just point me in the direction of my bedroom, I'll remove my prejudiced self from your noble presence."

Reese was too stunned by her remarks to say anything. Mary came to her rescue. "Go back to the main room and up the stairs. It's the last door on the right."

"Thank you." Faith remembered her manners, even if Reese had forgotten his. "It's a pleasure to meet . . . you both." Her voice cracked. She turned to stare through Reese. "Please send Joy upstairs as soon as she comes in. She'll need to wash up." She pushed back her shoulders and hurried out of the kitchen, through the main room, and up the stairs.

Mary waited until she heard the bedroom door close before she spoke. "You were very cruel to her, Reese."

"Cruel?" Reese was astonished. "It was no more than she deserved for—"

"Being surprised?" Mary asked softly.

"You saw the expression on her face. She was shocked to find Indian women here." Reese began to pace the length of the kitchen.

"She was surprised to find anyone in the kitchen cooking a meal for her, just as I would be surprised to return to my home and find someone cooking for me. She didn't expect it. She didn't mean to be rude."

Reese stopped pacing and stared at his cousin. Sweet, docile, even-tempered Mary was angrily defending a woman she had just met. A woman who wasn't even Cherokee. Even now, Mary was pointing a wooden spoon at him. "Did you tell her about us? Tell her we were here?"

"I told her I had a housekeeper," Reese defended himself.

"Just as I thought," Mary said smugly.

"What does that mean?"

"It means you didn't tell her anything about your family or how we live. It means that you left your new bride in ignorance and expected her to understand. Very typical."

Reese winced at her words.

But Mary continued. "This is her house now, Reese. According to Cherokee law, the house belongs to the woman. And that woman upstairs has every right to put your shoes outside the front door. You embarrassed her, hurt her feelings in her own kitchen and in the presence of relatives. You were wrong. You should apologize. You need to go up there and make peace with your bride."

Reese opened his mouth to protest, to tell them Faith wasn't his real bride, simply a temporary one, that there was no reason for all the fuss, but when he saw the look of grim determination in Mary's eyes, he thought better of it.

Sarah rounded the corner of the table to stand next to her daughter. She spoke a few words in rapid Cherokee, frowning up at Reese as she spoke.

"Well, I guess that makes it unanimous." Reese expelled a slow, martyred sigh before heading toward the stairs. He hated to admit he was wrong. He hated to apologize to Faith, but Mary had a point. Perhaps he had been hasty in his judgment. He hoped she wasn't crying. He didn't think he could handle her tears. He sighed again, running his fingers through his hair. It had been a bitch of a day! A day that appeared so promising at dawn when he'd been making love to Faith. God, but it had gone downhill since then. It bothered him to think how badly the day had turned out. And if it bothered him, how must Faith feel?

Reese shook his head as if to clear it. He hadn't thought about anyone else's feelings in a very long time. He paused in front of his bedroom door, then turned the knob. He expected the door to be locked, but it swung open.

Faith lay on her stomach, fully clothed, across the reassembled bed. She didn't move when Reese opened the door. She didn't bother to acknowledge his presence.

"Faith?" He took a couple of steps into the room.

"Please go away." She didn't turn over.

"I was told to come up here and apologize."

"Fine. Now go away."

"I came to apologize." Reese moved next to the bed. "Did you hear me?"

"I heard you." Her voice was dull, flat.

"I said I was sorry!" Reese was rapidly losing patience with her.

"No," Faith corrected him wearily. "You said you were ordered to apologize to me."

Reese was uneasy with the situation. "Well, at least I know how to follow orders."

"Then follow mine: Go away and leave me alone."

"No."

Faith rolled over to look at him. Her gray eyes brimmed with tears. Her face was blotched and swollen from the ones she'd cried earlier. "Why not?"

"Because you haven't said you forgive me."

"I forgive you." She said the words, but her heart wasn't in them. "Now please leave me alone.

I'm too tired to fight with you."

She should have forgiven him by now, Reese thought. She should be telling him how sorry she was for all this fuss. Faith had said the words, but she didn't mean them. For some reason he couldn't leave it alone. "I won't leave until I know you've forgiven me."

"Forget it. There's nothing to forgive."

"Faith, I—" he began.

"Leave me alone! Don't you see? You were right. I *was* shocked! I've always prided myself on my lack of prejudice, and yet I was shocked to find Mary and Sarah in your house. Shocked to find they were relatives! Do you know what kind of person that makes me?" Faith choked on her words, choked on the bitter taste of self-recrimination.

"Human."

"What?" She met his gaze, her gray eyes wide with astonishment.

"I said it makes you human." Reese sat down on the bed. "All human beings have prejudices of some kind." He moved to touch her, but she rolled away.

"But to stare the way I did. I knew it was rude, but I couldn't stop."

"Have you ever seen an Indian before?" he asked gently.

"No, but that's no excuse for being—"

"Curious." Reese pulled her into his arms. She didn't roll away. "I was Joy's age when I first saw a black man. I was terrified. I ran crying to my mother."

"But why? There's nothing to be afraid of. People are people."

"That's exactly what my mother said. She said it was foolish to fear something as natural as skin color. It was like fearing a red-haired man because his hair was different from mine and not fearing a black-haired man because my hair was also black. Skin color is superficial. The blood underneath is the same."

"I'm ashamed." Faith began to cry in earnest. "I feel so foolish! When I saw Mary I remembered asking Charlie how he came to settle in Wyoming. And now I realize he must have followed the trail from Georgia to the Indian Territory. Oh, Reese"— she clung to his shirt—"how he must have suffered coming all that way. I'm so sorry. I didn't mean to . . . but you never said anything, and then"—she sniffed, and Reese handed her a handkerchief— "when I met Mary she looked at me so . . . I thought you didn't tell me because you were ashamed of me. . . . Maybe you should have chosen someone else. I mean, I haven't a cent to my name, and I'm dressed in rags . . . and I shamed you in front of your family."

"Ssh." He brushed a kiss across her forehead. "Ssh, sweetheart, you haven't shamed me." He kissed the tip of her reddened nose. "And Mary likes you very much."

"She does?"

"She does. In fact, she ordered me to make peace with you."

"She didn't." Faith hid her face in his shirt.

Reese touched the underside of her chin with his finger, tilting her face up so he could see her eyes. "She did. She chased me around the kitchen with a wooden spoon"—Faith smiled at the image—"and ordered me to come upstairs and make peace with my bride."

Faith's smile died on her lips. She stiffened in his arms and tried to pull away. The lie hung between them.

"Well, now you're safe." She smiled brightly. "I'm not your new bride. I'm only rented. Temporarily."

"Faith, I'm sorry." He tried to kiss her. She avoided his lips. Reese stared at her face. He saw the pain in her eyes. For the first time he damned his contract and his elaborate scheme. "Faith, please . . ."

Faith studied his face. She saw the look in his eyes, and for the first time she was glad of the contract and his crazy plan. It was too easy to love him, and much too painful. She pulled his face down to hers and kissed him, telling him with her lips the things she couldn't say aloud.

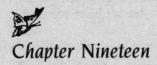

Chapter Nineteen

THE TRAIL T was home to four families, all relatives of Reese. The arrangement of the ranch resembled that of a plantation, and at supper her first night, Faith learned it functioned in a similar manner.

Charlie, Sarah, and Sam lived in a log house behind the main house. Reese's grandparents, Duncan and Elizabeth, lived in another cabin close to Charlie and Sarah. Mary lived by herself in a cabin several hundred feet away. The cabin next to the smithy belonged to Joe, the blacksmith. He was also part Cherokee, from another clan, a relation by marriage. His wife was dead. He shared the cabin with his two children. The ranch hands shared a dormitorylike building called the bunkhouse.

The Cherokee were a communal society as well as a matriarchal one. Everyone worked for the good of the ranch, and the ranch provided food, clothing, and shelter for the people who lived there. Reese had even provided a schoolhouse for the children. Mary was the teacher. She had three pupils—the blacksmith's eleven-year-old twins, Jimmy and Kate, and fifteen-year-old Sam. The lessons were taught in English and in Cherokee. Faith quickly decided Joy should become Mary's fourth pupil.

Mary tentatively broached the topic of school and the other children at supper. She was surprised to learn Joy hadn't been enrolled in school in Richmond.

"The school system was rather chaotic after the war," Faith explained. "I was afraid to send her. I started her lessons back in November, but I've been very lax."

Reese looked at Faith across the length of the long dining table. "We can hire a governess if you like."

"Why spend the extra money," Faith asked, "when she can go to school right here? I'm sure Mary is as good a teacher as any governess."

"Better," Reese told her. "How many governesses do you know who speak Spanish, French, English, and Cherokee?"

"Don't forget Latin," Mary reminded him, laughing at Faith's stunned expression.

Reese explained. "It's a family joke. Before David and I went off to school, my father hired a British schoolmaster to tutor us. Mary put up such a fuss at being excluded that my father decided she should be allowed to attend our lessons. Mary excelled in all the romance languages. She did better in Latin than either one of us."

"Do you teach all those languages?" Faith asked.

"Only English and Cherokee," Mary told her. "Unless you want the works," she added hopefully.

"Or happen to be her brother," Sam groaned.

"Joy and I want the works," Faith announced.

"You?" Reese was astonished. "Are you serious?"

"Why not?" Faith asked. "My education was interrupted by the war," she said defensively. "I would like to complete it, and I hate being the only person on the ranch who doesn't speak the Cherokee language. I want to talk to Sarah."

"Are you certain about this?" Reese wanted to know.

"Yes."

"Good," Mary announced. "Joy can start school in the morning. Faith, you can join us in the afternoon for languages."

The decision made, Faith worked at blending her life, and Joy's, into the everyday routine of the ranch. She spent her mornings learning the workings of the main house. She stood through hours of dress fittings while the seamstress Reese brought from Cheyenne measured, pinned, and stitched a suitable wardrobe for her. Faith selected patterns, fabrics, and notions and set to work on a wardrobe for Joy, including a gray corduroy riding habit. Though she longed to be smartly outfitted aboard a horse, Faith omitted a riding habit for herself. She didn't have a horse to ride and couldn't bring herself to ask for one. But as long as weather permitted, she never missed an opportunity to participate in Joy's riding lessons.

Faith had balked when she realized Charlie was teaching Joy to ride astride. She stood at the edge of the corral watching while he held the pony on a lead, coaxing him through his gaits.

"She needs a proper saddle," Faith told him. "A little girl's saddle."

Charlie shook his head. "Sidesaddle's too dangerous."

"That's ridiculous. I learned to ride in a lady's saddle. I've ridden that way all my life."

"In Richmond?"

"Yes."

"You can stay alive in a sidesaddle in Richmond," Charlie said. "But out here it'll get you killed."

"But—"

"Faith, let me teach the young 'un to ride western style first. Then if you still want her to know how, we'll teach her the 'proper' way."

Faith looked at Joy bouncing on the back of the pony, skirts flying, her blond braids swinging from side to side in rhythm with the pony's trot. "Look at me, Faith! I'm riding Brutus!" Joy waved and almost lost her seat as Brutus trotted a bit faster. She giggled.

"Keep both hands on the reins, lass," Charlie warned. "Else you'll be dusting off your skirts."

Joy giggled in reply, but dutifully placed her hand back on the reins.

Faith remembered her own riding lessons—the constant striving for perfection, the straight back, the perfect seat, the hours of torture as she strove to maintain her balance on her proper ladies' saddle. Joy looked carefree. She enjoyed her sessions. Surely that was more important right now than propriety. For a moment she was envious. Riding astride looked like fun. She smiled at Charlie. "We'll teach her the western style first."

Charlie reined the pony in. "That's enough for today, lass. Time to wash up for breakfast."

Joy protested. "I hafta groom Brutus."

"You go get ready for breakfast," Faith told her. "I'll groom Brutus for you."

Charlie raised an eyebrow.

"I don't mind," Faith said. "I'll enjoy spending time in a stable again."

Charlie lifted Joy off the pony and swung her into his arms. "Let's go, lassie. Mary'll be after me with her ruler if you're late for school."

Faith led the shaggy pony back to the barn.

Reese found her there a little while later, seated astride the pony, her toes almost touching the ground as she trotted up and down the length of the barn. Faith's back was to him. She was laughing at Brutus's futile attempts to dislodge her by scrubbing his side against the stalls.

"It will take more than that to get me off, you mean little imp," Faith warned. "I've kept my seat on better mounts than you."

"What a picture that conjures up," Reese said.

Faith whirled the pony around, almost losing her balance at the sound of Reese's voice. Embarrassment flooded her face. "What are you doing here?"

Reese's gaze traveled from the toes of her dusty boots up the length of her legs, hips, and waist, lingered a moment at her breasts, then focused on her face. "I came to see what was keeping you. I never dreamed I'd find you astride the pony."

Faith heard the husky tone, recognized the heat in his eyes, and tried to smooth her skirts down over her exposed legs. She wet her lips. "I promised Joy I'd groom Brutus for her."

"Groom him for what?" Reese approached the pony, eyeing him warily, careful to keep out of the reach of his teeth.

"Groom him," Faith repeated. "I was going to brush him, but then I thought how much fun it would be to ride astride instead of in a sidesaddle."

"Oh, it is." Reese's eyes darkened. "Fun to ride astride."

"I never have before." She looked almost guilty as she attempted to slide off Brutus's back.

Reese slid his hands around her waist and eased her off the pony. "Oh, yes, you have. Numerous times." He pulled her to him and kissed the corner of her lips. "But never in a barn. Until now."

"Reese, we can't," Faith murmured, already kissing him back and beginning to unbutton his shirt.

"Of course we can." He backed her into one of the clean stalls.

"Reese! Faith! Are you in there?" Sam's voice carried through the stables. "Breakfast."

"Maybe tomorrow," Reese muttered.

Faith shook her head. "I don't think so."

"Reese!" Sam called again, his voice closer.

"We'll be there in a minute, Sam. We're just putting Brutus away." Reese grabbed Brutus's reins before leaning over to kiss Faith one last time. "Meet me here after breakfast. I'll teach you to ride astride. We'll practice every morning."

"On a horse," Faith insisted.

"We can do that, too." Reese led the pony into his stall. "If you insist." He turned to face her. "But only if you're a good girl and practice."

"Reese . . ." Faith tried to warn him.

"And sometimes we won't even need a horse." He leaned toward her. Brutus leaned forward, too, opened his mouth, and took another chunk out of Reese's arm. "Dammit!" Reese spun around to confront his attacker. The pony shied away, looking bored, uninterested.

Faith took a sugar cube out of her pocket and held it out to Reese.

"Don't reward him for biting me!"

"I'm not." Faith smiled at him. "I just thought you might like to make friends with him."

"Not a chance," Reese grumbled.

"We might be spending a lot of time in this barn. . . ." Faith let her words trail off.

"On second thought . . ." Reese took the proffered treat, then grudgingly extended his hand to Brutus.

REESE ANNOUNCED HIS intentions at breakfast. "From now on I'll be giving Joy her riding lessons."

Charlie looked up from his plate.

Reese explained. "Faith wants to learn to ride as . . . western style. I promised to teach her."

"Do you have the time?" his uncle asked. "I can teach her as well as the little one."

"I'll teach her—them," Reese amended quickly. "I'll find the time."

"Okay by me," Charlie added. "But if you change your mind . . ."

"I won't." Reese smiled down the table at Faith. "I just wanted everybody to know that Faith and I will be spending some time together each morning after breakfast." Reese finished his meal, excused himself, and got up from the table.

Faith did the same, carefully heading in the opposite direction from Reese, her face a becoming shade of pink.

Charlie waited until they'd both left the table, then addressed the others. "Sam, Joe, boys, find something to do away from the barn after breakfast from now on." Joe and the two ranch hands nodded in understanding.

"But, Pa," Sam protested, "I clean the stables every morning after breakfast."

"Get up a bit earlier and clean 'em before breakfast," Charlie ordered.

Sam groaned.

Reese's grandfather reached over to pat his youngest grandson on the shoulder. "One day," Duncan promised Sam, "you'll understand and appreciate such thoughtfulness."

IN THE DAYS that followed, Faith fell more in love with Reese and with the people living at the Trail T. She studied them all, learning the many ways each person contributed to the ranch. The kitchen was Sarah's domain, the meals a communal affair. The children ate early, in the kitchen. The adults, including the two ranch hands, sat down to supper at the huge dining table. That was a Jordan family tradition, begun by Reese's father. Benjamin Jordan had spent his childhood eating alone under the supervision of a nanny who ate with the staff in the kitchen. Benjamin hadn't been invited to sit down with his parents until after his sixteenth birthday. There was no such formality at the Trail T.

Mary taught school. It was her first love, the thing she did best. Charlie was the ranch ramrod, supervising the men. Sam worked with the horses. He had a special affinity for the animals. When he wasn't doing his lessons, he was working in the barn or the stables. Joe was the blacksmith. He made many of the household tools and kept the horses well shod. Reese's grandmother, Elizabeth, tended her vegetable and herb gardens in the spring and summer and cared for the chickens and geese in the winter. And Duncan, Reese's grandfather, who was past seventy but spry, kept the family traditions. It was his job and his passion.

Faith felt an overpowering need to belong, but she was careful in the tasks she chose. She didn't want to intrude, disrupt, or usurp anyone else's role. She spent her first few weeks on the ranch searching for her place, her vital role. And then she found it in Reese.

She noticed Reese groping for his right jacket pocket as they returned from their morning ride.

Faith laughed. "Don't you remember, Reese? It's gone. Brutus stole it." Reese's first confrontation with Joy's pony had been weeks ago.

Reese looked down at his side. He'd been trying to stash his cigars in a pocket that didn't exist. "I keep forgetting." He turned to look at her. "My favorite jacket. I'll have to remember to order a new one."

"A new one?" Except for the missing pocket, it was practically brand new.

"To replace this one."

"Why not replace the pocket instead of the jacket?"

Reese shrugged. "It's simpler to buy a new one." He awkwardly tucked his cheroots into his left pocket. "Come on." Reese dismissed the subject of the jacket. "There's something I want to show you." He turned to leer at her. "In the barn."

By the time Reese had shown her the mare ready to foal in the back stall, Faith had forgotten about his jacket pocket. But she remembered it later that night when she found a crumpled sheet of paper on the floor near the bedroom dresser. Written across the front in Reese's bold scrawl was a list of things he needed to do. At the top of the list were several items: telegraph bank, Washington, Senator Darcy— and so on, in order of importance. And at the bottom, added in pencil: shirts, cigars, brandy, jacket.

Faith smiled. It was late. After supper Reese had gone to help Charlie and Sam with the mare. In his haste to change out of his good clothes, Reese had dropped his list. Knowing he would miss it, she tiptoed downstairs to his study. It wouldn't hurt to check his supply of cigars and brandy while she was there.

"I THOUGHT YOU'D be upstairs sleeping," Reese explained, stamping the dirt from his boots in the kitchen doorway. He'd seen the lamplight glowing in the window, smelled the aroma of coffee being kept warm on the stove, but he hadn't realized Faith was there until she raised her head from the table.

Faith straightened in her seat and wiped the sleep from her eyes. "I made some coffee for you." She got up to pour him a cup.

"Thanks." Reese wearily shrugged out of his coat.

"I warmed some leftover roast and potatoes, too. Are you hungry?"

Reese grunted. Faith moved closer to take his jacket. Reese held up his hands to ward her off. She looked so soft and clean in her white flannel nightgown and heavy robe, while he . . . "Don't get too close. I smell."

Faith wrinkled her nose. He did smell. His clothes were covered with dirt and blood and other substances she chose not to identify.

Reese tossed his jacket across a chair on his way to the sink. He pumped water into the basin and was about to wash his face when Faith stopped him.

"Wait!" She tipped a kettle over the basin. A stream of boiling water mingled with the ice cold. A cloud of vapor drifted upward. Reese stared at her as she swirled the water, testing the temperature as if he were a child. "All right." She set the kettle on the stove, then handed Reese a towel and a bar of soap.

He continued to stare, unable to comprehend the incredible luxury. He'd been washing in cold water for years. He couldn't remember anyone waiting up for him with coffee and hot water.

Faith smiled at him. He noticed that her braid hung over one shoulder. "Reese," she prodded gently, "wash up. I'll fix you a plate." She turned back to the table. "How's the mare?"

"What?" He sloshed water over his face.

"How's the mare?" She pulled one of his shirts from a sewing basket. "Put this on." She handed it to Reese as he moved to sit down.

"The mare is fine. We lost one of the foals, though. She had twins." His words were softly spoken.

"I'm sorry." Faith set a plate in front of him along with his cup of coffee. She sat down across from him.

"Aren't you having anything to eat?" Reese looked over at her.

She pulled another shirt from the basket and opened a small box of buttons. Her gold thimble glinted in the lamplight as she worked.

Faith shook her head as she bit the end of the thread. "I'm not hungry. But I thought I'd keep you company." She smiled and tried to gauge his reaction. "If you don't mind."

Mind? Reese thought. *Mind?* When there was a warm, sympathetic woman smiling at him, listening earnestly to his every word? He stopped eating. He watched as she bent her head over her sewing, and carefully sewed a button into place, then laid the shirt aside. She stood up.

He dropped his fork and reached across the table to catch her wrist. "Stay. Please."

"I'll pour us some more coffee," she told him. "Then you can tell me all about it."

Her invitation was irresistible. He told her all about the foaling process. Then when he thought he'd bored her to tears, she asked a question about the ranch, and he launched into a discussion of management practices. He talked until his throat felt scratchy and strained. And still Faith listened, calmly sewing on buttons and mending tears in a small mountain of garments, most of them his. She tossed the last shirt into the basket, then sat up straight and stretched her aching muscles.

"You're tired," Reese said.

"And so are you."

"I've kept you up too late." His brown eyes were dark, filled with expression.

"I enjoyed it." Faith got up from her chair and began bustling around the kitchen to dispel the sudden tension. "I need to cheek on Joy. There's hot water in the reservoir. I pulled the tub from the cupboard into the kitchen, in case you wanted a bath, and I hung your robe next to the tub. Would you like some more coffee? Some brandy?"

Reese shook his head.

"Well, I'll leave you alone to bathe." She hesitated in the kitchen doorway. "If you need me, just call. I'm going to make sure Joy's all right."

"Faith?"

"Yes?"

"It won't take me long to bathe. If you want to wait, we could check on Joy together. Before we go to bed." His voice was low, husky, endearing.

Faith swallowed the lump in her throat. Her heart surged with happiness. "I'll wait," she told him. "If you're sure you don't mind?"

"I'm sure."

An hour later they tiptoed up the stairs to Joy's room. Faith smoothed the wisps of hair off Joy's sleeping face and planted a kiss on her forehead. Reese fingered the plaits of her blond braid, tucked her dolls close beside her, and pulled the covers up tight, just as he did every night. Quietly he followed Faith out the door.

In his own room, in his own bed, Reese slept with his arms around Joy's sister.

FAITH HAD FOUND her niche, carved it out of her concern for Reese and the other people of the Trail T. She did as she had always done. She made the huge ranch house a home. She gradually took over the role of taking care of Reese. She performed the small tasks that made his life more comfortable. Each night there was plenty of water in the stove reservoir. She made sure his cigar box was always full and the ashtrays empty. She filled the brandy decanter from the casks in the cellar, straightened his desk, kept the scuttle full of coal for the fire in his office. She waited up for him when he worked late, ready to make him coffee or a late night snack, to listen, or to make his body sing with passion until the wee morning hours. Faith took her responsibilities seriously. She cared for the ones she loved. And she did it so subtly, so carefully, she didn't realize Reese was aware of it. Until one morning almost five weeks after her arrival.

The morning she missed breakfast.

"Where's Faith?" Reese asked as he entered the dining room and took his place at one end of the table.

"She's not feeling well," Mary responded. "I took some hot tea up to your room earlier."

"Why didn't you tell me?" he demanded.

"Faith said you were working, that I shouldn't bother you. She said she'd be fine." Mary's reply was calm.

"She wasn't ill last night," Reese said. "What could be wrong with her? Unless . . ." He pushed back his chair and hurried out of the dining room. He took the stairs two at a time. He knocked once on the bedroom door before entering. "Faith? Are you ill? Should I send for the doctor?"

Faith was curled into a miserable ball in the center of the bed. She rolled to one side to face him. There was a mark in the center of her bottom lip where her teeth had gripped it. "Oh, Reese, it's nothing."

Reese sat down on the bed beside her. "It must be something." He smiled at her. "I've never known you to miss breakfast. Have you been sick? Vomiting?" He tried to keep the hopeful note out of his voice in deference to her misery.

Faith shook her head. Her eyes filled with tears.

Reese's smile disappeared along with his hopes. "Then what is it? You can tell me."

"It's my time," she whispered, blushing furiously.

"What?"

"It's my time," she said a little louder. "Time for my monthly. It started this morning."

"Oh." It was all Reese could think to say. She wasn't pregnant. He had failed. They had failed.

"Reese," Faith said softly, "I'm sorry for causing you so much trouble this morning."

"It's no trouble. I missed you at breakfast. I thought you might be . . . you know . . ." He faltered.

"What?"

"I thought you might be pregnant. Morning sickness is one of the symptoms. When you didn't come down for breakfast and Mary said you were ill, I thought . . ."

Her face brightened. "I might still be." She was hopeful.

At first Reese thought she was joking. Then he realized she really didn't understand. "No, innocent, you can't be." And he explained why.

She blushed again, even redder this time, because she was so ignorant. She had heard these things whispered about her entire life, but being unmarried, she had been sheltered from the realities of life until her mother died giving birth to Joy. Faith had accepted responsibility for Joy from the day she was born, but a doctor had delivered her and a wet nurse had fed her. "I'm sorry, Reese." Faith realized how disappointed he was. She wanted to be as disappointed, but a small part of her was secretly glad. The longer it took to conceive his child, the longer she would be able to share his life. Once she conceived and delivered her child, she would be forced to honor the terms of the contract. She would have to walk away from Reese and the baby, when all she wanted was to stay. "I know how disappointed you are."

"It's all right," he told her. "We can try again as soon as you're feeling better. These things take time, I guess." He smoothed her hair away from her face. "Is there anything I can do? Anything you need?"

"No, I'm fine." She sat up in bed and swung her feet to the side. "I'll get dressed. We're missing breakfast. Yours will be cold."

Reese stopped her. "You climb right back into bed, and stay there until you feel better. Get some sleep. You didn't get much last night." He smiled, remembering.

"Neither did you."

"I don't need much," he said, "and I'll have a chance to catch up for a few days." He touched her lips with his own. "Get some rest." He tucked the covers under her chin.

"How is she?" Several voices spoke at once when Reese reentered the dining room.

"She's fine," he assured them.

"Well, what's wrong with her?" Charlie wanted to know. "Should I send somebody for Dr. Kevin?"

Reese shook his head, "No, it's . . ." He looked around at Sam, Joe, and the ranch hands. He cleared his throat. "I . . . um . . . overreacted," he whispered to Sarah.

Sarah nodded, then spoke to Charlie in Cherokee. He shifted uncomfortably in his seat, his face stained with embarrassment.

"Well," Charlie said, "if that's all it is, Sarah can fix it." He spoke to Sarah. She nodded in agreement and left the kitchen.

"What's the remedy?" Reese couldn't contain his curiosity.

"You'll see." Charlie smiled. "I'm an old hand at this. I have two women of my own." He looked fondly at his daughter, Mary, and his wife, Sarah, who returned carrying Reese's decanter of French brandy.

She filled a small pot of tea from the large pot on the table, added a generous helping of honey, then topped off the pot with brandy. Sarah placed it on a tray with a plate of fried bread and handed it to Mary.

"She'll sleep like a baby," Charlie predicted, "and feel much better when she wakes up."

The other men seated at the table took careful note of the remedy.

It was the last time Faith needed it. She didn't miss another breakfast.

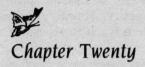

Chapter Twenty

THE PACE OF the ranch was slow in winter, and the weather unpredictable. The days were short, and the nights long. But there was still work to be done. Reese spent long hours at his desk tending to the management of the ranch and his other business interests. There was much to be done before spring, when most of his time would be spent rounding up the herd of Texas longhorns roaming the open range.

Faith spent her time tending to the hundred little tasks and details Reese was too busy to tackle. The rest of her time she devoted to Joy and to her lessons. Her nights belonged to Reese.

The arrangement worked well. Neither Reese nor Faith questioned the duration of their relationship. It was too easy to pretend the marriage would last.

Trail T Ranch
Cheyenne,
Wyoming Territory
March 1870

Dear Aunt Tempy, Aunt Virt,
Hannah, and Agnes,

Joy and I are well. Wyoming is beautiful,

241

though the weather is unpredictable. One moment the sun is shining and warm, and the next there is snowfall of blizzard proportions. Cheyenne, the largest town nearby, is small and new—a real western boom town, not at all like Richmond.

Joy is the proud owner of a Shetland pony named Brutus. She is learning to ride and enjoys it very much, though I fear she'll never have a proper seat. We ride together when weather permits, but only on the ranch grounds. The countryside is lovely, but there are all sorts of dangers. I've enrolled her in the school here on the ranch. Mr. Alexander's sister, Mary Alexander, is the teacher. She excels in teaching languages. Joy and I are learning French and Spanish.

Everyone living here on the ranch is family, except Joy and me. They are all very nice people. Sarah is quite a cook. Hannah would like her. And Mary and I sew together.

My work is very easy, even enjoyable. I enjoy taking care of the children and supervising the staff. In addition to Joy and my charge, there are two other children on the ranch. Taking care of them is very simple.

The year is passing very quickly. I will be home before you know it. I enclose drawings of the ranch and its inhabitants from Joy. Most of the sketches are of Brutus. We send our love, and we hope everything is going well. How is the new roof? Take care of yourselves.

My best to all,

Faith

Faith quickly sealed the letter, hiding the half-truths and vague descriptions. She wanted to write the complete truth, but evasions were necessary. She couldn't bear to describe Reese or her feelings for him in a letter that would be read by the Richmond Ladies Sewing Circle and repeated by Aunt Virt to gossips like Lydia Abbott. She didn't dare reveal the true nature of their relationship. Aunt Tempy knew the truth. That was enough.

Thinking of Tempy, Faith pulled out another sheet of paper. She wrote a brief note meant only for Tempy's eyes: "It's done. I'll keep you informed as time passes. Love to you, Faith." She folded the note into an envelope and addressed it to Temperance, then placed it with the other for mailing.

MARCH DRIFTED INTO April, the days passing, one much like the other until the morning of the second week. Faith awakened in Reese's arms, sat up in bed, and barely made it to the basin in time.

Reese was one step behind her, holding her head, wiping her face when the spasms ended. "Better?"

She nodded, reaching for her toothbrush and tooth powder.

"I was hoping we would skip this stage," Reese murmured, smoothing back her tangled hair, kissing her ear. He poured a glass of water from the pitcher and handed it to her.

Faith rinsed her mouth. "What stage?"

"The morning sickness," Reese told her. "Sweetheart"—the endearment had become second nature to Reese—"you and I are going to have a baby."

"How long have you known?" she asked.

"Just as long as you have." He scooped her up in his arms and carried her back to bed. "Your body has changed. Your breasts are tender. Your waist is a bit thicker."

Faith frowned at him, her hands going to her waist.

Reese smiled. "It's a subtle change," he assured her. "Only a thorough and extremely ardent lover would notice it. Were you hoping to keep it a secret?" He wouldn't have blamed her if she'd contemplated it. It had been a relief not to have to think about the contract for a while. But the brief respite was over. Faith was pregnant.

"No," she answered softly, "I wasn't trying to keep it a secret. I just needed a little time to get used to the idea." She glanced up at him, hoping she hadn't upset him. It had been such a relief not to think about her reason for being in his bed.

Reese simply nodded his head, understanding. He needed time to adjust as well.

"Do you think anyone else knows?" Faith asked.

"Sarah might suspect, but I don't think anyone else knows for sure." Reese lowered himself to the edge of the bed, leaned over, and brushed her forehead with his lips. "Would you feel better if we kept this to ourselves a little longer?"

Faith nodded.

"Then that's what we'll do," Reese promised. He got up from the bed and began to dress. A sudden realization took him by surprise. "Except for David. Faith, we have to tell David." Reese cringed at the thought of her reaction.

"Yes, I suppose we do," she agreed. "It is part of

the contract." Her voice quavered a little when she answered.

The tremor bothered Reese. He rushed to reassure her. "But we won't tell anyone else. Not yet, okay?"

"Okay." Faith managed a smile.

"Do you feel up to eating breakfast?" Reese asked. "I worked up quite an appetite last night," he teased.

"I think I can manage," Faith told him. Her face had regained most of its color. She looked much better as she rolled out of bed and reached for a dress.

Reese handed her a dressing gown. "No need to get completely dressed. You can come down to breakfast in your robe this morning."

"I'm not going to breakfast in my dressing gown," Faith protested uselessly as Reese swept her off her feet and into his arms. "And you certainly aren't going to carry me down!"

Her words were prophetic.

The smell of fried steak and eggs hit her nostrils before Reese was halfway down the stairs. The blood drained from her face. She swallowed hard, muttered a strangled "Reese!" then clamped her jaws firmly shut.

Reese bolted back up the stairs. Once again she barely made it to the basin.

"I guess breakfast is out," Reese murmured as he tucked her back into bed.

"You go," she urged, burrowing under the covers.

"If you're sure?"

"Go." Faith managed the one word.

Reese leaned over and touched her cheek. "Sleep. I'll send up some tea and toast later."

Faith groaned.

The other members of the family were already seated when Reese entered the dining room.

"What was all the ruckus?" Charlie asked. "We heard you run up the stairs. Where's Faith?"

"Faith isn't feeling well this morning," Reese announced.

The men seated at the table looked at one another, then at Sarah. She nodded meaningfully. Charlie smiled, walked over to Reese, and slapped him on the back. "Congratulations!"

Reese started to protest, but his grandfather's actions stopped him. Duncan pushed back his chair and raised his coffee cup. "I think we might have a wee nip of Scots whisky with our coffee." He looked to his wife, Elizabeth, for approval. She nodded. "This is a day of celebration. Soon we'll be welcoming another member of this family into the world." His words were softened by a noticeable burr. "We must plan the formal celebration!"

Faith was oblivious to the rumble downstairs. She curled up and slept, believing her secret would be safe a little longer.

Chapter Twenty-one

ALL OF THE people who lived on the Trail T threw themselves into the preparations for the celebration. Although she wasn't involved in the actual planning of the party, Faith had been twice as busy as usual seeing to Reese's comfort and overseeing the household details. Everything had to be perfect for Faith's introduction to Reese's friends and associates, many of whom were traveling great distances to attend.

The celebration at the Trail T ranch would be the highlight of the Wyoming social season. And although she wasn't really looking forward to it, she knew Reese was. She thought it a shame David would miss it. He'd sent his congratulations and apologies, but business in Washington had detained him.

The night of the party was clear and cool, a beautiful early spring evening. The lamps sent pools of golden light spilling out of every window in the main house. A fire roared in the stone fireplace to chase the chill away. The carpets had been rolled up in the dining room and main parlor and the connecting doors opened to make room for dancing. A small orchestra, brought in from Chicago for the occasion, played at one end of the room. A buffet table, groaning under the weight of food and drink, lined the far wall.

Reese escorted Faith to the landing at the top of the stairs. He paused so that Faith could get a bird's-eye view of the illustrious gathering. She was nervous. He could feel her cold hands through her dyed kid gloves.

"It's all right," he said soothingly, his gaze slowly caressing her. "You look beautiful."

"I do?"

He grinned, allowing her to read his face, the smoldering desire lighting his brown eyes. Reese nodded. "I do like that dress."

"I thought you must," Faith told him, her gray eyes shimmering, "when you asked me to wear it."

It was the burgundy silk dress she had worn to Senator Darcy's New Year's Eve reception. It fit her perfectly once Madame LeClerc's earlier seam adjustments were carefully snipped, allowing an extra inch on either side for her expanding waist and bust. Reese had even laced her into her corset himself, to prevent someone else from lacing her too tightly.

She sneaked a peek at him from beneath the cover of her long lashes. "And I had my heart set on making a grand entrance wearing something new and daring."

"Believe me, sweetheart," Reese teased, "in that dress, your entrance can't be anything but grand. And daring. You do fill it out quite nicely." He ogled the display of her creamy white breasts from his enviable vantage point above her. The

dark crevice separating them beckoned to him. His
tongue tingled from the need to test its depths.
He felt his body tighten in response to the view.
Reese forced himself to think of his guests and
the party. He lifted one of Faith's gloved hands
to his lips and kissed it. "Let's make that grand
entrance."

Faith took a deep, calming breath, then allowed
Reese to lead her down the stairs. "I don't understand why we had to have such a large party," she
whispered. "Wouldn't a private family celebration
have been enough?"

"Afraid not, Faith," Reese said. "I can't risk snub-
bing anyone right now. I have a lot of business
interests in the territory and a lot of money at stake.
Politics being what it is in Washington right now, I
don't need new enemies." There was a major push
to build Wyoming's population and to expand the
business interests there, and Reese was one of its
most successful businessmen and a tireless sup-
porter of statehood.

Reese introduced Faith to the guests. "Ladies and
gentlemen, may I introduce my"—he hesitated—
"my cherished helpmate, companion, and mother
of my child, Faith Collins . . . Jordan."

Faith stared up at him. She barely heard the
the clamor of congratulations and the scattered
applause as he led her onto the dance floor. Her
attention was solely focused on the man beside
her. He had called her his cherished helpmate. She
wanted that to be a reality. Her most fervent hope
was to have him ask her to stand beside him in
a church and for the rest of their lives. She hated
the half-truths she wrote in her letters home and

allowed his family to believe, and she knew Reese hated them even more.

She hated the gold ring she wore on her left hand. It wasn't hers; it belonged to someone else. She hated knowing that everyone believed Reese had slipped it on her finger. But most of all, Faith hated the contract. Hated her signature at the bottom, hated everything it stood for. Sometimes she even wished she hadn't conceived. It hurt too much to live a lie.

The party seemed to drag on for days. The pleasure she'd found in Reese's words faded with each introduction, each dance. Each time she shook someone's hand or smiled into someone's face, she wondered what these people would think when she abandoned her husband and child. What would they say about her then? What gossip would they invent? What would Reese say? She wished with all her heart that Reese hadn't insisted on having this party. She didn't want to know these people or remember their kindness. She pulled away from him, stumbling in her haste to leave the dance floor.

"Faith, what is it?" He looked down at her, alarmed by the sudden pallor of her face. "Are you sick?" She hadn't been eating well. The bouts of nausea persisted. He had noticed that she hadn't eaten a thing tonight.

"No." She shook her head, panting for breath. Bright spots appeared before her eyes. She panicked. "I c-can't . . . breathe. . . ."

Reese caught her in his arms as she slipped toward the floor. He swung Faith up into his arms. "Somebody find Kevin. He's here somewhere," Reese shouted as he headed up the stairs.

Faith opened her eyes. She was in bed. She pushed herself up against the pillows, glancing around, automatically searching for Reese.

"Here I am." Reese spoke from a straight-backed chair next to the head of the bed. Her burgundy dress was draped over the back of the chair. Reese was leaning against it, crushing the silk.

"What happened?" Faith asked.

"You fainted." He held up her frilly white corset, the laces neatly sliced in two. "I suspect this had something to do with it. I shouldn't have let you wear it."

Faith smiled. "I had to wear it. I couldn't have fastened your favorite dress if I hadn't."

Reese's face darkened a bit. He had asked her to wear the damned dress. "Well, since you won't be wearing this anytime soon"—he tossed the corset aside—"I'll just have to order you another burgundy dress in a larger size."

"Maybe even two or three." Dr. Kevin McMurphy leaned against the doorway smiling at the couple. He walked to the bed and sat down on the edge. He lifted Faith's wrist and looked down at his pocket watch, counting heartbeats. When he finished, he looked at Faith. "It must have been a boring party. I understand you fainted to get out of staying to the end. I hear you gave Reese an excuse to leave as well. Sorry I missed it, but I was called out to treat a gunshot wound." This time the doctor lifted Faith's hand to his mouth and kissed it. "I'm Kevin McMurphy. Dr. Kevin to friends and patients."

"Dammit, Kevin, quit flirting," Reese ordered. "She's not impressed."

The doctor looked so wounded at Reese's remark that Faith giggled.

"That's better," Kevin pronounced. "Nothing like a little laughter to stain a lass's cheeks." His voice was a musical Irish lilt. "Now, lass, what happened?"

"She fainted," Reese answered shortly.

Dr. McMurphy shot Reese an annoyed look. He turned back to Faith and addressed his questions to her. "Were you light-headed? Did you see spots? Did you have trouble catching your breath?"

"Yes," Reese said anxiously, looking at the doctor. "What's wrong with her?"

Kevin smiled. He was devilishly handsome. He had black hair lightly sprinkled with gray. His face was sun-bronzed, his dazzling, dark blue eyes framed by a web of lines. Black Irish, Faith thought, recalling the phrase from the depths of her memory. His eyes were sparkling with merriment as he looked at Reese. "If the rumors I'm hearing are true, I'd guess she's expecting a baby."

Reese sucked in a breath. "That's why she fainted?"

"Could be. I'll know more if you'll be quiet and let me examine her," he told Reese. "You always were an impatient cuss. Go wait outside in the hall, if you please."

"I don't please," Reese answered bluntly.

"Then keep quiet while I examine her." Dr. McMurphy questioned Faith as he worked. He asked about her eating and sleeping habits, daily routine, morning sickness, and her routine prior to the party.

Faith answered truthfully.

"How old are you?" Kevin asked.

She didn't answer.

"Twenty-three," Reese answered for her.

"You're thirty-one," Kevin told Reese. "I know how old you are. I'm asking your wife. Pipe down." He studied Faith's downcast eyes. "This is no time for vanity. Are you twenty-three?"

Faith didn't look at Reese when she answered. She couldn't meet his eyes. "I'll be twenty-five in five days."

"What?" Reese burst out.

"I said pipe down," Kevin reminded him. He poked and prodded a few minutes longer, then tucked the sheets back around Faith.

"Well?" Reese demanded, when Kevin finished the examination.

"She's pregnant," Kevin confirmed. "About three months along, give or take a couple of weeks."

Reese relaxed in his chair. "That's it?"

Kevin focused his sharp gaze on Reese. "No, that's not it." His voice was as sharp as the look in his eyes. "She's tired. She's not sleeping well, and she's not eating enough. She's suffering from morning sickness, her legs and ankles are swollen, and she's a tiny bit older than most first-time mothers." He softened his gaze as he looked at his patient. "She's bleeding, and she has no business riding around on a horse or dancing around the room trussed up in a damned whalebone cage!"

"Bleeding?" Reese echoed.

"Just a bit. Probably nothing to be alarmed about, but more than I'd like in any case." Kevin looked at his patient. "We'll keep you in bed awhile and use the time to fatten you up a bit."

"How long?" Faith fastened her gray gaze on the doctor's face.

"Until I'm sure this baby's going to stay anchored. The child is a bit young to be making an appearance this soon." Kevin frowned at the rapid whitening of her face.

"Are you saying my baby's in danger?" Faith's eyes seemed much too large for her face.

"I'm saying it could be in danger," he corrected. "Keeping you off your feet for a week or two is a precaution. You follow my instructions and we'll deliver ourselves a healthy baby. Understand?" He looked first at Reese, then back at Faith.

"We understand," Faith answered for both of them.

"Good. Now you get some rest. I'm going downstairs to the party. I'll check on you tomorrow." He motioned to Reese.

Reese nodded his head, then bent down and pressed a kiss on Faith's lips. "I'll be up in a little while." He followed Dr. Kevin McMurphy out of the bedroom.

"How is she?" Reese asked as soon as he stepped out into the hall. "Is the bleeding serious?"

"Probably not," Kevin answered, "but I would rather not take chances. That means she's to stay in bed. I don't want her on her feet until the danger is past. And, Reese"—the doctor's sharp blue gaze bored into Reese. "If you can't keep your hands off her at night, then for her sake, and the baby's, stay out of her bed."

Reese nodded, his expression grim.

"It doesn't have to be for the duration, just until

I know the baby is going to stay put." Kevin smiled at Reese.

"If it means keeping Faith and the baby safe, I'll do it, Doc," Reese told him, "but I don't have to enjoy it."

"No," Kevin agreed, "I didn't say you had to enjoy it." He clapped Reese on the shoulder. "Let's go down and rejoin the party. We must let your guests know Mrs. Jordan is fine." Kevin started down the hallway, but Reese hesitated, looking back over his shoulder. "Let her rest awhile, Reese. You can look in on her later."

Reese followed Kevin down the stairs.

The last of the local guests had departed and the remaining guests had been assigned rooms for the night before Reese was able to return to the master bedroom. He tiptoed up the stairs and, after stopping to check on Joy, moved down the hall to the room he shared with Faith. She turned to look at him as he opened the door.

"I thought you'd be asleep," Reese said, walking over to the bed. He could see her red-rimmed eyes and knew she'd been crying.

"I waited up for you," Faith said. "How was the party?"

"It disintegrated into a political gathering after you left." He sat down on the bed.

"I'm sorry." Faith looked up at him, her gray eyes wide with concern.

"Don't be." Reese brushed her forehead with a kiss. "I missed you." The words slipped out. He hadn't meant to say them.

"I missed you, too. Very much." Faith held out her arms to him.

Reese leaned down, barely touching her lips with his. Faith held on, trying to deepen the kiss, wanting the reassurance only his touch could give.

"No, Faith." Reese pulled away from her, then eased off the bed. He couldn't trust himself not to touch her, not to make love to her. And he couldn't endanger her or the baby.

"Where are you going?" Faith was alarmed.

"Back downstairs," he said. "I have some paperwork to do. Try to rest. I'll see you in the morning."

"Reese, please stay with me. I'm frightened," she confessed.

He could see the fear in her eyes. Reese knew she needed reassurance. He wanted to give it, but he couldn't. He was too afraid he would lose control. Too afraid he wouldn't be able to stop at holding her. Afraid she wouldn't let him stop. But she was too precious. The life she carried was too precious to risk. "I have to go back downstairs." His voice was brusque, husky, but he offered no explanation.

She blinked back tears. "Yes, of course. I'm sorry."

"I told you before, there's no need to apologize. Is there anything I can get for you? Anything you need?"

I need you to hold me. I need you. She wanted to scream the words at him, make him understand, but she said nothing. She shook her head.

He lingered for a moment in the doorway. "Then I guess I'll see you in the morning."

Faith didn't speak. She turned away.

Reese closed the door. He could hear her sobbing

into her pillow, calling for someone. It tore at his heart. Her words were muffled, and he couldn't make out the name, but he knew who she needed. He went down to his study and wrote out a telegram. He would ride into Cheyenne first thing in the morning.

Chapter Twenty-two

REESE RODE OUT at dawn, headed for Cheyenne. After spending a miserable night on the leather sofa in his study, he had chosen to skip the family breakfast. There would be plenty of time to answer questions later. First he had to send for help. Faith needed someone with her, and until Reese was certain he could trust himself, he couldn't be that someone. He nudged his horse into a canter, determined to set a new record for the trip into town.

Reese was waiting for the clerk when the telegraph office opened at half-past eight. He handed the telegram to the clerk along with several coins.

"I want you to notify me as soon as you get a reply. I'll be across the street having breakfast." Reese touched the brim of his hat, then exited the telegraph office.

Dr. Kevin McMurphy tied his black medical bag to the back of his saddle, mounted up, and trotted his Arabian mare briskly out of Cheyenne. He was headed on his daily rounds. He had promised to check on several patients this morning—a child with an injured ankle a mile outside town, the gunshot wound on the Jackson spread, and Faith Jordan at the Trail T. He kicked his mare into a

259

faster gait. If he made good time, he could make it to the Trail T in time for a late breakfast.

"Good morning," Kevin said, as he tapped at the door to Faith's bedroom. "Sarah said you were awake. May I come in?" He sounded very cheerful, his voice very Irish.

Faith sat up, propping herself against the pillows. "Yes, please."

The doctor walked to the bed and studied her face. The dark circles under her eyes were very pronounced, her nose was red, and those big gray eyes were red-rimmed and swollen. "Spent the night crying, didn't you?"

Faith nodded.

He flipped back the covers and gave her a quick but thorough examination. "The swelling in your ankles is down. Very good." He looked at his patient. "You stayed off your feet." He smiled down at her. She smiled back. Kevin froze. Faith's smile stunned him. He looked past the woman on the bed, seeing the face he'd dreamed about for so many years. She had smiled at him like that—a small, tremulous smile that had knocked the breath right out of him. He shook his head. There was a resemblance in the clear gray eyes, the slope of the nose, her mouth. But his love had been blessed with glorious red hair and a sprinkling of freckles. He remembered her so vividly. A sixteen-year-old beauty. Mother of God, but it frightened him to think how much he still loved her after all these years!

"Doctor?" Faith's eyes were puzzled. "Is something wrong?" Her voice rose at the end of her words.

He shook his head. Faith could see the sprinkle of silver in his black hair. "No, lass." His eyes creased at the corners as he pulled his mouth into a sad smile. "You reminded me of someone. Someone I knew a long time ago."

"In Ireland?" Faith blurted out her thoughts.

"No, in America. I met her just after I arrived. I was thinking you resemble her."

"I'm flattered you think so," Faith said softly.

Kevin looked down at the woman on the bed. She was twenty-five and married to one of his closest friends. He was forty-eight and acting like an old fool. He knew it, but couldn't help it. Faith Jordan made him think about love again. He pushed aside the thoughts, then cleared his throat. "That's enough Irish melancholy for today."

"How did you meet Reese?" Faith asked suddenly.

So that was the way the wind blew, Kevin thought. Served an old fool right for having thoughts he shouldn't have. This young woman was in love with her husband.

Kevin McMurphy sat down on the edge of the bed. "I met Reese during the war. I patched him up a couple of times, and David, too, once. The last time was at Gettysburg when Reese took a saber cut across the hip. Nasty business. It took him several months to recover. We became friends and talked quite a bit. I brought him books, art supplies, that sort of thing. After the war we kept in touch. I was in Washington for a while, then briefly in Petersburg. I ran into Reese in Washington. Cheyenne needed a doctor. He asked me to come out here."

Faith studied the doctor as he spoke. He was a mystery. There was something about him, something she couldn't put her finger on. Her brain nagged at her. He reminded her of someone. The term "black Irish" crept into her mind each time she saw him. She wasn't attracted to him, though he was a handsome man, but she couldn't deny her unexplainable curiosity.

"My home was in Richmond," Faith volunteered. "I met Reese in Washington. I was there . . . visiting. And here I am."

"About to have a baby." Kevin was all doctor once again. "If you continue to follow orders, I think we'll be able to keep the child safe." He stood up, closing his black bag. "I'll check back again later," he said before closing the door behind him.

Faith was left alone. She slept. She read a book Mary brought her. She even practiced her Cherokee on Sarah, but she was bored. For someone accustomed to being busy, the enforced idleness was a trial. Faith became short-tempered, irritable.

"Faith?"

She opened her eyes.

Joy stood in the doorway clutching her slate and primer. "Miss Sarah said I could come see you."

Faith smiled and patted the place beside her in the bed.

Joy scrambled up. "I missed you, Faith."

"I've missed you, too, sprite." Reese's pet name for Joy slipped out.

"Are you sick?" Joy's large gray eyes were worried. Frown lines wrinkled her forehead.

Faith pulled her closer and hugged her. "Not really. I'm just a little tired." She took a deep breath, searching for the right words. "You see, Joy, in a few months I'm going to have a baby. I have to stay in bed for a while. And rest."

"Before you have a baby?"

"Uh-huh." Faith nodded.

"Will you have a little girl baby?"

"I don't know," Faith confided. "I'd like that, but Reese wants a little boy."

"Is he having a baby, too?" Joy was confused, upset at the prospect of being displaced.

"Uh-huh. It will be my baby and Reese's."

"Will I still be your little girl?"

A sheen of tears sparkled in Faith's eyes. "You'll always be my little girl."

"Weese's too?" Joy asked.

"Of course." Faith nodded. "Reese will always love you."

"Will he love your baby as much as he loves me?"

Faith smoothed the wisps of blond hair off Joy's forehead, then traced the worry lines with her fingertip. "Yes, he will." She looked at Joy. "Reese will love the baby just as much as he loves you, but that doesn't mean he'll love you any less. Do you understand that, sweetie? He'll love both of you."

"Will he buy the baby a pony like Brutus?"

"No." Faith had to hide her smile at Joy's noticeable relief. "I promise you Reese won't buy the baby a pony for a long time. And it won't ever be a pony like Brutus."

"Cross your heart?"

Faith drew a cross over her heart.

"Good." Joy beamed up at her sister, her confidence in Reese's affection fully restored. She pulled her slate onto her lap. "You want me to draw you a picture?"

"That would be nice."

"Okay." Joy bent her head over her task.

"What will you draw for me?" Faith asked.

"A picture of Brutus."

Faith smiled. What else?

Joy stayed most of the afternoon. The doctor visited again. Even Charlie and Duncan stood awkwardly at her bedside, attempting conversation, but there was no sign of Reese.

Faith's worst fears were realized. She had hoped she could make him need her, but she'd failed. He didn't need her. Didn't love her. Faith tried to halt the flow of tears. They were tears of self-pity, but she couldn't seem to stop them. She curled herself into a ball and cried herself to sleep.

When she opened her eyes once again, it was dark outside and Reese was sitting in the chair next to the bed. Faith blinked twice to make sure she wasn't dreaming. "Reese!"

Reese gritted his teeth against the breathless sound of his name on her lips. He had heard her say his name that way many times when she cried out her pleasure—her satisfaction. His body responded as always to the sound and the image. She moved closer to him, but he didn't kiss her. Instead, he told her abruptly, "I've brought you something to keep your mind off having to stay in bed." He picked up a brown paper package.

What she really wanted was his kiss, but her eyes brightened at the sight of a gift. He had been thinking about her.

"They're for the baby. I hope you like them."

The light in her eyes dimmed. Her reply was polite, mechanical. "I'm sure I will. Thank you."

He unwrapped the package and placed the contents on her lap. Inside the paper were pieces of fabric in various shapes and colors, most of the patterns in cotton flannel. "I had the dressmaker cut them out for you. I thought you might like to sew a few things for the baby." He held up one half of a gown. "I brought your sewing basket and all the things the dressmaker said you'd need," he added awkwardly. He had wanted to do something for her that no one else had thought to do. While the others brought her books, newspapers, and homework to review, he had thought of the baby. Faith enjoyed sewing. She was always mending his shirts and reattaching his buttons. Now she could sew for someone besides him and Joy. She could make things for the baby.

"Thank you. They'll keep me very busy." Faith's eyes were dull, her voice soft.

"Faith, are you all right?" His chocolate brown eyes were full of concern, but Faith couldn't tell if it was for her or the baby. "I thought you liked sewing. I thought you'd like staying busy."

"Oh, I do," she replied absently, "and this way you won't have to pay anyone else to make clothes for your child. It's very economical."

He flinched at her words. He hadn't meant his gift to imply that he was attempting to save money. "Are you sure you feel all right?"

"I'm fine. The doctor came twice today."

"I know. I spoke to Kevin."

"Then you know I'm much better," Faith told him.

Reese nodded. "That's what the doctor said," but he wasn't so sure he agreed with Kevin. Reese didn't think she was any better.

"Will you be here tonight?" Faith's question sounded casual, but Reese knew it was not. The deliberate lack of emotion in her voice told him how important the question was.

"I'm afraid not." Reese didn't elaborate.

"More paperwork?"

"Something like that."

"I see," she replied, drawing the covers up around her as if to shield herself from his view. "Then I guess there's nothing more to say." She dismissed him.

Reese sat there looking at her. He was stunned. She acted angry, hurt. Surely she understood the sacrifice he was making by staying away from her. Surely Kevin had explained the risks. "Faith, I . . ."

She looked at him coldly. "Good night, Reese," she said. "Pleasant dreams."

He got up from his chair and stalked out the door.

FOUR DAYS LATER, the morning of Faith's twenty-fifth birthday dawned clear and cool with visible signs of warming. It was a welcome sight for the men of the Trail T. They stumbled into the main house for breakfast after three days of rounding up cattle on the open range in numbing cold and fresh snowfall.

A freak winter storm had dumped several inches of white powder snow on the ranch. The cows were dropping their calves, and the newborns were in danger of freezing to death. All able-bodied men were working long hours to round up the cattle and rescue the calves.

Reese hadn't seen Faith during those long days. He'd bunked with the hands in a shack on the range. This was his first morning home. He sank into a chair and gratefully wrapped his hands around a cup of Sarah's strong, hot coffee. Most of the herd were safely bedded down inside the holding pens.

"How's Faith?" Reese asked Mary as soon as he pulled his wool scarf from around his face.

"Lonely, bored, missing you," Mary answered bluntly.

Reese was silent.

"Well?" Mary asked.

"What?" He stared at his cousin.

"Aren't you going to say anything?" she demanded.

"Has Kevin been in to see her today?"

Mary heaved a dramatic sigh. "Not yet, but I expect him this afternoon. He's been here nearly every day."

"Doesn't he have any other patients?" It bothered Reese to know the handsome Irishman was spending so much time on the Trail T. He'd asked Kevin to cheek on her. He hadn't asked him to move in!

"Faith invited him for supper tonight," Mary told him.

"She what?" Reese slammed his cup down into the saucer. Drops of hot coffee splashed the back of his hand.

"Faith invited Dr. Kevin to stay for supper. It's her birthday, you know," Sarah replied in Cherokee, setting a plate in front of Reese.

"Yes, I know it's her birthday." Reese muttered an obscenity beneath his breath. "I telegraphed David several days ago. Has he sent a reply?"

"On your desk," Mary told him. "It came yesterday."

Reese shot up from his chair and hurried into his study. He ripped open the telegram and scanned the contents. David was brief. He and Tempy would arrive in Cheyenne today on the 4:15 P.M. train. Reese walked back to the kitchen and finished his breakfast. "I'm going to try to get some sleep," he told Sarah. "Will you wake me in a couple of hours?"

Sarah nodded her head, then went about her business.

Reese stood up and started back to his study.

"Aren't you going up to see Faith?" Mary asked the question everyone in the kitchen was dying to ask.

"I'll see her at supper," Reese answered, then stomped into his private retreat and slammed the door.

Four hours later, freshly bathed, shaved, and dressed in a clean suit and overcoat, Reese climbed into the surrey. Joy, bundled into her heavy coat and mittens, sat next to him. The temperature had risen above freezing, but the hard-packed dirt roads were still solid. Reese prayed the train carrying David and Tempy would arrive before the ground began to thaw and the roads turned to mush.

He hadn't planned on Joy's company, but decided to bring her along when she threatened to tell Faith. He had forgotten what a tyrant Joy could be when she wanted something. She was in the barn

feeding lumps of sugar to her pony when Reese
ordered the team hitched to the surrey. He was
going somewhere and Joy was determined to go
with him.

Reese had made a tactical error when he attempted to dissuade her by explaining why he was
going to town. Joy seized the opportunity. When
the promise of a licorice whip failed to buy her
silence, Reese was forced to bring her along. He'd
been outmaneuvered by a five-year-old expert.

Joy was immune to Reese's bad mood. She
climbed over his thigh then settled herself on
the wedge of seat between his legs. Placing her
red-mittened hands over his gloved ones, Joy pretended to guide the vehicle into town.

THE TRAIN PULLED into the station right on
schedule. Tempy could hardly wait to alight from
the railroad car. She danced on her tiptoes, searching for Reese. David Alexander chuckled in amuse-
ment.

"Conduct unbecoming a grown woman?" Tempy
asked, hearing the rumble in David's chest and
sneaking a glance at his amused expression.

"Not at all." David shook his head, trying to
appear serious despite his obvious laughter. "I
think it's entirely appropriate for an aunt who
dearly loves her nieces." He had visited Richmond
several times over the past few months and come to
know the ladies of the sewing circle fairly well. He
knew Temperance Hamilton best of all, especially
after spending four days traveling alone with her.

David smiled at the memory. Virtuous Jessup
had pitched a fit over that prospect.

"Temperance Hamilton, are you seriously considering traveling all the way to Wyoming alone with *him*?" Virtuous had asked, outraged.

"Faith is ill," Temperance replied calmly.

"But what will everyone think?" Virtuous persisted. "He looks so different and he's a Yankee to boot."

"I don't care what anyone thinks. My . . . Faith needs me." Tempy was adamant. "I'd travel with General Sherman and a whole band of Yankees to be with Faith." Tempy's hand flew up to cover her mouth, suddenly cognizant of the fact that David Alexander was privy to the heated exchange. "No offense intended, Mr. Alexander."

"None taken, ma'am." David inclined his head.

"Well, Temperance, you were never one to care much for proprieties," Virtuous sneered. "First an Irishman and now a Yankee!"

"Virt!" Hannah and Agnes gasped in horror.

"Right!" Tempy blanched at her sister's unexpected attack, but she stood her ground. "And I won't care much for proprieties when I trounce you in front of Mr. Alexander, either, Virtuous May! Now get out of my way. I'm tired of arguing with you. You're wasting time." Tempy picked up her bag and smiled sweetly at her older sister. "Do keep in mind while I'm gone that if something happens to Faith, the money you're so pleased with will be forfeit. Think about that, Virt, while I worry about your niece!" Tempy pushed past her sister and followed David Alexander out the door.

Temperance Hamilton was petite like her niece, but David now understood where Faith's temper came from. She had inherited it from Temperance.

He smiled at the thought of that. He'd become quite fond of Faith's aunt.

"There he is!" Her cry of recognition brought David back to the present. "Joy's with him and . . . Oh, dear Lord, she's got on a black coat? I hope Faith . . ." She leaped down from the car to the platform, pushing through the startled onlookers in her frenzied haste to reach Reese.

David was just a few steps behind her. He had spent the better part of the journey assuring Temperance that her niece was fine, but the older woman was convinced Faith was seriously ill. She had repeatedly reminded David of her niece's sick spell before departing from Washington. David had done his best to persuade her that there was no reason to worry, but apparently he'd failed. Miserably.

"Faith? Is she—" Tempy burst out, colliding with Reese's hard chest just as he stepped down from the surrey.

Reese reached out to steady the woman. Her eyes were wide, bright, and frantic with worry. Her gaze darted about his face searching for the truth. Her heart hammered against his chest, her breasts heaving with exertion. "She's resting, at the ranch," Reese said softly.

"Thank God!" Temperance slumped against him with relief.

"Didn't you get my telegram?" Reese held the woman close. He glanced over her head, to find David standing behind her.

"Yes," David answered. "I even showed it to Temperance, but she's concerned about her niece."

"I can see that," Reese answered dryly. "I'm bowled over by her concern."

"The little girl is wearing a black coat," David said. "Miss Hamilton thought . . ."

"It's her warmest," Reese explained. "I never dreamed . . ." He looked down at the older woman. She had regained her breath and most of her composure. "I apologize to you, Miss Hamilton, for giving you such a fright. Faith is fine. In fact, she's much better." His voice was soft.

Temperance managed a weak smile. His gaze was warm, even tender, when he looked at her, the frown between his brows confirming his genuine concern.

Reese gave Tempy his best smile of assurance, then turned to Joy. "Say hello to your aunt, sprite." He lifted Tempy up to sit beside Joy.

Joy hugged Temperance, then began bombarding her with news of the ranch.

Reese spoke to David. "Climb in. I'll see to the luggage."

"We left in a hurry," David told him. "We each brought one bag. I told Miss Hamilton she could buy whatever she needed when she got here."

"Fine," Reese agreed absently. "I'll get your bags and we'll be on our way. I need to make one stop before we leave town."

Tempy interrupted Joy's nonstop chatter. "Is that necessary, Mr. Jordan? I don't mean to pry, but I'm anxious to see my . . . niece." She leaned forward.

Reese grinned, then turned his charming smile on Temperance Hamilton. "Very necessary. Today is Faith's birthday, and in addition to you, I have a couple of other gifts to pick up."

Tempy sat back in her seat. "Oh, my goodness, how could I have forgotten? I didn't even bring a gift!"

David laughed aloud. "My dear Temperance, you are the gift!"

Tempy looked at David, then to Reese for confirmation.

Reese nodded, his cocoa-colored eyes sparkling. "The best gift I could hope to give her."

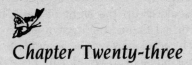

Chapter Twenty-three

"IS EVERYTHING READY?" Reese asked as he entered the kitchen of the main house.

"Yes," Sarah answered. "She thinks we've forgotten her birthday." She lifted the large sheet cake from its resting place on the worktable. "All I have to do is take this to the dining room."

"Good," Reese told her. "David and Faith's aunt Temperance are hiding in my study. They're part of her surprise."

Sarah's face lighted up with happiness at the mention of her son's name. Reese smiled down at his beloved aunt. "And part of yours, Aunt Sarah."

Sarah wanted to hug him, but didn't dare display that sort of childish affection for a grown man. She rapped him on the arm with her wooden spoon instead. "You should have told me," she chided.

"And spoil your surprise?" Reese asked. "Not likely. You go and spend some time with David. I'll take the cake into the dining room and then go upstairs and get the birthday girl." Reese smoothed a stray hair back from Sarah's face as he moved past her.

Faith looked up from her book as Reese entered the bedroom a few minutes later. Her gray eyes hungrily scanned his face. It had been days since

275

she'd seen him. She missed him. "Hello."

"Hello yourself," Reese answered, his brown-eyed gaze soaking up the sight of her. She was wearing a ruffled flannel nightgown and a quilted bed jacket. Her black hair was loose and falling over her shoulders. She looked wonderful. He moved to the foot of the bed for a better view.

"I haven't seen you lately," Faith murmured. "I thought you'd forgotten all about me." She turned back to the page in front of her, pretending a lack of interest in him.

"I've been out on the range for the past few days. The snowstorm was hard on the cattle. The newborn calves were in danger of freezing. We had to get them in." He felt awkward standing there in front of her.

"Really? I hadn't noticed the weather," Faith lied.

Reese didn't know whether to shake her or burst out laughing at her bald-faced lie. How could anyone not notice snow whirling past the windows and a fifty-degree drop in temperature? "Well," he said, deciding to play along, "I guess you've been busy." He sneaked a glance at her to gauge her reaction. "Sewing baby clothes and all."

Faith glared at him. The baby clothes were still a sore point with her. She'd done nothing but sew on the tiny garments for the past three days. How dare he imply otherwise on the one afternoon she'd decided to read? It was her birthday after all, even if no one on this godforsaken ranch remembered it! "As a matter of fact, I have been very busy. And I'm busy right now."

"Too busy to join us downstairs for dinner?" Reese asked softly.

"What?" She was startled by his invitation.

"You did invite Dr. McMurphy to supper tonight, didn't you? Or perhaps you'd rather he dined up here with you?"

"Yes. No," Faith faltered.

"Which is it?" Reese's tone of voice was harder, almost cutting as he tried to curb his spurt of jealousy.

"Yes, I did invite him," she answered, "and no, I don't want him to join me here." She looked up at Reese. "I'd like to eat downstairs with the rest of you. If it's all right."

"It's fine with me," Reese told her. "Kevin said it would be all right if someone carried you downstairs. I'm the someone. Take it or leave it." He glared at her, demanding an answer.

"I'll take it!" Faith practically bounced up and down on the bed.

"You'll need this." He thrust a gray velvet robe at her.

"Can't I get dressed?" Faith pleaded. "It won't be too hard if you help me."

On the contrary, Reese thought, he wouldn't be anything but hard if he helped her dress. Looking at her was bad enough. He cleared his throat. "One thing at a time. The doctor didn't say anything about letting you dress for supper. Take it or . . ."

Faith opened her mouth to protest, but a glance at Reese stopped her. "Leave it." She finished his ultimatum for him.

"Well?"

"I'll take it." She removed her bed jacket and took the robe.

When she was securely wrapped in velvet, Reese scooped her up in his arms and carried her down the stairs to the dining room.

"Surprise!" The dining room erupted with shouts the minute Reese walked through the door. "Happy birthday!"

"Oh!" Faith stared at the familiar faces. The members of Reese's family were crowded into the dining room, but her one invited guest was absent. Reese lowered her into a dining room chair.

"I don't know what to say," Faith began. "I thought you had forgotten." She looked at Mary, then at Sarah.

"We know," Mary groaned, looking for all the world like a long-suffering martyr.

"Thank you," Faith said simply. "Thank you all."

"Look, Faith!" Joy bounced up and down next to Faith's chair. "Sarah made you a birthday cake!" She pointed to the large confection of flour, eggs, and sugar. "And we all got you presents. Can we open them now? And eat the cake?" Joy's eyes sparkled greedily.

Faith glanced at Sarah, then down at her young sister. "We probably need to have supper first. The cake will spoil your appetite." It was hard to contain her own excitement. She hadn't had a birthday cake since her sixteenth birthday. She looked up at Reese. "Where's Dr. McMurphy? I thought he was here."

"That was a ruse to get you downstairs." Reese couldn't help the frown marring his handsome face. "I hate to disappoint you, but the doctor sent word that he's been delayed. He said not to hold supper for him. He'll be late."

"Then I guess we should start." Faith was hurt by the hostile tone in Reese's voice. Some of her delight in the wonderful birthday surprise was muted.

"Thank goodness!" David announced from the doorway of the dining room. "I'm so hungry I could eat a bear!"

"David!" Faith exclaimed, excited once again. "This is a surprise! How did you get here?"

"By train," David answered. "Reese sent for me."

"How is everyone in Richmond? Is everything settled? How are my aunts? How is Aunt Tempy?"

"Why don't you ask her?" David stepped aside to allow Temperance Hamilton entrance.

"Aunt Tempy!" Faith cried, tears of joy shimmering in her eyes. "Oh, Aunt Tempy . . ."

Temperance ran to her niece and hugged her tightly.

"How did you get here?" Faith wanted to know.

"I came with David." Temperance smiled, smoothing Faith's hair away from her face. "Happy birthday, darling."

"You came with David? Reese sent for you?"

"Of course," Tempy told her. "How else?"

Faith looked up at Reese.

"Surprise," he said.

A lump formed in Faith's throat. Tears slipped down her cheeks. She tried to thank him, but words failed her. She simply stared at him, her love for him shining in her eyes.

Reese stepped forward and took her hand. He raised it to his lips and tenderly brushed the knuckles with his lips. "Happy birthday, Faith."

The last of the supper dishes had been cleared away, and most of the gifts presented to the birthday girl, before Dr. Kevin McMurphy entered the dining room. Faith looked up as he stepped inside the doorway. She greeted him warmly. "Dr. Kevin, I'm so glad you made it. We waited to cut the cake." She extended her hand in his direction. "Come in, come in. There's someone special I'd like you to meet. Reese surprised me by sending for her." Faith took Kevin's hand in hers.

Reese glared at the couple from his vantage point halfway across the table. The room was full of people standing together in little groups, laughing and talking. Celebrating. Reese sat at one end of the table. Alone. His good mood had deteriorated with Kevin's entrance. He had another present for Faith, but he wanted to give it to her when he could be assured of some privacy. Reese shifted in the hard chair and angrily tossed back the remainder of his brandy.

"Aunt Tempy," Faith called, over the noise of the group. "The doctor's arrived. I want to introduce you."

Temperance was laughing at something Mary said when Faith called to her. She turned. Her laughter died on her lips when she saw the man standing next to Faith. Tempy's face whitened in shock. Blood roared through her brain. Her knees trembled. The cup and saucer slipped from her fingers and shattered against the hard floor.

Tempy opened her mouth. Her lips formed his name. "Kevin." Then, like a flower gracefully bowing to a strong wind, she swayed. Seconds later Temperance followed the cup and saucer down to the hard floor.

"Aunt Tempy!" Faith shouted, jumping to her feet.

"Mary, Mother of God! Temperance!" Kevin gently pushed Faith back into her chair. "Someone get my bag. I need some smelling salts." He hurried to Tempy's side. "Step back," he ordered David, Mary, and Reese who hovered over her. "Give her some air."

A few seconds later Sam handed him his medical bag. Kevin uncorked a vial of smelling salts and passed it under Tempy's nose.

Unnoticed by the crowd gathered around Temperance, Faith left her chair and worked her way through the group to stand at Reese's side.

Tempy's eyes opened. She looked up into the dark blue eyes of Kevin McMurphy and smiled. "Am I dreaming?" she asked. "Kevin, is it really you?"

"In the flesh." Kevin helped her sit up, then get to her feet. She leaned against him. He curled a protective arm around her.

"Aunt Tempy?" Faith moved to stand in front of her aunt. "Are you all right?"

Tempy looked around and saw the concerned faces, but her gaze drifted back to Kevin. "Too much excitement," she murmured, embarrassed.

"She's had a long day and a tiring journey," Reese said. "It's probably exhaustion."

"That's a possibility," Kevin agreed amiably. "But more than likely, it was seeing me again."

"Again?" Reese asked.

"You know each other?" David asked.

"Oh, yes." Kevin hugged Tempy close. "Once, long ago, I married the lass." He smiled down at the woman cuddled against his side. "And I intend to repeat the procedure as soon as possible."

Temperance blushed, looking younger and prettier than her forty-one years.

Kevin bent and lifted her into his arms. "For now I'm taking her to her bed. Which one is it?"

"I'll show you," Mary volunteered, leading the way.

"But her husband was Kevin O'Malley!" Faith protested.

"Well, lass," Kevin paused to explain, "so was I. In another lifetime."

"What?" Reese demanded, following Kevin halfway out of the dining room.

"I'll explain it all later," the doctor promised. "Right now, Temperance and I have some catching up to do." His handsome mouth curved into a tender smile as he gazed at Tempy. "Don't we, love?" He nodded a dismissal in Reese's direction and proceeded up the stairs with Temperance cradled in his arms.

"Well, what do you know!" Charlie exclaimed, amazed by the sudden turn of events. He plopped down in his seat at the table.

"What *do* you know?" Reese returned to the dining room and looked at Faith.

"Only that Aunt Tempy eloped with a Kevin O'Malley when she was sixteen," Faith told them. "My grandfather Hamilton caught them in Baltimore, put Kevin on a ship bound for England, then sent Aunt Tempy to stay with relatives until the scandal died down."

"Kevin has been spending a lot of time with you lately," Reese reminded her. "Did you tell him about your family? Did you know he was your aunt's long-lost beau?"

Faith stared up at him. "No!"

"Did you suspect it?" He stood over her. His hands imprisoned hers on the arms of the chair.

"How could I?" Faith countered, wondering why Reese had decided to interrogate her. "She only mentioned him once or twice. She knew him as Kevin O'Malley, not Dr. Kevin McMurphy. Why are you questioning me? What difference does it make to you?"

"Not a bit," Reese admitted. "But it might make a lot of difference to you. You might decide to change your mind about . . . *things*." He emphasized the last word, forgetting the curious friends and relatives gathered around, forgetting everything except this unexpected wrinkle in his well-laid plan.

"What things?" Faith demanded to know. "Why should it make a difference to me? It's fine with me as long as Aunt Tempy is happy."

"Why don't we discuss this later?" David, suddenly understanding the drift of the conversation, smoothly interrupted.

Reese ignored him. "Kevin mentioned marriage." He leaned closer to Faith to emphasize his point. "That means settling down. It means your beloved aunt might be my closest neighbor. It means you might want to visit her someday."

"Well, of course, I'll want to"—Faith stopped, suddenly remembering—"visit." The last word nearly died on her lips. If Tempy decided to marry Kevin and stay in Wyoming, visiting would be out of the question. The contract explicitly forbade Faith to venture anywhere near the Trail T, Reese, or the baby. She sat back in her chair, stunned. She might lose Tempy as well as the baby. "Oh, no!" she whispered.

"Isn't it wonderful?" Mary asked, reentering the dining room. "Two romances on one ranch. First Reese and Faith, and now Temperance and Dr. Kevin."

"It's just grand," Reese retorted dryly. He wondered how Kevin and Temperance were spending their private minutes alone. He wanted to do the same thing. He wanted to swing Faith up into his arms and carry her off to bed. Sleep was the last thing on his mind. And he sure as hell didn't feel like celebrating.

"I think it is grand," Mary repeated. "Two weddings and a new baby coming. All in one year! We should celebrate. It's Faith's birthday! It's time to—"

"Cut the cake," Joy cried. "I want some birthday cake. Weese. You promised!"

He looked pointedly at Faith. "Ask your sister, sprite," he advised Joy. "It's her birthday and her cake."

Joy turned her hopeful expression on Faith. "Can we please cut the cake? I want some birthday cake."

Faith hesitated, but she couldn't disappoint Joy and the other children who had waited patiently to taste the sweet dessert. "Why not?" she capitulated. "Sarah, if you'll pass me a knife, I'll do the honors." Sarah handed her a knife. "Do you think we ought to save a couple of pieces for Dr. Kevin and Aunt Tempy? Or wait for them to come down?" she asked Reese.

"Just cut the cake."

"But, they might want . . ." The hostess in Faith and the years of southern training protested this lack of manners.

"Faith," Reese began before Joy decided the matter.

"Aunt Tempy!" Joy shouted at the top of her lungs. "Dr. Kevin! Faith is going to cut her birthday cake! Are you coming down? Or do you want us to save you a piece?"

"That settles that," David interjected, moving to stand beside his mother.

But it didn't. Joy wasn't taking any chances. She demanded an answer. "Aunt Tempy! Doctor—"

"We're right here, lassie." Kevin spoke from the stairs. "We hear you."

"The whole ranch heard her," Sam declared, with fifteen-year-old wisdom. "She probably started a cattle stampede."

"Did not!" Joy argued childishly.

"Did too!" Sam forgot his dignity and argued back.

"Children . . ." Mary chided.

Sam turned to look at his sister, mortified because she'd called him a child in front of the others. He opened his mouth to protest.

Tempy walked over to Faith who sat, knife poised above the cake. "Faith darling, we apologize for interrupting your birthday celebration." She glanced over her shoulder at Kevin. He winked at her. "Why don't you cut the cake now, before—"

"Before Joy pitches a fit," Sam muttered.

"Or this happy family occasion turns into a brawl," David added as Joy stuck her tongue out at Sam.

Sam retaliated by swatting Joy's bottom.

"Yeah," Reese muttered ungraciously, glaring at Kevin for spoiling the party and ruining his plans. "Cut the cake."

Faith did as he asked, first cutting slices for the children.

Sarah volunteered to fetch coffee for the adults and milk for the children. She nudged her husband in the ribs, motioning for him to help her. He stood up somewhat reluctantly as he moved to help his wife. "Let's hurry. I don't want to miss a minute of this."

Only the children were oblivious to the tension permeating the room. It was almost as palpable as the creamy, rich icing atop the birthday cake. Faith's movements as she sliced the cake were jerky and uncertain. Reese seemed to be staring a hole through her as he angrily poured yet another glass of brandy. His behavior was unsettling.

Faith managed a halfhearted smile as she lifted slices of cake onto plates for the adults.

Sarah and Charlie returned carrying trays of fresh coffee and glasses of milk. Sarah placed the first cup of coffee in front of Reese.

He glared at her as she removed his brandy glass and set the cup and saucer in its place.

The silence in the room was deafening as the cake and beverages were passed around. Faith let her gaze rake the room as she looked for some way to start a civilized conversation.

David answered her silent plea, smiling sympathetically. He invited Kevin and Temperance to sit next to Reese. "Why don't you tell us how you met?"

"Well," Kevin began, launching into his story. He had immigrated to America from Ireland. Unable to hang his doctor's shingle in the face of extreme anti-Irish prejudice, he had found work as a horse trainer on the Hamilton plantation. "I met Temperance." The love echoed in his voice as he said her name. "And I proposed marriage." Kevin's handsome face darkened with remembered anger. "But her father wouldn't hear of his daughter marrying a dirty Irish horse trainer. So—"

"We eloped," Tempy said softly, "to Baltimore. My father tracked us down. He had . . . had Kevin . . ." Her voice cracked remembering her father's cruelty. She took a sip of her coffee.

"He had me beaten unconscious and signed onto a ship bound for England and then China. I was gone for five years. When I got back to England, I worked passage back to the States. I headed straight for the Hamilton plantation." He shrugged his shoulders. "You know what they say about hardheaded Irishmen. I bearded the lion in his den and got clamped in the Petersburg jail for my efforts. Old man Hamilton . . ." He felt Temperance cringe at his side and corrected himself. "Temperance's father told me she'd gone to live with relatives and that the marriage had been annulled."

"It had," Temperance announced. "I was sixteen when we eloped. My father had it annulled and sent me to Philadelphia. I stayed there for a while. I was only allowed to return home when my sister Prudence became ill. She was carrying a child."

"Me," Faith interjected.

Tempy smiled at Faith, then continued her story. "I moved in to take care of Pru until she was back on her feet. By that time . . ."

"I was out of jail, but barred from living in Virginia. Hamilton had powerful friends." Kevin looked around at his audience. "Maybe I could have done more, but I didn't relish spending more months in jail."

"You did everything in your power." Tempy patted Kevin's hand, reassuring him.

"I left, set up practice in a little town on the Pennsylvania-Maryland border, and made inquiries. I knew Hamilton had sent Temperance to Pennsylvania, but I didn't know where. There wasn't much call for an Irish doctor. I tended more animals than people until the war. I volunteered as a surgeon, giving my full name Kevin McMurphy O'Malley. My full name wouldn't fit in the space on the army forms. Some clerk shortened it. I became Dr. Kevin McMurphy to the United States Army, and though I tried to correct the error, Kevin McMurphy I stayed."

Tempy reached over and clasped Faith's hand. "He hunted for me after the war."

"I didn't know to look in Richmond. I didn't know Temperance's sisters or their husbands. I went to the plantation," Kevin explained.

"And of course there was nothing left of it except the chimneys of the house and part of the orchard," Temperance finished, reminding Faith of the state of the plantation.

"I believed Temperance was dead." Kevin's voice was husky, filled with emotion.

"And I knew something had happened to Kevin. I knew he must be dead or he would have found me, hardheaded Irishman that he was." She gazed lovingly at the handsome doctor. "We would never have found each other if it hadn't been for you, my dear." Tempy patted Faith's hand. "And you, Reese." She smiled at Reese. "Thank you for bringing me here to surprise Faith. Thank you for giving me my . . . nieces." She choked over her words. "And my love."

"What do you plan to do now?" Faith asked.

"Marry him again." Tempy glowed. "This time for good."

"Oh," Faith said.

"Oh, is right," Kevin added. "And if you're a very good girl, I might let you get up for the wedding." He winked at Faith. "A matron of honor should stand up for the bride."

"When's the happy day?" Reese demanded, already planning how to celebrate the occasion.

"As soon as we can talk to the priest," Tempy confided. "We've already waited long enough."

"Twenty-five years," Kevin said. "Twenty-five long, lonely years."

Duncan Alexander stood up and rapped his fork against his empty coffee cup. "This calls for a wee nip of good Scots whisky."

"Scots!" Kevin roared. "For an Irishman's engagement?"

"Well," Duncan conceded, laughing, "the boy"— he looked at Reese—"likes brandy, but he might have a bottle of inferior Irish whiskey tucked away somewhere next to that poisonous French brew."

Chapter Twenty-four

"WELL, ARE YOU terribly embarrassed about us?" Temperance asked Faith as they sat stitching baby clothing on the front porch of the Trail T. "Because your aunt Virt is just going to have a conniption when I write her about it."

"Of course I'm not embarrassed about your marrying Kevin. You've been married for nearly three months. Why worry about what Aunt Virt thinks? She's two thousand miles away."

"Faith Elizabeth Collins," Temperance said, "have you heard a single word I've said?" She followed Faith's gaze to the corral where several of the men, including Reese, were branding the last of the summer calves.

"You asked if I was embarrassed about . . ." Faith wrinkled her brow in frustration, trying to remember Tempy's exact words.

"Well, go on," Tempy prodded. "What did I say?" She smiled a knowing smile. "You can't tell me because you don't know. The whole time I was confiding in you, you were busy lusting after Reese."

Faith blushed to the roots of her ebony hair. "Tempy!"

"Don't Tempy me. It's true." She placed her sewing in her basket and reached over to pat Faith's hand. "And don't look so embarrassed. It's perfectly natural. I lust after Kevin all the time. In fact, I've done it so much since we've been married that I think"—she lowered her voice to a mysterious whisper—"I'm pregnant."

"What?" Faith sat up in her chair, giving Temperance her undivided attention. "Are you certain?"

"Not entirely." Temperance laughed softly. "But I'll be sure to have the doctor examine me completely after I break the news."

Faith giggled. "You haven't told him?"

"I don't know how to approach the subject."

Faith looked at her aunt. Temperance was glowing with health and happiness. She looked years younger than her age, while Faith, glancing down at her own protruding abdomen, felt tired and fat and old. At nearly seven months, she had lost her gracefulness and, she feared, any attraction Reese had felt for her. She turned back to Tempy. "I'm sure you'll find a way."

"Just as I'm certain you'll find a way to tell Reese."

"Tell Reese what?" Faith asked, curious as to where Tempy was leading the conversation. "He already knows I'm expecting. It was part of the deal."

"But he doesn't know you love him. As I recall, that wasn't part of the deal."

"Am I that transparent?" Faith didn't bother to deny the truth.

"Only to those who know you well," Tempy assured her. "And I've known you since the day you were born."

"Just as I hope you'll know my baby." Faith

turned to her beloved aunt. "Tempy, I've made a terrible mistake. I can't do it. I can't give up Reese, my baby, and you. I can't go back to Richmond alone."

"I don't think you'll have to." Tempy spoke her thoughts aloud.

Faith turned her attention back to the man in the corral. A calf bawled its displeasure as Reese branded its left hindquarter, singeing the hair, burning the teardrop-shaped mark into the calf's tender hide. She marveled at the calves' ability to recover so quickly. Reese had left a similar, if invisible, mark on her, and Faith doubted she would ever recover. "He doesn't love me," she admitted aloud for the first time.

"I think he does," Tempy told her. "Kevin thinks so, too."

"He hasn't touched me since I fainted at his party." Faith folded the baby gown she'd finished embroidering and set it aside.

"Do you want him to touch you?" Tempy's clear gray gaze seemed to bore into Faith's. Her brows were pulled together in a frown.

"Yes," Faith answered simply. "I do."

"Then, my girl, I'm afraid you'll have to take the first step."

"What do you mean?"

"He's probably afraid to touch you."

"Reese afraid? That's impossible," Faith scoffed.

"Not really," Tempy told her. "Not after Kevin warned Reese not to touch you."

"Dr. Kevin did that? When?"

"When he felt you were in danger of losing the baby."

"Did Kevin tell you that?"

"In a roundabout way," Tempy said. "I happened to mention that Reese seemed to be bad-tempered and unapproachable at our wedding. Kevin said that was pretty common for a man who got . . . you know . . . whenever he looked at his wife and wasn't doing anything about it. He's . . ." Temperance whispered a word that Faith was sure her aunt had never uttered before. "It's up to you to do something about it."

"Did Dr. Kevin say it was all right?" Faith's eyes began to sparkle in anticipation.

"Yes." Tempy smiled. "He even told Reese after our wedding, but Reese obviously doesn't believe him."

"Or he no longer finds me appealing." Faith turned to her aunt. "Look at me, Tempy! What man would find this bulk attractive?"

"That man over there who keeps sneaking glances this way." Tempy nodded in Reese's direction. "The man who hasn't yet realized he's in love with you."

Faith followed Tempy's gaze. Reese stood up, wiping the sweat from his face with a red bandanna. He had removed his shirt, and the perspiration on his body shimmered in the sunlight. He looked wonderful.

Reese glanced over at the porch. His eyes met Faith's. Her mouth went dry at the look of hunger in his deep chocolate-colored eyes. She swallowed convulsively. Her breasts began to heave in response to her shallow breathing and rapid heartbeat. Tempy was absolutely right. Faith did lust after Reese. And it was time she did something about it.

She smiled at Reese, then very deliberately wet her lips with the tip of her tongue before she turned back to face Tempy.

Reese felt the impact of her tiny gesture across the length of the yard. His heart seemed to slam into his ribs. He shifted his weight from one leg to the other to accommodate the sudden swelling in his groin. He could almost believe she'd done that on purpose. He shook his head. No, not Faith. She was still too much of an innocent. She just didn't realize the effect she had on him. Even now. Especially now.

He ached to touch her. He wanted to feel her full breasts and place his hand on her stomach. Reese wanted to feel his child move within her, to share the miracle. But he didn't dare. He wasn't about to put Faith or the baby at risk. Reese was determined to prove he was not a rutting beast. He could control his desire. He would.

"Reese!" Charlie shouted. "Are you gonna stand there ogling the ladies all day, or are you gonna help brand these beeves?"

Reese jumped at the sound. He had no idea how long he'd been standing in the sun mooning over Faith like a schoolboy. He shrugged, then turned back to Charlie and the bawling calves. "I guess I'm going to help brand these damn cattle."

One of the cowhands snickered. "Yeah, but later on tonight, you can bet he'll be brandin' his wife."

Reese glared at the cowboy, then bent to pick up one of the white-hot branding irons resting in the fire. He shook his head as if to clear it, but the cowboy's remark stayed with him throughout the rest of the afternoon.

*   *   *

DR. KEVIN MCMURPHY drove up to the main house of the Trail T an hour or so before supper to collect his wife. He had spent the day checking the progress of his patients on the neighboring ranches. Temperance had been thrilled at the opportunity to spend an entire day with Faith, but now it was time to head home to the house they occupied outside Cheyenne.

"Are you sure you won't stay for supper?" Faith asked, accompanying Tempy and Kevin onto the porch.

"Well . . ." Kevin began. Sarah's cooking was always a temptation.

"Thanks for the invitation, darling," Tempy said. "But if we stay for supper, we'll have to spend the night, and Kevin always sleeps better in his own bed." She winked at Faith.

"What she means to say, lass, is that you'll sleep better without us," Kevin teased. "Temperance makes quite a bit of noise at night. She's always moaning and groaning."

Temperance blushed, but smiled happily at her husband's teasing. "Good night, Faith, and say good-bye to the others for us. Oh, and good luck." She took Kevin's arm and let him lead her to the buggy. He lifted her into the seat and climbed in beside her. Kevin flicked the reins, and the buggy began to roll down the driveway. Temperance blew kisses at Faith until she walked back into the house.

"What was that all about?" Kevin wanted to know.

"What?" Temperance was all innocence.

"Why would Faith need good luck?" he asked.

"She's planning to seduce Reese tonight."

"She's what?" Kevin yanked the horses to a halt.

Temperance studied her husband's features in the waning light. "He hasn't touched her since you warned him not to."

"Mary, Mother of God, that was months ago!" He couldn't believe his ears.

"Exactly." Temperance nodded to emphasize her words.

"Well, no wonder the boy's been stalking around like a wounded bear. I told him it was fine when I let her get up for our wedding."

"He obviously didn't believe you."

"Of all the thickheaded . . . That baby is fine. So is the mother . . . And they call the Irish hardheaded." Kevin urged the horses into a walk.

"Which is why I told Faith she had to make the first move," Temperance said. "She's planning to do it tonight. That's why . . ."

"We couldn't stay for supper." Kevin shook his head. A tiny chuckle escaped his lips, then turned into a full-fledged laugh. "You two planned his seduction this afternoon? I don't believe it!"

"Believe it." Temperance leaned over and kissed her husband on his handsome mouth.

"What else did you plan today?" Kevin whispered when Temperance released him. "Did my name come up?" he asked hopefully.

"As a matter of fact, it did," Temperance said. "We were trying to decide how I should break the news to you."

"News about Faith and Reese?" He sounded so disappointed Temperance almost burst out laughing.

"No, about you and me."

"What about us?"

"I suspect we're going to have a baby."

Temperance almost fell out of her seat as Kevin sawed back on the reins. The buggy jolted to a stop. He sat perfectly still for several moments before speaking. "Are you certain?"

"Pretty sure." She smiled mischievously. "But I can't be absolutely certain until the doctor takes a look at me."

"The doctor is looking at you," Kevin said softly.

"And what does he have to say?" Temperance was serious. Kevin's acceptance was vitally important to her.

"He's overwhelmed. I never . . ." A lump formed in Kevin's throat; tears shimmered in his eyes. He could barely grasp the miracle. "I'm going to be a father. We're going to have a baby!" He felt like shouting, like laughing and crying and dancing! He understood, for the first time, how his patients felt when he gave them the news. "Oh, Temperance." He leaned over and kissed her gently, reverently. "This is something to celebrate. How do you feel? Are you all right?"

"I'm fine." She laughed. "I feel wonderful."

"A father," Kevin sighed, immensely pleased with himself and with Temperance. Until a sudden thought crossed his mind. "I'm forty-eight. Do you think I'm too old to be having a baby? For the first time?"

Temperance smiled at him, softly, gently. "That's something else I want to talk to you about. There's something I need to tell you. Something you need to know. . . ." She began to speak, her voice filling the interior of the carriage, then spilling out into the night as the buggy carried them home.

When Temperance finished speaking she sat in the buggy waiting silently for Kevin to say something.

Kevin sat next to her, holding her hand, digesting the astonishing news. He climbed out of the buggy and held up his arms for Temperance. He didn't speak until he'd opened the front door, entered the house, and carried Temperance into the bedroom. He placed her in the center of the double bed. "As I said, this calls for a celebration!" he said, ripping off his tie and unbuttoning his shirt.

Temperance held out her arms. "Oh, Kevin . . ." The tears rolled quietly down her cheeks. Tears of joy. And love. Love for the hardheaded Irishman who had fathered her children.

"Mary, Mother of God, woman! Why didn't you tell me sooner?" He blew out the lamp and climbed into bed beside his wife.

THE MAIN HOUSE of the Trail T was quiet. Reese blew out the lamps in his study, closed the door, and started up the stairs to the bedroom he currently occupied. He had long since given up trying to sleep on the leather couch in his study. He had moved into the bedroom next door to the one he had shared with Faith.

Reese opened the door to his bedroom and stepped inside. He began peeling off his clothes as he walked across the room. A small fire burned in the grate. Faith, he thought. At least a hundred times every day he meant to thank her for the little comforts she provided, but somehow he never managed to say the words. He was afraid to acknowledge the numerous ways in which she made life more comfortable for him. Reese was afraid he might not be able to do without those comforts once she left. He decided it was better not to say anything at all.

So he pretended he didn't realize Faith was responsible for the hot baths waiting at the end of the day, the endless supply of his favorite cigars and Napoleon brandy. He chose to dismiss the idea of Faith caring for him. But secretly he enjoyed the fires burning in the grate at night, warming his room, and the fresh clean sheets on his bed. He appreciated her light, woman's touch. He wanted to feel it again.

Reese turned to his bed and flipped back the covers. A thousand times during the day he must have thought about making love to Faith in a thousand different ways. He sat down on the edge of the bed and removed his boots. God, how he wished he could bury himself inside her. He squeezed his eyes closed, trying to block out the image of Faith naked in his bed. He wanted to hold her. He ached to hold her, to smell the soft fragrance of her hair. He sniffed the air. He wanted her so badly he could smell the scent of her. Reese kicked his boots aside and stretched out on the bed.

"I was beginning to think you were never coming to bed." A soft cloud of lavender enveloped him as her soft voice echoed through the room. Faith moved from her chair in the corner of the room to sit beside him on the bed.

"Faith?" He cleared his throat, moving closer to

the edge of the bed as she advanced. "What are you doing here?" He squinted in the semidarkness, making sure he was in the right room.

"Waiting for you." Her lips brushed a flat nipple as she shifted her weight, leaned closer, and bent to kiss his chest.

"What is it? What do you want?" God, her mouth felt good. He wasn't sure he could stand much more. His flesh quivered as she leaned across him to kiss his other nipple.

"Isn't it obvious?" Faith moved to her knees, crawling over one of his legs, imprisoning him beneath her. Her rounded stomach pressed against his. "I want you, Reese." Her mouth burned a trail from his chest along his flat belly.

Reese gasped, half in pleasure, half in pain, as her tongue darted inside his navel, then swirled through the dark thatch of hair below. His hands moved up to tangle in her hair. "No, Faith." He pulled her closer as he spoke. "You don't know what you do to me."

Her hand found him. She wrapped her fingers around the length of him and, leaning closer, kissed him there.

He jerked in reaction, groaning his pleasure.

"I know exactly what I do to you." She let her tongue glide up his shaft, then down again. "You do the same thing to me."

"Faith." He murmured her name. It was half prayer, half curse. "Faith!"

She raised her head, leaned over him, and kissed his mouth. "Let me love you, Reese." Her hands caressed him. "Let me show you how it feels." Her mouth followed her hands.

Reese gave himself up to the pleasure. He didn't question the miracle that had brought her to his bed. He simply enjoyed it. He lay back and let Faith work her magic. She brought him to a stunning climax. Then, sometime later, Reese worked his magic on her.

They made love, slept, and loved again, gently, tenderly, until the morning light filtered in through the curtains.

"Reese?"

"Hmm?" He opened his eyes. Faith was propped up on one elbow, a pillow wedged underneath her arm, staring down at him. She looked beautiful.

"I've never thanked you for all the things you did before I came out here," she said. "Christmas, the pink bedroom for Joy, the money . . ."

"Ssh." Reese pressed a finger against her lips. "There's no reason to thank me. I didn't do it out of generosity. I did it because I wanted you."

"Well, thank you just the same," she said. "It made the ladies, Aunt Tempy, and Joy very happy. I . . ." She broke off, wincing.

"Faith, what is it?" Reese was alarmed.

She smiled. "Your son is trying to kick his way out of there." Faith lifted one of Reese's hands and placed it against her belly. "There. Feel it?"

"Yes, I do." Reese's face was awash with pleasure. "He's so strong. Does it hurt?"

"Only once in a while when he catches me off guard." She removed Reese's hand from its resting place and, raising it to her face, kissed his palm. "Thank you," she said, the tears, glittering in her gray eyes, "for giving me the chance to experience this."

"Christ, Faith." Reese pulled away and rolled to his side. "Don't thank me. For God's sake, don't thank me for doing this to you. I've watched you for months now." He got up from the bed and began to pace, naked, back and forth across the bedroom floor. "Don't you think I know how you feel about this? Don't you think I realize what this is doing to you? And now Tempy is married to Kevin. Damn, I wish . . ." He turned to face her, frustration lining every inch of his handsome face. He could stand anything except her tears. If only he had met her first. Before Gwendolyn.

"Reese," Faith said firmly, "we made a deal. We signed a legal, binding contract. You don't have to worry about me. I won't let you down. I'll honor it."

"Dammit, Faith!" Reese's face darkened until he seemed ready to explode. "You—"

"What will you tell the baby about me?"

The abrupt question startled Reese. "What do you mean?"

"I mean, what will you tell your son about his mother?" Faith placed her palm over her abdomen.

"I guess I'll tell him she died when he was born."

"What?" Faith gasped.

Reese stared at her. "What would you have me tell him? That his mother abandoned him at birth? That a piece of legal paper forced her to abandon him? That I forced her?"

Faith shook her head. "But death is so final."

"He'll love a mother who died giving him life." Reese's logic was brutal. "He wouldn't find it so easy to love one who abandoned him. For whatever reason."

"Then there's only one more thing I need to ask of you." Her voice was barely a whisper.

"Anything," he said without hesitation. If she asked him to tear up that damned contract, he'd do it. Gladly.

"We've only got two more months left," she reminded him. "And they'll be the hardest. I'll need all my strength to get through them."

"I know." He didn't want to be reminded.

Faith took a deep breath, swallowed her pride, and placed all her cards on the table. "For the time we have left, please, Reese, do you think you could stay with me? Pretend to love me so I can do what I have to do?"

"Damn," he muttered. He felt as if she'd stabbed him through the heart then ripped it from his chest.

Faith watched the different emotions flicker across his face. She wanted to call back her words. She fervently wished she'd never voiced her hopes. "Please, Reese, forget it." Her voice was barely above a whisper. "I shouldn't have said anything. It's just . . . I'm frightened a little. I'm sorry. It was too much to ask. Forgive me."

Reese said nothing. He couldn't. The words he wanted say lodged in his throat. But, Reese couldn't make himself say them aloud. He wanted permanence. She wanted him to pretend. He jammed his legs into his denim trousers, snatched his shirt from the floor, and grabbing his socks and boots from beside the bed, stalked out of the room.

He slammed the door as he left. It vibrated in its frame. Faith buried her face in Reese's pillow and wept. She couldn't make him love her, and it seemed he couldn't bring himself to pretend.

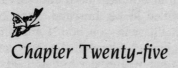

Chapter Twenty-five

HE FELT LIKE kicking himself as he marched down the stairs. Reese could hear Faith weeping, knew he'd hurt her again. He hadn't meant to, but he'd hurt her just the same. He hadn't known what to say to her. Her words had taken him by surprise. Her brutal honesty had shocked him to the very depth of his being. Damn him! He had let her beg for his affection, then beg his forgiveness for asking.

Reese marched through the kitchen and out the back door, slamming it in his wake. He was a fool, he berated himself, a damn fool. Why couldn't he do what she asked? Why the hell couldn't he go along and pretend? Why? Because he was tired of pretending. Sick to death of living a lie. He needed to talk to someone—someone older and wiser. Someone who could help him straighten out the mess he'd made of his life. He knocked on the door to his grandfather's cabin.

Duncan answered the door.

"Grandfather, I need to talk to you," Reese said without preamble.

"We were just on our way over for breakfast," Duncan told him.

"I need to talk to you alone, Grandfather." Reese frowned at Duncan, then at his grandmother, Elizabeth. "I'm in trouble. I need your advice."

Elizabeth smiled at her husband. "You counsel him, husband. I'll send you both some breakfast from the main house." She smiled at her grandson. "Your grandfather will give you better advice on a full stomach." She patted Reese's arm as she walked out the door.

Duncan ushered his grandson inside, urging Reese to make himself comfortable. "We'll talk as we eat," he told Reese when Mary arrived a few minutes later, carrying a tray with enough food for two hungry men.

Reese nodded his agreement, but waited until his cousin left the cabin to begin.

"How can I help ye?" Duncan asked, reaching for a piece of fried bread and the honey pot.

"I've done a terrible thing," Reese admitted. "I've dishonored myself and someone I care about." Reese bowed his head and waited for his grandfather to speak.

"I can't believe ye would do such a thing," Duncan told him.

Reese took a sip of steaming coffee. "I have, Grandfather. And I feel very bad about it."

"Then ye must make it right so ye'll feel good about yourself again, laddie," Duncan pronounced simply.

"That's the problem. I don't know how to make it right. I don't know what to do. Help me do the right thing," Reese said.

Duncan studied his grandson. Reese had always made him proud. It was hard for him to believe

Reese could dishonor himself or anyone else. But Duncan could tell from the look on Reese's face that he felt he had dishonored someone. There had been very few times when Reese had sought his counsel. His grandson was a proud, confident man, sure of himself and his place in the world. If he came to Duncan seeking guidance, it was because Reese felt he needed it. This was a serious matter.

"Tell me what it is ye've done," Duncan said. "Then maybe I'll know how to help ye."

Reese poured more coffee for himself and his grandfather, then settled back in his chair and began to talk. He told Duncan the truth about his grand scheme to gain a legal heir without having to declare his feelings before God and man. Reese hadn't had to wait at the altar for a bride who might or might not show up. He had simply purchased a mother for his child. His emotions hadn't been involved. It was a logical business transaction. He'd paid Faith enough money to ensure her appearance before a judge.

Reese finished relating the events, then sat quietly staring into the fireplace, waiting for Duncan to speak. His plan, which had once sounded so clever to his ears, now sounded tawdry, like the scheme of a swindler.

"Ye mean you didn't stand up with the lass? Ye sent your cousin in yer place?" Duncan was outraged. "Ye mean to tell me that ye plan to take the lass's child and keep it? For money? And never allow her to see it again?"

Reese nodded his head without speaking.

"I can't help ye with this, lad." Duncan shook his head. "I'm heartsore and disappointed in ye.

There's only one way ye can make this right, and I canna do it for ye. Do ye understand?" Duncan's voice rose in agitation. His gaze sought the gaze of his grandson. Their eyes met and locked. "Ye must face your greatest fear."

Reese understood what his grandfather was telling him, but he wasn't sure he could do it.

"It will be easy if you love the lass," Duncan assured him. "Ye do love her, don't ye?"

"I don't know," Reese confided. "I don't know what love is anymore. I loved Gwendolyn. . . ."

"Bah! That shallow creature?" Duncan scoffed. "Ye didn't love her. Ye loved the idea of marrying her. Of thumbing yer nose at high society." He stared at Reese. "She didn't hurt yer heart, laddie." He gestured for Reese to keep quiet when he opened his mouth to defend himself. "She hurt yer pride."

"What should I do about Faith?" Reese stood up, tossed the dregs of his coffee into the fireplace, and began to pace. Deep in his heart he knew what to do, but he wanted Duncan to confirm it.

"I dinna raise a fool," Duncan reminded him. "Ye know what to do. Marry the lass for real. Beg her on yer knees if ye have to. Or send her home—with her child."

"I can't." A desperate, tortured expression filled Reese's eyes.

It broke Duncan's heart to see that look, but he refused to pity his grandson. Duncan turned his back to Reese. "Then I'll have nothing more to do with ye until ye come to yer senses."

Reese walked to the door.

"One more thing, lad." Duncan didn't turn to face Reese, but called over his shoulder. "I'll have yer word that ye won't touch the lass unless ye plan to marry her."

"Grandfather . . ."

"Yer word, mon."

"You have it," Reese said, lowering his head as he walked out the cabin door.

SOMETHING WAS WRONG. Faith could feel it in the air. There was a definite rift in the family. Over the past two months the atmosphere surrounding the dining table had been tense, strained. Duncan and Elizabeth no longer came to the main house for meals. Their food was delivered to their cabin on trays. And Reese stalked around the ranch like a wounded animal, lashing out at his loved ones, acting as if he'd lost his best friend.

Faith hated to see the pain on his face. She wanted to go to him, to soothe him, but she was afraid, unsure of her welcome. Reese hadn't shared her bed since the night she'd surprised him. Faith ached to help him, but she was too wary, too disheartened, to risk his wrath.

She knew she was partly responsible for the crisis in Reese's family. She could see it in the pitying glances cast her way, sense it in the way her name was spoken, but she had no idea what had caused the turn of events.

Faith decided to confront Mary as they worked inside Elizabeth's glass-enclosed herb garden, harvesting the last of the fall crop of herbs and filling the ground with flower bulbs and spring seeds.

Mary did the actual digging and planting. In her ninth month of pregnancy, Faith was relegated to handing Mary the tools and bulbs.

Faith searched for a diplomatic way to broach the subject, then decided to be blunt. "Mary, will you tell me what's going on? I know something is wrong."

Mary wiped her hands on her apron, then sat back on her heels. "It's not for me to tell."

"Please. I know it concerns Reese, and I think it concerns me as well. I have a right to know."

"Reese has dishonored himself and someone we all care about." She studied Faith's taut features. "I don't know the details. I don't want to know them, but I do know that until Reese regains his honor Grandfather won't speak to him or sit at his table."

"Reese would never dishonor himself," Faith declared hotly, "or anyone else! Your grandfather is wrong." She stretched her arms above her head, then lowered them and began to rub absently at the ache in her back.

"Reese told Grandfather himself," Mary said.

"Then Reese is wrong," Faith insisted stubbornly. "Who does Reese think he's dishonored?"

Mary didn't answer. She reached for a trowel and began digging another hole in the ground.

"It's me, isn't it?"

Mary looked up and met the worried gaze of her friend. "Yes."

"I knew it," Faith whispered. "That stupid, thick-headed Scots-Cherokee and whatever else man!" Faith said, borrowing Aunt Tempy's favorite phrase and expanding on the theme. "And just how does he think he dishonored me?" she demanded.

"He didn't marry you," Mary answered. "He sent my brother in his place. That's all I know about it," she said, hoping to fend off any more questions. "He didn't bother to stand up with you in person."

Faith's temper soared. It was bad enough to pretend to be something she wasn't. Now, thanks to Reese, everyone on the ranch knew she wasn't truly his wife! "The marriage was legal! David said it was perfectly legal. I never wanted to get married in the first place. Who said I'd stand up in a church with Reese Jordan anyway? He never even gave me a ring. How does he know I'd have him even if he asked?" she stormed, walking back and forth in front of Mary's neat row of plants.

"He doesn't," Mary said. "And I don't know if he'll ever be able to bring himself to ask you to stand up in church with him."

Faith swung around to face Mary. "Why?"

"He's afraid."

"That's absurd. Reese afraid of a church?" Faith scoffed at the idea, but a tiny voice in the back of her mind reminded her of the truth of Tempy's words when she'd told Faith Reese was afraid to touch her. She dug her fist into the small of her back to relieve the tension knotted there. "I don't believe it."

"He's not afraid of the church. He's afraid of being humiliated again. Of being stood up at the altar."

"What woman in her right mind would leave Reese waiting at the altar?" Faith asked, half amused by the incredible thought.

"A woman who was determined to humiliate him. A woman who used Reese to set an example for all other 'half-breed' upstarts who thought they could take their place in 'polite' Boston society," Mary explained. "A proper lady. Her name was Gwendolyn."

"That . . . that . . ." Faith searched her vocabulary for a word bad enough. "Bitch!" she swore. "To humiliate him because . . . No wonder he felt he had to hire a mother for his child."

"You love him, don't you?" Mary interrupted Faith's vengeful tirade.

"He's a stubborn fool." Faith turned and looked toward the house. "But so am I. I love him with all my heart." Reese was inside working in his study. "I should have told him months ago," she realized. "I don't know if it will change anything, but at least he'll hear the words before I go." Faith started out of the greenhouse, then stopped in her tracks. Slowly she turned to face Mary, her face a mask of confusion.

"What is it?" Mary jumped to her feet, alarmed.

"I'm wet," Faith whispered, embarrassed. "There's water trickling down my leg."

"Dear Lord," Mary murmured. "It's the baby." She grabbed Faith by the arm, urgently guiding her to the kitchen door. "Can you walk?"

COULD SHE WALK? It seemed to Faith, she'd been walking for hours. She had kept a steady pace around the bedroom since long before Dr. Kevin arrived with a noticeably pregnant Temperance beside him. Faith had been walking since the agony began. She was tired, so tired. And it hurt so much. She just wanted to lie down and rest, but Sarah wouldn't hear of it. She and Reese took turns walking Faith around the room.

They were arguing about it. She could hear Kevin insisting that Sarah let Faith lie down. Sarah shook her head, speaking rapidly in Cherokee, refusing to consider the idea.

"What's she saying?" Kevin asked Reese, who was busy supporting most of Faith's weight. "I can't understand her when she gets excited."

"She says no," Reese told him. "She says it's too early to let Faith lie down." Reese's face was whiter than Kevin had ever seen it. Faith's labor was exacting a toll on him, too. "She says Cherokee women walk until the pains get very close." He repeated his aunt's words, but privately he agreed with Kevin. He wanted Faith's ordeal to end. He pleaded silently with Sarah to allow Faith to lie down.

"Faith is not Cherokee, dammit!" Kevin exploded. "Besides, I'm the doctor!"

"The baby is part Cherokee." Temperance touched his elbow. "Faith said she wanted her child born in the Cherokee tradition."

"Temperance, the baby is not doing the walking," Kevin pointed out. "Our . . . Faith is."

Faith panted through another strong contraction. "Walk," she whispered to Reese when it was over. "Walk." She took a step, determined to walk.

"All right," Kevin conceded. "She can walk for a while longer. But when I think she's had enough, she's going to bed. Understand?"

Everyone nodded obediently except Sarah, who ignored Kevin's blustering and went about preparing for the child's arrival.

"Enough!" Kevin roared half an hour later, when Faith's contractions were so close together she could barely move. Reese had been half carrying, half dragging her for the past twenty-five minutes.

Sarah shook her head.

"Don't shake your head at me, woman!" Kevin warned. "She's going to bed!" He nodded at Reese, who lifted Faith into his arms.

Still Sarah shook her head, speaking hurriedly and gesturing with her hands.

"She says the bed's too soft," Reese translated. "She says Faith should squat down."

"Absolutely not! I'll not have my first grandchild fall on his head trying to be born!"

"What?" Reese turned his attention from Faith to Kevin. His chocolate-brown gaze met Kevin's blue one. He turned to Tempy. She nodded in confirmation. "Holy Mary, Mother of God!" Kevin's favorite oath sprang from Reese's lips.

"That's right, lad," Kevin said. "My grandchild," he repeated for emphasis. "Faith is our daughter. Mine and Temperance's." Kevin spoke clearly, confidently. "Now, my boy, gently place *my* daughter on that bed so I can bring your child into the world."

Reese spared a glance in Sarah's direction, but did as he was told. He was too shocked by Kevin's pronouncement to do otherwise. Taking a great deal of care not to hurt her, Reese lowered Faith to the bed.

"Now," Kevin ordered, rolling up his sleeves and washing his hands, "step back out of the way."

Reese stood firm. The baby might be Kevin's grandchild, although he still wasn't totally convinced of that, but dammit, it was his child! He refused to leave Faith to endure the agony by herself.

A short while later Reese wished he'd had the good sense to leave. Every one of Faith's screams of pain stabbed him right through the heart. He became paler by the minute. And just when Reese thought he'd faint and disgrace himself completely, his child was born.

"Temperance, my darling," Kevin crowed. "We've got ourselves a grandchild." He eased the baby out of the birth canal, laughing and crying at the same time, as the infant let out a lusty squall.

Faith heard Kevin's words, but she was too tired to make sense of them. Later, she promised herself. Later she would sort everything out. But first she wanted to see her baby. She wanted to see the miracle she and Reese had created. Just once before she closed her eyes. "What is it?" she asked, pushing herself up, trying to see.

Temperance hurried to her side, the infant tucked securely in her arms. "You have a daughter, Faith," Temperance told her. "A beautiful little girl." Gently she placed the baby in Faith's arms, then helped Faith sit up against the pillows. Temperance opened the blanket covering the tiny bundle so Faith could get her first look at her baby's tiny face.

Faith studied the baby. Tempy hadn't exaggerated. She was beautiful with her crown of ebony hair and tiny features. "She has blue eyes."

"Black Irish," Kevin announced proudly. "Just like her grandpa."

"All babies have blue eyes," Temperance reminded the proud grandfather.

"I always pictured them as being brown," Faith told them. "Chocolate brown, like her father's." She looked up at Tempy.

"Perhaps they'll turn brown as she gets older," Temperance attempted to reassure her daughter.

"But then I won't be here to see it," Faith whispered, tears clouding her vision. "Where's Reese?"

"I'm here," Reese said, from his position near the fireplace. He walked to the bed and sat down on the edge.

Faith held the baby out to him. "Come meet your daughter." She thrust the baby into his arms. "She belongs to you."

Reese opened his mouth, tried to stop her, but Faith wouldn't let him. "I hope you're not disappointed because she's a girl. I know you wanted a son, but she can still be your heir. David will know how to draw up a suitable contract."

The baby wriggled in his arms, and Reese tried to hand her back to Faith. "Take her, Faith," he pleaded.

"I can't." Faith smiled at Reese through her tears. "It hurts too much. You'll have to learn how to cope with her, Reese. She's yours now. I've delivered her to you." She turned away from him.

"Faith . . ." Reese began.

She shook her head.

Temperance stepped forward and took the baby from Reese. "Faith's tired, Reese. Let her rest. You can talk to her later."

"But I lo . . ." He tried his best to say them, but the words stuck in his throat.

"Let her sleep," Sarah said to him in Cherokee. "You can tell her what you feel tomorrow."

Chapter Twenty-six

"ARE YOU SURE you won't change your mind?" Tempy asked, watching as Faith packed her trunk.

"You didn't change yours." Faith turned to look at Tempy. Her mother. She hadn't meant to say that, but after six weeks she was still coming to terms with the fact that Temperance had given her into her sister Prudence's care.

"I've tried to explain that I didn't have a choice," Tempy repeated. "You had to be raised as Prudence and Edward's natural daughter. That was the price they charged for taking you in. I accepted those terms so I could be near you. I couldn't tell you. I couldn't risk having them turn you out. Please try to understand, Faith."

"I understand why you couldn't tell me the truth in the beginning," Faith said. "But after they died . . ." Faith folded another dress and placed it in the trunk. "All of the others knew, didn't they? Aunt Virt, Hannah, and Agnes? You could have told me."

"Yes, they knew. We all grew up together. They were aware of my so-called disgrace. I wanted to tell you after Prudence died. I ached to tell you, but

I was afraid. Afraid of jeopardizing our relationship, yours and mine." Tears sparkled in Tempy's gray eyes. "How could I tell my niece that she was really my daughter after nearly twenty years? How could I expect you to understand why I stood by and allowed others to raise my daughter as their own?"

"But I do understand," Faith said.

"Now you understand," Tempy told her, "because you're about to make the same mistake I made. You're about to leave your daughter the way I left you."

"You never left me!" Faith said fiercely. "You always loved me. You were always there when I needed you." Faith folded another dress and placed it in the trunk.

"I'm still here," Tempy reminded her hardheaded black Irish daughter, "and your father as well."

"And here you'll stay. David is going back to Richmond. I'm sure he plans to start divorce proceedings."

"Has Reese said anything?"

"No."

"Then you don't really know why David's going back."

Faith looked up from her chore and met her mother's worried frown. "The point is he's going for some reason. It has to be because of the divorce. Joy and I are going with him."

"Your father and I will go with you," Tempy decided.

"Aunt . . . Mother, you're pregnant. You shouldn't be traveling across the country. You must stay in Wyoming. Reese might need help with the baby."

"The baby, the baby!" Temperance exploded. "Won't you at least give your daughter a name before you leave?"

"That's for Reese to do."

"I named you," Tempy confided, "and I made Prudence promise to keep the name. Your daughter should have something you've given her. What better than her name?"

"Her father." Faith was openly crying. "She'll have her father. I'm giving her Reese. Don't you see? He needs someone to love. Someone of his own. Someone he can love without fear of rejection."

"What about you?" Temperance demanded. "What about your needs?"

"I need to know they have each other." Faith hugged her mother. "And I need to know you and Kevin are looking out for them."

"I can't promise to do that," Tempy told her. "You're my child, Faith. My flesh and blood. If you go to Richmond, I'll go with you." Temperance stood firm. "I won't give you up again. I can't."

"You have to stay here, Mother," Faith replied. "You have a family here. A home. A husband who dearly loves you. And in a few months you'll have another child to love."

"Not as much as I love you." Tempy brushed away her tears.

"Every bit as much as you love me." Faith smiled at her. "This is your home now. Not Richmond."

"My home is where my family is," Tempy said.

"Your family will be here."

"Except you," Tempy said. "You won't be here."

"I have to go," Faith explained. "You know that. I signed a contract. I have a legal obligation. I must abide by the terms of the contract, just as you honored your agreement with Aunt Prudence."

"I was sixteen. I was forced to submit to my father's will. But, Faith, this is different. I don't believe Reese would fight you. I don't think he would really try to keep you from seeing your baby. He won't enforce the terms of the contract." Temperance walked over to her daughter and put her arms around her.

"What if he does?" Faith asked. "What will happen to Aunt Virt and the others if he does? I can't put the house in Richmond at risk. It's their home."

"Oh, Faith, my brave darling Faith. We can hire a lawyer to break the contract."

"And drag Reese's good name through the mud? And mine as well? No, Mother." Faith closed the trunk, then sat on top of it. "I love Reese. I love him enough to abide by his conditions. To give him whatever he wants." She looked Temperance in the eye. "He wants his child. And Reese Jordan wants me out of his life."

"I think you're wrong, Faith."

"Not this time," Faith said sadly. "If he'd ever mentioned wanting me to stay before the baby was born, I'd stay. But now . . . it's too late. He never once mentioned love. He never suggested . . ."

REESE PACED THE confines of the nursery, his tiny little girl cradled against his shoulder. Her mother was leaving in the morning, and he couldn't bring himself to ask her to stay. He'd had every opportunity. He'd followed her around like a puppy dog for the last six weeks, hoping for a chance. And he'd missed it. He'd missed lots of them, he reminded himself. He'd had the past year to rip up the contract and ask Faith to stay with him.

So why hadn't he?

"Because I'm afraid," he whispered in his daughter's ear. "I'm afraid she doesn't love me." He'd never dreamed he would turn out to be such a coward. He'd never been afraid to risk anything before, but he realized he'd never risked his heart.

"What if all she feels for me is desire?" He gently patted the infant's back, burping her as the wet nurse had instructed him.

He didn't think he could survive Faith's rejection, but then again, how could he stand to lose her?

"I thought you'd make the difference," he confided to the sleeping baby. "I thought I was so clever. I thought she'd beg me to let her stay once she found out about you. And then, when she didn't, I was sure everything would be fine once you got here. Faith would take one look at you and refuse to leave without you. Then I'd have her. I could wave the contract and the marriage papers and forbid her to take you. And she'd stay. We would be a family—me, you, Joy, and your mother. I'd have everything I ever wanted," Reese explained, "without having to say the words, without having to risk anything. It was such a clever plan. And I was such a fool. I should have known better." He sat down in the large rocking chair and began to rock. "Your mother is a fine and honorable woman. And she's determined to honor that damned

contract whether I want her to or not." He kissed
the top of the baby's head. She smelled faintly of
lavender, like her mother.

"That's why I'm hiding out in the nursery with
you," Reese continued talking to his infant daughter. "I know she'll come to see you before she leaves.
She loves you very much. And when she comes
to see you, I'll be able to talk to her. I'll be able
to give her the ring I meant to give her for her
birthday. And I'll be able to tell her something very
important. I have to explain how I feel. It won't be
easy, but I hope she'll understand how much . . ."
His voice broke. He tried again. "I hope . . ." The
words choked him. Reese cuddled the baby closer,
hiding his face against her tiny body, afraid she'd
be frightened by the sight of his tears.

FAITH FOUND THEM asleep in the rocking
chair. As she eased the baby out of Reese's arms,
she noticed the dampness on his cheeks. He had
obviously comforted his daughter, soothed away
her tears, by rocking her to sleep. Faith smiled
at the thought. He would be a good father. His
daughter would never lack for love.

Faith tiptoed to the cradle, half hoping Reese
would awaken.

There was so much she wanted to say, so much
she wanted to tell him, but she couldn't. She wanted
to stay. She wanted him to ask her to stay. She
wanted to beg him to let her stay and love him, even
if he couldn't pretend to return her love. She kissed
the top of her daughter's head as she tucked her into
the cradle. "I love you so much," she whispered. "I
love you both so much, but I can't stay. I can't ask

him to marry me. He doesn't love me. There was someone else, someone named Gwendolyn, a long time ago. She hurt him badly, and now he won't allow himself to love anyone else. He's afraid to trust." Faith gently rocked the wooden cradle back and forth. "Your daddy is afraid to love me, but he loves you very much. As much as I do. So promise me you'll take good care of him. Grow up and be happy. I wish I could be with you. I hope you'll forgive me one day. And I hope . . ." Her tears clogged her throat, making her words inaudible. "One day you'll read this and understand how much I love you, how much I love your daddy." She slipped the envelope into the cradle next to her daughter's tiny fist.

Written in Faith's clear, precise handwriting on the outside of the envelope was one word. A name: Hope.

Faith kissed her daughter one last time, then on impulse lightly brushed Reese's ebony hair with her lips.

She hurried out of the nursery, down the stairs, out the front door, and into the buggy. Tempy and Kevin would drive her to the railway station. She'd decided not to wait for David. She would be in Richmond, ready to learn the terms of the divorce, when he got there.

The mail train to Omaha would leave the station at nine. And when it pulled out, Faith planned to be on it.

REESE DISCOVERED THE note when he woke sometime after midnight. He felt no qualms about ripping it open and reading the contents.

She was gone. Reese sank back down into the rocking chair. He'd missed his golden opportunity. She'd come to the nursery, then left without waking him.

For the first time in his adult life, Reese couldn't think what to do. Reese Jordan, the master strategist, the man with a proven plan for obtaining his goals, was lost. And all because Faith had left him.

Reese got up from the rocker and began to pace the nursery again. He couldn't believe his stupidity. He'd worked so hard to win her, then pushed her away. He'd pushed her away, when what he wanted most of all was to have Faith share the rest of his life.

Reese had to get her back. He had to think of something—some way, some plan—to keep her.

He crumpled Faith's note in his fist, then tossed it into the fire. Hope wouldn't need the letter. She'd grow up knowing how her mother felt. He hurried out of the nursery and raced down the hall.

"Get up!" Reese stood next to David's bed. He reached down to shake his cousin's shoulder.

"What time is it?" David struggled out from under the covers.

"Never mind that. Get dressed and get the buggy. I'm going to get Grandfather."

David sat on the side of the bed and reached for his trousers. "Where are we going?" He pulled his pants on.

"Faith is gone," Reese told him. "But I'm going to bring her back. We're going to the telegraph office in Cheyenne."

"Now?" David glanced at the clock.

"Can you think of a better time?" Reese countered. "She's already got a head start. Hurry!" Reese slammed the bedroom door. The sound of his booted feet echoed through the hall as his shout ripped through the silent house. "And, David, don't forget to bring the baby—and the nurse!"

"I don't want to go to Wichmond," Joy protested irritably, shifting on the hard bench seat. "I want to go back. I don't want to leave Brutus. Or Sam. Or Weese," she repeated for what seemed like the thousandth time.

"Neither do I, angel, but we have to," Faith explained, her voice tight.

"Well, I don't like it," Joy said.

"It's just for a visit," Tempy promised. "If you don't like it once we get there, you can come back with Uncle Kevin and me."

"Truly?" Joy's face brightened.

"Of course," Kevin told her.

"Will Faith come, too?" Joy asked.

"I hope so," Temperance said simply. "She can live with us if she likes, but it would be better if she lived with Reese and the baby." She stared at Faith, daring her daughter to contradict her.

The train whistle sounded.

"How much longer till we get there?" Temperance asked her husband. "I need to walk around."

"You shouldn't have come," Faith said. "This traveling can't be comfortable for you."

"You weren't going to leave me behind," Tempy answered. "Besides, I know you don't really want to face your aunt Virtuous alone." She smiled at Faith. "We always handle her better when we stick together. And I'll bet she turned three shades of red when she got my last letter."

"Or green with envy," Kevin teased. "Because you've managed to snag a handsome husband."

Tempy laughed, then shifted in her seat. "A well-to-do husband. My sister Virtuous isn't impressed by handsome men."

"Unlike some women I know." Kevin winked at Faith.

"She's only impressed with wealthy ones," Tempy continued.

"Then you ladies are lucky that we ... I ... fit the bill. Virt should be most impressed." Kevin glanced at Faith to gauge her reaction to his gaffe.

She pretended not to notice. Just as she pretended this was simply a trip home from an extended vacation. Kevin was worried about her. If only she'd cry. If only his fool son-in-law would come to his senses. Kevin grasped Temperance's hand.

She looked up at him. "How much longer?"

"We should be stopping for breakfast in just a few minutes." Kevin snapped his pocket watch closed just as the train roared into the Pine Bluffs station.

"Come on, Faith." Joy pulled at Faith's hand.

"I think I'll stay here," Faith said.

"You'll do nothing of the kind," Temperance protested. "You're going to eat breakfast with the rest of us."

"I don't—"

"You heard your mother," Kevin chided. "Get going."

Faith pushed herself up from the bench and allowed Joy to lead her into the aisle and down the steps of the train.

A young man stood on the platform shouting, "Telegram for Faith Jordan. Telegram for Mrs. Reese Jordan."

It took Faith a moment to realize he was shouting her name. Her married name. "Here!" she called, waving a hand.

"That's us!" Joy cried, gleefully jumping up and down. She held up the coin Faith handed her.

The messenger took the money from Joy, but was careful to hand the envelope to Faith.

She ripped it open and read the message, then clasped it to her breast, laughing and crying at the same time.

"What does it say?" Kevin demanded.

Faith held it out to him. It was typically Reese, simple and to the point:

STAY WHERE YOU ARE. I LOVE YOU. HAVE COME TO MY SENSES. I NEED YOU. YOUR DAUGHTER, HOPE, NEEDS YOU. AM BRINGING DAVID, GRANDFATHER, AND THE PREACHER. YOU PICK THE CHURCH. ACCORDING TO OUR CONTRACT, YOU STILL OWE ME A SON. WILL YOU MARRY ME SO WE CAN BEGIN NEGOTIATING THE TERMS? LOVE, REESE. P.S. DID I MENTION THAT I LOVE YOU?

Epilogue

FAITH STAYED AT the Pine Bluffs station. She was pacing the length of the platform as the train from Cheyenne rolled to a stop. She hurried forward.

Reese was the first person off the train. He held out his arms as soon as his boots hit the platform.

Faith rushed into his embrace. "I love you!" he whispered into her hair. "I love you." Reese pulled her into his arms, smothering her face with kisses before his warm mouth located her lips. "Let's get married. Now. Today."

"Oh, Reese." Faith was overwhelmed by the rush of emotions she felt for this man. "I thought David was going back to start the divorce proceedings. I thought you wanted to be rid of me. You never—"

He kissed her again to stop the flow of words. "I was afraid," he admitted. "Afraid you wanted to leave me. I was trying to find the courage to tell you how much . . ." He pulled her tighter into his arms. "Promise me you'll never leave me again. Stay with me. With us." Reese looked around for the first time. Kevin, Tempy, and Joy stood watching them. David and Duncan were exiting the train. David held Hope against his chest. Reese took his daughter from David and handed her to Faith. "We love you. We need you. We missed you. Say you'll marry me . . . again."

"I will." Faith cuddled Hope close and smiled up at Reese.

"Today?" He looked hopeful.

"Oh, Reese." Tears formed in Faith's eyes. "I can't. Not like this."

"What?" Reese took a step backward, staring at Faith as if he'd never seen her before.

Faith stood on tiptoe, tilted her face up for another kiss. "I love you, Reese, more than anything on earth, but I don't want another haphazard, spur-of-the-moment ceremony. I deserve more than that this time. *You* deserve more." She smiled at him, then kissed him again to show how much she did love him. "Thank you for bringing a preacher. But we won't be needing him today."

Reese's stomach seemed to sink. He understood all too well what she wanted. He cleared his throat. "I suppose you want a big wedding."

"Uh-huh." She kissed the scar on the underside of his chin.

"With lots of guests."

"Uh-huh." Faith stood on tiptoe, straining to reach his lips.

Reese bent over slightly to accommodate her. The baby wiggled in her arms. "And I suppose you want me to wait at the altar while Kevin escorts you down the aisle?" There wasn't an ounce of enthusiasm in his voice.

"Something like that," Faith agreed.

"All right." Reese sighed heavily. "But there is one thing you must do for me."

"What's that?"

"Tell me again how much you love me," he ordered.

"My darling Reese, I love you," Faith told him. "I'll love you until the day I die."

"That's all I wanted to know." He reached down for Joy, who had run forward to grasp him around the knees. Then he opened his arms for Faith and Hope. He couldn't stop smiling. His fondest dream had come true. They were a family.

THE WEDDING TOOK place two weeks later at the Roman Catholic church in Cheyenne. The priest who had married Temperance and Kevin officiated.

Reese smiled at the memory. It was the town's most colorful and unusual wedding ceremony to date.

David Alexander, Reese's best man, stood alone at the altar.

Mary and Sarah were two of Faith's attendants. They had worn beautiful gowns which incorporated the Alexander's red and green Highland plaid and traditional Cherokee wedding garb.

Typically, Joy had stubbornly refused to wear any color except pink.

Temperance was dressed in a velvet gown of brilliant emerald green, and though her gown was artfully sewn, it failed to hide her pregnant state. Kevin sat beside Temperance. He held their eight-week-old granddaughter on his lap.

Faith's aunt, Virtuous Hamilton Jessup, and the two other members of the Richmond Ladies Sewing Circle had put up quite an argument against having a public ceremony. Virtuous pitched a fit at the train depot.

Reese understood how she felt. He'd put up quite an argument himself. But there was no dissension in the family ranks during the ceremony. And Reese was grateful that the very proper Richmond ladies did not allow their shock to mar the proceedings. And they had to be shocked. Because . . .

Faith wore burgundy silk. And because he marched down the aisle at her side. Her hand was firmly locked inside his elbow as she matched him stride for stride until she was practically running up the aisle.

Reese overheard the snickers of several guests and a comment about Faith being afraid he wouldn't show up at the church. But he didn't let those indiscretions bother him. He knew better, and so did the members of his family.

Reese smiled as he recalled the look on Faith's face as she recited her vows. Tears rolled down her cheeks as he removed the thin gold band she wore on her left hand and replaced it with a wider, heavier band. And he would never forget Hannah Colson's expression when Joy carefully delivered the first wedding band back to its rightful owner.

Tears had sparkled in his own eyes when the ceremony ended and Faith asked the good father to read a message to the guests. Reese would never forget the words. They were embedded in his heart.

"This is my public proclamation of love for my husband, Reese Alexander Jordan. I am honored to share my husband's Cherokee-Scots-English heritage. I am proud to stand beside the man I love and prouder still to bear his children." It was signed Faith Elizabeth Collins Jordan and duly witnessed and dated by the best man.

Agnes Everett and Hannah Colson had surreptitiously fanned the faint Virtuous Jessup when Reese Jordan made his own proclamation. He produced a thick sheaf of white documents from inside his suit pocket. David solemnly handed him a candle from the altar.

"This contract is declared null and void." Reese had set fire to the corners of the papers. And once the papers had blackened to crisp ash, he dropped the ashes onto a tray and offered them to his bride. "I love you, Faith," he whispered. "I'd like to renegotiate a contract favorable to both parties." He bent down and kissed his wife.

Their daughter howled throughout the ceremony, then howled even louder a half hour later when the priest sprinkled her with water. Hope Amanda Jordan, as she was christened, proved herself a person to be reckoned with. Just like her father, snickered half of the crowd. Just like her mother, snickered the other half.

And at the request of Faith's aunt Virt, Reese had a full account of the wedding, descriptively recorded and lavishly embellished by the local newspapers, sent to Richmond. Virtuous was cackling with glee at the idea of a copy residing in Lydia Abbott's mailbox.

Reese saw to it that no mention of Champ Collins ever appeared in print. He remained a well-guarded, well-loved family secret, his memory toasted with every bottle of champagne opened in the Jordan household.

Home is where the heart is . . .

If you enjoyed *Golden Chances*, don't miss the other thrilling tales of true and tender love from DIAMOND HOMESPUN ROMANCE . . .

Turn the page for an exciting preview of *Spring Blossom* by Jill Metcalf. Available now.

Treemont Farm, 1883

THE TREE-LINED ROAD to Treemont mansion had not changed a great deal. The oaks were older, of course, as was he. The crushed-stone path was as neat as he remembered, and the red brick edifice in the distance appeared the same. But the columns and dormers seemed more gray than white as the sun concentrated its beams there. Beyond the oaks the brush had sprouted up, adding to the deep shadows along the lengthy route.

Hunter Maguire pressed the soles of his booted feet firmly into the stirrups, stretching his long muscular legs by standing up in his saddle. The journey from his home near the James River had been tedious, although not overly long. He knew what really made him weary was making the decision to return to Treemont. But, being perfectly honest, he *was* in the market for a good stallion. So far his trip had been profitable, and he did not doubt that Alastair would have some good stock. A great stallion to match the two excellent mares already on their way to his home.

He relaxed once again in the saddle. Soon he would enjoy a thirst-quenching drink and, he hoped, a long hot bath.

Over the years Hunter had corresponded with
Alastair Downing occasionally, and the man had
extended to him an open invitation to visit Treemont. Curiosity, as much as the desire to find a
champion stallion, had fostered Hunter's decision
to return. He had often thought of the bright,
delightful Maggie. He wanted to see how she had
grown, wanted to know the woman she had become,
even though he understood that she could well be
married by now, though Alastair never mentioned
her in his letters. She had shown great promise of
becoming a beauty, and her spark for living had
touched Hunter in some way. A way that no other
woman ever had.

As he rode along the stone drive he removed
his hat and raked his long, lean fingers through
his straight black hair. Then, replacing the hat, he
surreptitiously scanned the trees to his right. The
house was near enough now, and he was certain
there was no cause for concern, but still . . . he felt
that he was being watched.

MARGARET DREW HERSELF up as thin and tall
as possible in order to remain unobserved, although
she was certain the thunder of her rapidly beating
heart would reveal her presence.

She'd heard the muted clip-clop of a horse's
hooves, and though it was childish, she was hiding
behind a tree. She frowned and considered why she
was really hiding as Hunter Maguire rode by her
secret place. He had taken her by surprise, of course.
That was a major reason. She just had not expected
to see him so suddenly, and she was not prepared
for a meeting.

She peered around the tree at his retreating back. He sat his horse proudly and confidently, his fine-cut coat moving slightly as he swayed with the rhythm of the horse's movements. He was still a fine equestrian.

Maggie ducked back behind the tree, frowning as she quickly looked about for an escape route. But when she dared to peek up the road again, he had vanished.

Maggie sensed the danger of exposure and moved deeper among the oaks where the shadows were darkest. The last thing she wanted was to meet Hunter Maguire here beside the lane, before she had prepared herself.

She darted to the safety of the next tree.

HUNTER HAD DUCKED between two giant oaks and tied his horse at the edge of the high brush. He then backtracked under cover of the scrub until he could emerge near the spot where he had spotted the spy. He had caught only a glimpse of a hat brim as he rode by and calculated the person to be short—either that or the man was squatting low as he watched.

Coming out from the thick underbrush, however, Hunter saw no one as he looked among the trees. It appeared his daylight stalker had moved on.

He cautiously stepped out onto the gravel surface of the road, his eyes darting warily from left to right. No one was in sight. Perhaps he was so tired he was imagining things. Perhaps what he had thought was a hat had been a tree limb or a clump of shadowed moss.

Shrugging his shoulders, he had started walking back to his mount when suddenly the horse charged out onto the road from between the trees. Hunter stopped in his tracks, his mouth falling open in amazement. His horse was being ridden away by a man in a black hat, black breeches, and a white shirt!

Horse and rider raced up the road toward the house, bits of cut stone flying upward in their wake. The man could be admired for his horsemanship, Hunter thought, as he watched his transportation fleeing. But then his thoughts turned far less charitable. He now had one hell of a long walk ahead of him!

As the figure grew smaller, Hunter once again halted in his tracks. The rider's hat had flown off in the wind, and long white-blond hair billowed out behind her.

Her!

He grinned slowly as he realized he had been duped. Duped by a small woman, at that. "Maggie," he said softly. Strangely, her trick amused him despite his weariness and the long walk ahead. She'd obviously lost none of her fire.

If you enjoyed this book, take advantage of this special offer. Subscribe now and get a

FREE
Historical Romance

No Obligation (a $4.50 value)

Each month the editors of True Value select the four *very best* novels from America's leading publishers of romantic fiction. Preview them in your home *Free* for 10 days. With the first four books you receive, we'll send you a FREE book as our introductory gift. No Obligation!

If for any reason you decide not to keep them, just return them and owe nothing. If you like them as much as we think you will, you'll pay just $4.00 each and save at *least* $.50 each off the cover price. (Your savings are *guaranteed* to be at least $2.00 each month.) There is NO postage and handling – or other hidden charges. There are no minimum number of books to buy and you may cancel at any time.

Send in the Coupon Below   To get your FREE historical romance fill out the coupon below and mail it today. As soon as we receive it we'll send you your FREE Book along with your first month's selections.

- -

Mail To: **True Value Home Subscription Services, Inc., P.O. Box 5235**
120 Brighton Road, Clifton, New Jersey 07015-5235

YES! I want to start previewing the very best historical romances being published today. Send me my FREE book along with the first month's selections. I understand that I may look them over FREE for 10 days. If I'm not absolutely delighted I may return them and owe nothing. Otherwise I will pay the low price of just $4.00 each: a total $16.00 (at least an $18.00 value) and save at least $2.00. Then each month I will receive four brand new novels to preview as soon as they are published for the same low price. I can always return a shipment and I may cancel this subscription at any time with no obligation to buy even a single book. In any event the FREE book is mine to keep regardless.

Name _____

Street Address _____ Apt. No. _____

City _____ State _____ Zip _____

Telephone _____

Signature _____
(if under 18 parent or guardian must sign)

Terms and prices subject to change. Orders subject to acceptance by True Value Home Subscription Services, Inc.

750

ROMANCE FROM THE
HEART OF AMERICA

Diamond *Homespun* Romance

*Homespun novels are touching, captivating
romances from the heartland of America that
combine the laughter and tears of family life
with the tender warmth of true love.*

__GOLDEN CHANCES 1-55773-750-9/$4.99
    by Rebecca Lee Hagan
__SPRING BLOSSOM 1-55773-751-7/$4.99
    by Jill Metcalf
__MOUNTAIN DAWN 1-55773-765-7/$4.99
    by Kathleen Kane (Sept. 1992)
__PRAIRIE DREAMS 1-55773-798-3/$4.99
    by Teresa Warfield (Oct. 1992)